C000254916

MURDER UNJOYFUL

ANITA WALLER

Print ISBN 978-1-913942-08-3

ALSO BY ANITA WALLER

For my son Matt, for his total dedication to Doris,
and to all my Kat and Mouse fans
who have loved the five books in this series.

Incandescent trees hide presents bought.
A tale of a saviour's birth,
A child
Empowered to save the earth.
A fear insidious, a vengeance sought.
A cry for help amidst darkness
Developing feelings fraught.
Unjoyful.

PROLOGUE

Julie Clark stared through the windscreen, watching the useless wipers battle against the relentless downpour. She had been sitting there for nearly an hour, conscious of the man in the back seat, unmoving, unspeaking apart from occasionally repeating her husband's name, followed by that of her five-year-old son: Greg Clark, Oliver Clark.

Not Ollie, as they had been calling him since the day he was born, but Oliver. The name somebody who didn't love him would use. She wrapped the image of Ollie's beautiful face around her brain, and felt tears prick her eyes.

She was waiting to kill someone. She didn't know his name; the man in the back of the car hadn't told her that. She had been locked in a cellar for three days with no food and water until an hour earlier, when he had brought her a bottle of water and her clothes.

Her mind returned once more with clarity to Monday morning, wondering if she could have done anything differently to change the course of events that was going to alter her life forever. Or extinguish it.

She had walked Ollie to school, nipped into the supermarket

I

for some milk and a quiet coffee in Morrisons' café. On her way back to the car she had been bundled into an open boot. It was as simple or as complicated as that. She guessed nobody had seen it; certainly, nobody had helped.

She remembered nothing of the car journey beyond the cloth that was held against her nose and mouth as she fought desperately to keep out of that car boot, before oblivion stopped the fight.

Her next conscious memory was of the cellar, extremely cold, not damp, and definitely not inviting. She had a colossal headache and was naked. One blanket had been left for her to either use as a mattress or a cover.

Screaming for help had no effect. She didn't know where she was but she guessed it was isolated. There was a complete absence of traffic sounds. And there was no contact for three days with anyone, beyond a five-minute recording piped into the cellar hourly, constantly repeating the words: Greg Clark, Oliver Clark.

He watched while she put on her clothes, commenting about the smell of urine coming from a corner. She made no response; she expected to die.

The hourly recording had activated and she felt hot tears roll down her cheeks.

The man, who appeared to her to be of a similar age to her own thirty-one years, was tall, slim and had dark brown eyes; one of his eyes appeared to have a murky film over it. His hair was brown and slightly greasy, and he wore it long and pulled back into a ponytail. Pacing around the room as he waited for her to get dressed, his limp was imperceptible, but clearly there.

'They're going to die unless you follow my instructions to the letter. If you do everything I tell you to do, you will be allowed to live, as will your precious family. Is that understood?'

'Yes,' she whispered.

He handed her shoes to her. 'Put them on. Tie the laces tight, you will need to run when you have done what you have to do.' His Yorkshire accent was strong, but she had no difficulty understanding what he was saying. It was unbelievably clear.

Julie knelt down to secure the laces, her long blonde hair falling forward on to her face, obscuring her tears for a moment. Was he offering her a chance of an escape?

'Nice arse,' he commented. 'Shame we've got stuff to do.'

She froze, terrified of what was coming next, aware of her vulnerability. He pulled her up from the kneeling position by her hair and shoved her towards the door. 'It's open. We're going outside and it's raining.'

As soon as she stepped outside she realised it wasn't a cellar; it was a solid stone built barn, small, obviously used for storage to keep something dry, with no windows and a door with a massive padlock on it. A black Ford Fiesta was parked by the side of the building. The land around was bare of any other buildings except a rundown farmhouse; she sensed it was unoccupied.

'Get in.'

Julie felt the barrel of a rifle press into her spine, and a sob escaped. She sank into the driver's seat and waited while he climbed into the back seat.

'Okay,' he said, 'here's what's going to happen. You're going to drive following my instructions and you're going to pull up outside the gates on the road. This is a private house. Shortly after we get there a man will arrive. He lives there. You will be waiting in the shrubbery. You will shoot him in the head.'

Julie shook violently. 'I can't...'

'I know you can shoot. This has been researched. We have been following you for some time, Julie, and we know of your skills with a rifle. When you have killed him, you run and make your way home. If that man dies, your family lives. If you don't do this, Greg and Oliver will both be dead before morning. You will live long enough to know what you have done by disobeying me, and then you will die. Is that understood? The reason you give to the police for having been missing for three days needs to be amnesia following a massive pain in your head. When you get home tell them you've been sleeping rough in some woods because you didn't know where you lived, but you're starting to remember things again. They'll have no reason to link you with this crime. If I am even so much as questioned, all three of you will die, starting with Oliver. While you watch, of course.'

She nodded, unable to speak. Unable to think coherently.

'His name is Konrad Bialik. You won't know him, but many will. You are sending a message by doing this that will reverberate around the whole of the UK and beyond. This is his car.' He passed her a small piece of paper with the registration on it. 'It is a Land Rover with bulletproof windows. Do not shoot until he is out of the car. Now drive.' He handed her the keys, and she started the car.

He touched her shoulder. 'When I removed your clothes, if I had asked you for sex what would you have said?'

'No!' The word exploded out of her.

'Then I raped you.'

The shrubbery gave her ample cover. She had slipped in through the small gate to the side of the imposing front gates, open for the arrival of the Land Rover. Her mind was in freefall. There was no way out of doing this. The distance to the front door was considerable, and she now knew why it had to be a rifle and not a handgun. The rubber gloves he had given her to put on before handing her the rifle were a little too big, and she tried to pull them on tighter, afraid they would affect her handling of the weapon. The rain was streaming down her face, and she brushed her hand against her eyes, trying for better vision.

The Land Rover pulled up to the house, and she trembled. *Wait*, she thought, fear taking over. *Don't show yourself yet. You have to get this right.*

Bialik opened the car door and looked towards the house as the front door opened. He waved at the figure silhouetted by the light coming from the hallway, and Julie stood. She fired two shots and he dropped to the floor as the passenger door also opened.

Julie hesitated for a second, knowing she had to run, but every instinct in her wanted to help the man she had been forced to shoot.

The man standing in the shadows lifted his own rifle, aimed at her back, and fired. He smiled. *Fooled you, Julie Clark, fooled you.*

1

D I Carl Heaton pulled his wife of three weeks towards him. 'Come here, wife, let me kiss you.'

'You've kissed me. Several times.' Kat looked up into his grey eyes and smiled. 'Carl, today is Thursday, tomorrow is Friday and the day after is Saturday, you'll be home and we can go Christmas tree shopping. You're only going to Newcastle, not the North Pole, and it's a conference you've been chosen to attend so you have no choice. Now go, man.' She once more had a try at putting her long dark hair up into a ponytail – every time she tried, he kissed her and it came tumbling back down.

'But you'll be on your own. Martha's in Lapland, and I don't like to think you're home alone.'

'You make me sound like a film. And let's never forget I work for a living, so I won't be here till around five tonight, then my plan is Christmas present wrapping with you two out of the way, and an early night with a book and a hot chocolate. When you ring tonight, don't FaceTime me, I don't want you seeing things you can't see until Christmas morning. You can FaceTime me tomorrow.'

'You're a hard taskmaster, Kat Heaton.' He kissed her

7

soundly on the lips. 'I'll follow your instructions. Love you, Kat.' He reluctantly let go, pulled on a navy woollen hat over his short, slightly greying hair and kissed her again. A minute later Kat heard his car pull out of the drive. Immediately she missed him...

The journey to the office in Eyam was short, certainly within walking distance, but Kat decided to take the car because she wanted to pick up a couple of things from a toy shop in Bakewell. They had rung to say the wooden toys had arrived, so she figured the easiest thing to do was collect them while Martha was having five days with her Nanny, Grandy and Father Christmas, in Lapland.

Kat would take a couple of hours off, maybe try to persuade Doris, one of her two business partners, to go with her. Doris had not had a brilliant year following losing her long-time friend, and while occasional flashes of the old Doris still surfaced, the loss of Wendy had knocked Doris's ebullience and laughter out of the window.

Kat was the last to arrive; her hair had proved troublesome and she acknowledged that maybe it was her locks that were at fault, not her husband's kisses.

Luke Taylor, Connection's operative/receptionist, held open the office door as he saw her get out of the car, and smiled at her. 'Has he gone?'

'He has, a bit reluctantly.' She grinned. 'He sees Newcastle as not being on the same planet as the one I'm on, so by the time he gets there he'll be as grumpy as hell. Nan and Mouse already in?'

Luke nodded, and he pushed his dark brown hair back from his forehead.

'They are. Joel is in with Mouse, but he's heading off to Manchester in the next five minutes. They're currently on a conference call, so she'll not be long before that's done. Nan is in her own room, I've taken her a coffee in. You ready for one?'

'Thanks, Luke. I'll have it in Nan's room, see if she's feeling any happier. She was really down yesterday. I want to take her out for a couple of hours today.'

'It would have been Wendy's birthday.'

'How do you know these things? And how come I didn't know?'

'She mentioned Wendy's birthday when Wendy died, and things like that stay in my mind. I didn't say anything to Nan, left her to remember on her own, but I did buy her a little box of Ferrero Rocher to cheer her up.' He poured Kat's coffee. 'Go and dump your stuff in your office, and I'll take this into Nan's room.'

Doris Lester was feeling old. Her workout at the dojo the previous evening had temporarily invigorated her but she knew her thoughts were aging her. Wendy's death had made her all too aware of her own mortality. Stepping up her exercise regime had taken off any extra weight she had put on after their aborted holiday, but she missed Wendy.

She looked up as Luke brought in the extra coffee. 'Kat's joining you in a minute,' he explained. 'You need anything else, Nan?'

'No, I'm good. And thank you for my chocolates yesterday. You made an old lady a bit happier.'

'Huh. Old lady. I don't think so.'

. . .

His brown eyes softened as he looked at this woman who had nurtured his way through the beginnings of his career, who had trained him in surveillance, in talking to clients, in everything he needed to know to work at Connection. She may be old in years, he thought, but with her thick silver-grey hair and dazzling blue eyes, old would be one adjective he wouldn't use if asked to describe her.

He moved aside to let Kat enter, and went out to complete his main task of the day, decorating and squeezing a large Christmas tree into a small reception area without hampering disabled access.

He put some softly playing Christmas music on, and pulled out the cardboard box filled with Christmas baubles and tinsel. This year, he decided, they would go with a gold theme.

'You're sure you're feeling okay?' Kat sipped at her mug of coffee.

'I'm fine. I had a chat last night with my Hucknall friends, and Megan managed to cheer me up.' Doris was referring to friends she had discovered over the spring and summer. It had been an interesting evening when she had to explain to Mouse, Kat and Luke who they were, how her own husband had fathered two daughters with another woman, without Doris having suspected anything.

'Good, I'm glad you're keeping in touch with them. I liked Rosie.'

'And strangely enough, I think you would have liked Shirley. Her minimum fifteen-year life sentence – I don't know, Kat, it rattled me a bit.'

'Okay, let's put bad thoughts away. You fancy a run into Bakewell? I'm going to the toy shop to pick up some wooden toys for Martha, and I'll treat us to lunch.'

Doris's eyes lit up. 'That would be nice. I can look for a doll's cot while we're there. What's her other Nanny and Grandy getting her? I don't want to duplicate anything.'

'Their main gift they're having right now, the trip to Lapland, but Mum did say she would buy her a special little present from there to wrap up for Christmas Day, so I don't think she'll be buying her a doll's cot. You're safe with that. We've bought her a doll, about twelve inches long, and one of my ladies at church is knitting me loads of clothes for it so that Martha can undress and dress it.'

Doris smiled. 'I love Christmas now we have Martha. And thank you, a trip to Bakewell might nicely set me up. Has Luke told you we have an appointment booked in for tomorrow, and it's for both of us?'

'No. Does it need two of us?'

'He seems to think so. It's a couple, and the wife is in a wheelchair. He seems to think they want some sort of surveillance, but maybe more than that. If we use your room, Kat, there'll probably be enough space for the five of us. I'd like Luke to be in on it from the beginning. He's so patient and prepared to sit it out when it comes to keeping an eye on people.'

'That's fine. I'll make sure I'm in early and we'll move my desk nearer the window.' She finished her coffee and stood. 'You're sure you're okay? We'll go about half eleven if that's okay with you, and I'll warn Luke to expect us back whenever.'

She opened Doris's door and faint Christmas music drifted in from reception. Kat smiled. Her favourite time of year was here again. Her church's tree was already in place, and there was a joyousness within the congregation. Such a special time of year. Her shiver was a shiver of anticipation – her first Christmas as Mrs Heaton. This one would be... amazing!

Mouse's blonde head appeared around her door. 'I can hear Christmas music,' she said, a huge smile on her face, then closed her door. Kat looked at Luke, they both looked towards Mouse's firmly closed door, and laughed.

'Strange person,' Kat said, and went into her own office.

Bakewell was showing its festive face, with all its shops displaying Christmas trees and seasonal goods. Carrying bulging bags, Doris and Kat finally sank down gratefully onto two seats vacated seconds before by two more weary shoppers, and picked up the menu. They studied it for a moment, then both settled on steak and ale pie. Kat went to the bar to order and arrived back with two orange juices.

'About ten minutes,' she said. 'You okay? I've not tired you out?'

'You're kidding, and if I hadn't come here with you we'd never have found that little shop with the handmade stuff. I'm so pleased with that doll's cot, I can tell you.' She pulled out a package from her bag and opened it. 'And this is beautiful enough for a child, never mind a doll.' The coverlet was white lace and had a matching pillow. 'Who knew you could get stuff like this? I'm going to make her a couple of sheets for it, and Martha will be set up for looking after her new doll.'

'I'm pleased we found the cot first and were near enough to take it back to the car. At least we haven't had to struggle in here with it. I think I'm about done with Martha's gifts, so it's wrapping time tonight. I've warned Carl not to FaceTime me, I don't want him seeing anything.'

'You can do FaceTime?'

'Don't be cheeky, Nan. Of course I can, but not every time. Sometimes I cut him off.'

'Aaah, there's my real Kat.' Doris smiled. 'I thought we'd got an imposter in her place. Is everything sorted for the festive season with church?'

'It is. I'm not working Christmas Day, which means we can go to the service as a family, so I'm pleased about that.'

'Is the vicar any better?'

'He is. He's doing the Christmas Day stuff, but taking it easy up to the day. This pneumonia was pretty bad, but he seems to be pulling round now. I know it put a lot of extra work onto me, but it wasn't as though it was a long-term thing, I knew he would take up his duties again as soon as he could.'

Their meals arrived and twenty minutes later, after a major discussion about whether they wanted a treacle sponge, they left the pub and headed back to the car.

Kat loaded the boot, and they drove back, Doris still saying she would really have liked a treacle sponge but...

The tree in the office looked splendid. Luke had stuck to the gold theme, and it glimmered in the corner. He'd even placed a foot-high gold tree on his reception desk.

Kat's face lit up when she saw it all. 'Oh, Luke, it's beautiful. How on earth have you managed to do this? I didn't know we had all these decorations.'

'We didn't. Mum's going silver and blue, so I scrounged all her gold stuff, plus I sent Mouse upstairs to see if she had anything gold she didn't want. Looks good, doesn't it?' His pride was reflected in his smile.

'It's all my training, of course,' Doris said.

'I haven't had any training in putting up Christmas trees.'

'Yes you have.' She grinned. 'I distinctly remember saying it's time we had a Christmas tree in this office.'

2

K at felt surrounded, overwhelmingly so, by Christmas. A mad shopping splurge two weeks earlier had resulted in everybody on her list being at the crossing-off stage, job done, but now came the most difficult part, the wrapping.

She put the roll of shiny gold paper to one side, designated for wrapping the Christmas table presents, and pulled a Marks & Spencer bag towards her. It was full; when the cashier had said how much she had needed to pay, it had taken all her willpower not to gasp aloud. However, the girl with Tara on her name badge had noticed, and waited for the okay. Unsure of her current account balance after a day of Christmas shopping, Kat had meekly inserted her credit card into the card reader.

Four of the items in the bag were table presents. She had invited Carl's parents, her own parents, Doris, Mouse and Joel, making a nice even figure of ten to feed on Christmas Day.

But that required the wrapping of ten small gifts and Kat knew her wrapping capabilities were laughable. Did they do online courses in such things? YouTube. Her saviour for so many things. Kat designated the M&S bag to be the holder of the table presents, and pulled the rest of the gifts that had been in the bag towards her.

The beautiful angora sweater she had bought for Doris was a delight to touch and to wrap. It seemed to Kat that she used half a roll of Sellotape to secure the paper, and the bow looked more like a hangman's noose, but she hoped the large gift card diverted the eye away from the ribbon.

'Yes,' she exclaimed triumphantly, 'one down, one or two more to go.'

By the time Kat went to bed at a little after midnight she was too wound up to sleep. Everything except the table presents was wrapped and stored in a wardrobe in the spare bedroom away from prying eyes, but a visit to YouTube was definitely called for if she wanted her Christmas table to look special.

She opened her book, and when her alarm sang out at seven she woke to find the book on the floor and the bedside lamp still lit. A quick shower and an even quicker slice of toast saw her out of the house by half past seven. She walked down into the village centre and spent twenty minutes moving furniture towards the window of her office, in order to accommodate the wheelchair requirements of the promised clients. She set out water glasses and two decanters, then heard Luke arrive as she was finishing.

'Kat Heaton, what are you doing?'

'Setting up for the meeting this morning. Don't tell me they've cancelled.'

'No, but I would have done this.'

'Luke, you're an operative in your own right now. You have your own clients. You're not a junior any longer, and we don't expect you to do junior jobs. We do our own.'

'Kat, this is furniture removals.'

'I managed, honestly.'

He looked into her eyes. 'When this meeting is over, I put the desk and chairs away. Is that understood?'

Kat nodded, trying not to smile. All three women blessed the day Luke had come into their lives and their business. 'Shall we have a coffee?' she suggested quietly.

'You trying to deflect me away from being pissed off with you?' Luke smiled. 'It's not working. I'll get us a coffee, but I mean it, Kat. Don't move that desk, I'll do it.'

Luke saw the large people carrier pull up outside the office and watched as the driver steered the wheelchair down the ramp that extended from the rear of the vehicle.

He held the shop door open and welcomed Greg and Julie Clark. Kat appeared in her doorway and with a smile, guided them through. Doris stood and offered her hand to both of them.

Introductions over with and coffee requirements fulfilled, Kat placed the recorder in the centre of the table and explained they liked to record everything alongside taking notes, so they missed nothing.

Luke returned to his own desk; after a discussion they realised Luke's attendance would leave the reception unmanned for possibly some considerable time, so he had said he would listen to the recording later. He pulled the file that was his current baby towards him – a man wanting to know who his wife was seeing when he wasn't there. Luke had photographs to collate, a report to write, and an invoice to prepare. The divorce solicitors would find the file invaluable.

. . .

Julie Clark, at fifty, was beautiful. Hair that had once been long and blonde was now shoulder length and silvery white, framing an almost unlined face. Her grey eyes scanned the room, and she smiled.

'See,' she said, patting her husband's knee, 'this is what a tidy office looks like.'

Kat laughed. 'It doesn't always look like this, believe me. It all depends what sort of job we're working on as to the degree of tidiness in here. Today is a good day.'

Doris pulled her notepad towards her, and Kat switched on the recorder. 'So, perhaps you can introduce yourselves. Please call us Kat and Doris.'

'I'm Greg Clark, and this is my wife, Julie. I'm an accountant, have had my own business for many years, and we live in Hathersage. When we received the diagnosis that Julie would never walk again, we looked for a large house we could convert for her, and found a beauty in Hathersage. Julie lives as normal a life as possible, and we have a fully functioning home for my wife.' The pride in his voice was evident in every word.

Julie smiled. 'He loves me. Greg is perfect. I am alive because of him, but also because of our son, who also treats me as if I am glass. I lack for nothing except closure.'

Doris glanced towards Julie at that point, aware they were going to find out what had brought this middle-aged couple to their office.

'Closure?' Doris repeated the word.

'Yes.' A slight frown showed on Julie's face. 'Until I was thirty-one I lived a normal life. We had a five-year-old son, Ollie, we had an easy life and a business that was growing extremely fast, mainly because Greg is a nice man. He gets on with everybody, and they respond. They also remember him when they need tax returns and accounts doing. I worked part time in a flower shop owned by a friend, mainly making up bouquets, wreaths, that sort of thing, while she dealt with passer-by trade in the shop itself. It gave me flexibility for Ollie's school runs and school activities, and we lacked for nothing.'

Julie paused for a moment, gathering her thoughts. She took a sip from her coffee, then felt for her husband's hand. 'One morning in January 2000, a couple of days after school had restarted following the Christmas break, I took Ollie to school. It wasn't a working day for me, so I nipped into Morrisons for some milk, and went to their café for a coffee. I'd also bought a book while I was getting the milk, so I read a couple of chapters of that while I enjoyed my little moment of peace before going home to store the boxes with the Christmas decorations in. They needed to go back into the loft.' Again she paused. 'I'm telling you as much detail as I possibly can, I need you to know everything the police knew at the time. It shows my state of mind, everything that was happening in my life on that morning. I can only tell you my side of it up to a certain point, then Greg will have to take over.'

Again she sipped at her coffee. Kat and Doris waited patiently for her to recommence. Greg was still holding her hand.

'I've never been in that Morrisons' café since. I can't. I walked out of the building with a carrier bag containing a large bottle of milk, and my book, and a six-pack of Fudges, Ollie's favourite sweets at that time.' Julie gave a slight laugh. 'He still likes them now, and he's twenty-four. My handbag strap was across my body, and I remember fishing around in the bag to get my keys as I walked across the car park. I reached my car, opened the boot, and put the carrier bag in it. The vehicle next to me also had its boot open, but I didn't see anybody there, didn't think anything about it, if I'm honest. I reached up to pull down the boot lid and I felt a terrific thud on the back of my head. An arm went around my waist, and I was dragged to the car next door to mine. He bundled me into his boot and I tried to scream but he put a cloth over my mouth. I can only assume it was chloroform on that cloth because I know nothing from that moment until I woke up.'

Julie turned to her husband, seeking the support she needed as she repeated her story. He reached across the table and poured her a glass of water, then handed it to her. 'Drink this,' he said. 'We can stop if you want.'

'I can't. You know I can't. I'll be fine in a moment. Give me a little breathing space.' She drank the water, and replaced the glass on the table. 'I don't remember anything of the journey. When I woke my world changed forever.'

3

Julie indicated she wanted more water, and Greg refilled her glass. She once more drank deeply.

Doris sensed it was a delaying tactic. What Julie was about to tell them was going to be the most difficult part of the story. Doris tried to cast her mind back to the millennium year, to see if the name Julie Clark rang any bells, but it was an ordinary name, nothing different about it, a simple name, and she knew it wasn't in her memory banks. Maybe the story would be once Julie felt composed enough to relate the rest.

Julie placed the glass back on the desk, and took a deep breath. 'I woke up in a groggy state, not really able to think at first. I was naked, in what I thought was a cellar. It was cold, really cold, and it was dark. I had a blanket but nothing else. Nothing to sit on, sleep on, absolutely nothing. I used the blanket to wrap myself up, then to sleep on the bare floor with it wrapped around me. I saw nothing and no one for what turned out to be three days. I had no food, no water, and by the end I went to the corner that I had designated as my toilet and weed into my hand before drinking it. My throat was so dry it was stopping me breathing and I didn't know what to do. I had to stay alive for Greg and Ollie. Throughout all of this there was a recording. After a few times of hearing it, I worked it out it was on some sort of hourly timer, and all it said was "Greg Clark, Oliver Clark". Over and over and over again, for about five minutes, then it would stop and restart an hour later.'

'Do you want a break?' Kat asked, aware of how pale the woman across the desk from her was looking.

Julie shook her head. 'I've psyched myself up to do this, to ask for your help. If I stop I may lose whatever courage I have.' She rubbed her face with her hands. 'I'm okay. One afternoon, although I didn't know it was an afternoon, I heard something. Up to that point there hadn't been any sounds other than the recording, and fear hit me like a sledgehammer. The sound came from the left, and slowly a door opened. A man came in and looked at me. He was carrying a bag which he threw at me. His first words to me were "It stinks of piss in here". Then he said "Get dressed". He watched every move I made, made some comment about me having a nice arse, then told me to fasten my trainers carefully as I would have to run. All of this, ladies, is firmly fixed in my mind. Every word he said, exactly how he looked nineteen years ago, it's all in there. Luckily, it didn't seep into my brain that as he was letting me see his face, it probably meant he intended killing me.'

'You'd never seen him prior to this?' Doris asked.

'No, I'm sure I hadn't. He told me to go outside and get in the driver's seat. It was raining really heavily, but I still managed to see I hadn't been in a cellar, it was a small barn of some sort, and there was a dilapidated old farmhouse a short distance away. Then he told me I was going to kill a man. He didn't say the man's name at this point, but even if he had I wouldn't have known who he was. He said if I didn't kill him he would kill Greg and Oliver before the morning.

'He knew all about my shooting skills. I tried to say I couldn't shoot, but he stopped me straight away. Said he'd done his research and he knew I was a damned fine shot. I drove following his directions and we parked near to a house, a large house. I had to get out with a rifle, wait in the shrubbery of the garden until a Land Rover arrived, then shoot the man once he exited the car. By this time he'd given me a name, Bialik, but again I didn't know him.

'Fear was overwhelming me all the time this was going on. The lives of the two people I loved most in the world would end if I didn't shoot this man, and I had no choice. He came up with some convoluted thing about running home as soon as I'd shot the man, telling the police I'd had amnesia for three days to cover the time I'd been absent from home and the police had spent looking for me. He said they wouldn't link me to the crime.

'By the time I got out of the car I was feeling really ill, my stomach was cramping because all I'd had since my coffee in Morrisons was the bottle of water he'd provided an hour earlier. My body needed food and it was letting me know it. Anyway, the Land Rover arrived, I was hiding behind a large shrub, and this Bialik chap got out of the car. I seemed to be in slow motion, but I stood, took aim, and fired. He dropped to the floor, and I hesitated because all I really wanted to do was help the poor man. Then I felt a pain in my back that took all of my breath, and that's the end of my story.'

And that was when Doris remembered. The name Konrad Bialik had been known to her; he had wandered into her world through an assignment she had taken on for the Foreign Office, and he had seemed untouchable. He ruled through fear, his bodyguards would all have taken a bullet for him, and he supplied a large part of the universe with drugs. Any drugs. She had documented his life from his birth in a tiny village in Poland to his arrival in England and beyond. His contacts had been wide and varied, and her work had resulted in many arrests, but not his. He had died at the hands of a woman. The woman now sitting in Kat's office.

Doris made a note on her pad to reread the file on Bialik; knowledge was power as far as Doris was concerned, and she wanted a refresher on this evil man.

Kat switched off the recorder. The tension in her office was palpable; it was as if a cloud had seeped in and was slowly sucking the air into it.

'Okay,' she said. 'Let's take a break. Julie, you're drained. No further mention of this until this recorder is switched back on. Let's have fresh coffee, and try to relax a little.' She pressed her intercom and asked Luke to bring in four coffees, then changed the subject.

'I wrapped presents last night,' she said, 'and by the time I went to bed I felt as if I'd done a week in the office. I actually didn't realise how many stocking fillers I'd bought for our little girl – she'll need three very large ones.'

Julie smiled. 'Funnily enough, I still buy fillers for Ollie, and he's an adult now. In fact, he's managed to acquire a girlfriend, and Saskia also gets some. I mainly shop online because it's a struggle in crowds with the wheelchair, but I do like to occasionally go to places like garden centres where their array of gifts feeds my addiction to stocking fillers,' she said with a laugh.

The door opened and Greg held it while Luke brought in a plate of biscuits and four coffees. He handed out the drinks then placed the tray to one side before handing Doris a note. **Rosie rang. Nothing urgent. Only wanted a chat.** She acknowledged him, and he went back to his own desk.

They chatted about inconsequential things, sipping at their coffees and eating biscuits, until Kat judged Julie looked better. This had to be a massive ordeal for the woman, having to relive what must have been the worst period of her life, one that had changed everything for ever.

Kat judged it was time to start up the recorder again, and switched it on. 'Okay, let's carry on. Presumably, Julie, the pain in your back was a shot?'

She nodded. 'It was. It was meant to kill me, but I think my hesitation in not running immediately probably saved my life. Instead of killing me, it disabled me. I have no feeling at all below my waist. But Greg knows more about what happened next than I do really, so he can take over from here.'

Greg took a deep breath. 'Some of this is what I was told, and what came out at the trial. It seems that the house Julie went to that night was Bialik's home address. He apparently always drove himself, but always had at least one bodyguard with him. That night the bodyguard was reaching into the back to pick up some stuff Bialik had put on the rear seat, so didn't get out first. Bialik did, and Julie shot him. He died instantly, but then they heard a second shot almost immediately, and Julie went down. By they, I mean Bialik's wife and daughter. They had come out to meet him. He hadn't been home for three weeks and despite his criminal lifestyle, and the death rate soaring when he was around, he was a good husband and father. They sent for an ambulance, thinking they had two bodies on their hands. Julie was found to be still alive and was removed from the scene immediately.'

Greg took a sip of his coffee; the others waited for him to

carry on. It was clearly as difficult for him as it was for Julie to experience the whole trauma again.

'In the meantime, I was stuck at home with a five-year-old little boy crying all the time because he hadn't seen his mummy for three days. The first I knew of anything amiss was on what we call day one. Julie had taken Ollie to school. She had left him there safely but never went back to pick him up. The school rang me around half past three that first afternoon to say Julie hadn't arrived, wasn't answering her phone, and could I make arrangements for someone to collect Ollie. They called him Oliver so I knew they were pretty pissed off that he hadn't been picked up. I tried ringing, obviously, but she didn't answer. My first priority was to get Ollie, so I shot off to school, grovelled a bit and took him home.'

Greg Clark's face was white; it was clear he was struggling with the telling of the story. They waited, letting him arrange his thoughts.

'That three days of being without Julie were the hardest three days of my life, even harder than the year she spent in hospital. I had no idea where she was, if she was alive or dead. I reported her missing around seven on that first night. I'd been unable to contact her and I knew something was really wrong. She wouldn't have left Ollie for anything. Even if she'd walked away from me, she would have taken Ollie. For three days we were in limbo. The police had taken details and were starting to come around to thinking maybe there was something awry, when they turned up to tell me they had found her.'

Reliving the horror of that night, he paused again. 'They said it was touch and go, they didn't know if she would survive. They said she had been shot, that she was in the Northern General and she was in surgery. They had identified her by the picture I had given to them. I arranged for cover for Ollie, and I was taken to the hospital. And that began the longest month of my life.'

4

Julie smiled, and reached for Greg's hand. 'It was pretty long for me too. I knew he was still out there, the freak who had taken me, and I knew he knew I knew what he looked like.'

Everybody laughed. 'You knew a lot, then?' Doris said.

Greg grinned at Julie. 'She certainly did. When she was fit enough to help the police they brought some pictures in for her to go through. She found him almost straight away and six months later he was banged up in Strangeways. Julie gave evidence from her hospital bed and that sealed his fate, I think.

'The intervening years have been different to how we expected them to be back at the beginning of the millennium, but we have everything to make Julie's life as easy as it can be. She has access to the full house via a two-storey lift, and the doorways and rooms have all been reconfigured for her. We have what used to be a granny annexe built out in the back garden, and that has been turned into accommodation for Julie's carer and her daughter. They have been with us for ten years now. We have a good life. Ollie is a partner in the business and we work from home. We built an extension on the side for offices, and we live a fulfilling life.'

Doris was writing as he was speaking. 'So who actually lives in your house?'

'Julie and I, Ollie and Saskia... Saskia van Berkel, and in the annexe we have Tracy Worrall and her daughter Kaya. Kaya arrived with her mum, and she is now fifteen. We have two cats, Boris and Jeremy, and a tankful of fish. Platys. We started with two...'

'You still have something to tell us, don't you?' Kat spoke for the first time in a while. 'Has something happened?'

Julie and Greg turned to each other. 'He's been released, Paul Fraser.' Julie's eyes glistened as she said his name.

'Released?' The shock was evident in Kat's voice.

'Yes. On licence.'

'So he has to report to the police frequently?'

'He would if he hadn't disappeared.'

Julie could no longer hold back the tears, and Kat handed her a box of tissues. She dried her eyes, and blew her nose, then fished around in her bag.

'Greg, I need my inhaler. I think it's in the car. Can you get it for me, please?'

Greg stood and left the room.

'Please, can you stop the recorder for a minute.' There was an urgency in Julie's voice as she spoke to Kat and Doris. Kat pressed the off button.

Julie kept her voice lowered. 'I need to tell you something that Greg doesn't know and I don't want him to know. When we left that awful barn place, Paul Fraser said "If I had asked you to have sex with me what would you have said?" I screamed no at him, and he said "Then I raped you". I think I knew he had really, because I was so sore, but it devastated me. While I was in the hospital I developed a raging temperature, they did some tests and I had gonorrhoea. It could only have come from him. Greg knows nothing about that, I figured it would only upset him even more. They cured it, and life goes on, but I wanted you to have the full picture. This information is between us.'

The door opened as Greg returned holding the inhaler, and Julie used it immediately. She smiled her thanks, and took a sip of her water as Kat discreetly switched on the recorder once again.

'We will probably have lots more questions,' Kat said, 'but what is it you want from us?'

'To find him. Because he's broken the terms of his licence by not checking in, he'll go straight back to prison, but it's more than that. We're scared. We feel as though we're being followed, and that may be paranoia but it may be real. The police have said they'll have a car pass the house regularly, but that won't last long, will it? Connection, of course, is highly recommended by all and sundry, so we discussed it as a family at the weekend and decided to make an appointment with you to see what you say. Are we being stupid?' Greg finished speaking and glanced around the table.

'Of course you're not being stupid.' Kat spoke firmly. She could sense these two people were falling apart and needed reassurance. 'We will need to come and speak with everyone at your home, make sure they're aware of safety precautions they need to take every time they move, but eventually this man will be back in custody whether it be by our efforts or by the police finding him. Now, Doris and I, and probably Luke, will put together a plan this afternoon, make a note of any more questions we have, and we'd like to see you all tomorrow morning at ten. Can you organise with...' she consulted her notes, 'Saskia, Tracy and Kaya to be there, please? If he is following you, he'll be following all of you.'

Kat opened her drawer and removed a contract. 'I need you to sign this, and then pay a retainer fee to Luke. As you could potentially be in danger, this will be prioritised. Please take care today. Once you get home don't go out again until after we've been in the morning. Fortunately, it's a Saturday, so it won't impact on Kaya's schooling, but we will need a separate set of instructions for her. We'll also have to speak with her school. Be prepared for a long session tomorrow morning, we'll need to go through everything, get you all talking together and understanding what is needed, and if you think you have noticed anything – a strange car, a person somewhere where they shouldn't have been, a cyclist appearing at frequent intervals – make a note of it. Car registrations are always helpful,' she added with a grin.

Greg stood. 'Wait here, sweetheart, I'll go and give some money and the contract to this young man on guard duty. I'll be back in a minute.'

'Thank you,' Julie whispered. 'I've never told anyone that he raped me, only the hospital staff knew...'

'Don't worry,' Kat reassured the pale-faced woman in the wheelchair, 'it will go no further. Now, you will be vulnerable when you leave here as I assume it takes some time to settle you in the car. We will go out with you. Doris and Luke will scan the area and I'll be by your side until you drive away. After that you go straight home, and you get inside as quickly as you can. Make sure all doors are locked securely, and you hunker down for the night. One other thing... does your lounge have a bay window?'

'It does. A huge one. Costs an arm and a leg to buy curtains. Oh, you want me to keep the curtains closed?'

'No, I want you to get the biggest Christmas tree it can accommodate and get it set up as quickly as possible. Fill it with lights so that it blinds anyone looking in from the outside. This will give you some protection until you have to take it down. This is how you need to be thinking until this evil man is found.'

'We already have a massive one resting in the garage,' Julie said with a smile. 'A friend who grows trees gives us one every year – Greg does his accounts. We were going to put it up on Sunday, but maybe we'll bring it forward to tonight. Thank you so much for this help, Kat and Doris, already you're making us think differently.'

'You're welcome. Now go home and be safe. I'll probably be a bit harsh tomorrow,' Kat said, 'but rest assured it's only because you have younger people to consider, self-assured, and not really accepting of danger. They will be by the time I've finished with them. There will be at least three of us, and I'm going to discuss this with Beth, our other partner, so there may be four of us. It depends if she has anything else booked in. I really need you to take notice of Luke tomorrow. He does a lot of our surveillance work, so you need to be aware of what he looks like, how he works. If he needs to be in your house at any time, rest assured you won't really notice him, he quietly gets on with his job and produces results. Mouse – oh, sorry, Beth–'

'You call her Mouse?' Julie laughed.

'She's my granddaughter,' Doris explained. 'When she was born she was a little underweight, a scrawny little thing, and we all said she looked like a little mouse. The name stuck. We all call her Mouse now, so much so that when we say Beth it sounds unnatural. Beth deals with our corporate side, such as headhunting, interviewing for large companies, so rarely gets involved with the day-to-day details of what we do. She's winding down for Christmas, so may want to throw her two penn'orth into the mix. If not, it will be the three of us for as long as it takes.'

The door opened and Greg returned. 'Come on, Julie, the car is open and ready. Luke told me not to hang around, he's going to go outside with us, check nothing out of the ordinary is happening. This is real, Julie. I need to get you home.'

Julie picked up her bag, and Kat took hold of the wheelchair. 'Go and stand by Julie's door, Greg. I'll wheel her out. You be ready to get her in the car as soon as we're out there.'

He looked at Kat, fear evident on his face, then nodded.

Luke and Doris stood at either end of the car, immobile, their eyes watching everything around them while Greg made his wife comfortable. Kat squeezed Julie's hands and said goodbye. 'We'll see you at ten tomorrow morning.'

They all watched as the car pulled away, but nobody's eyes were really on that vehicle, they were all looking for any other random vehicles that set off at the same time. Nothing moved, so the three of them headed back into the office.

'Conference time,' Doris said. 'Luke, we might need a cup of tea while we make the plans for this one. Let's get you up to speed with everything.'

They moved back into Kat's room, and Luke quickly made the drinks. He carried them through, and sat down, wedging the office door open so he could see into reception. 'Nice man,' he said. 'Respect to him, with his wife like that for nineteen years.'

Doris nodded. 'We have a recording we need you to listen to, which will tell you the full story. I wish we'd known a little bit about what the problem was, because we would have had you in on discussions right from the start, but you were right, we did need someone on reception just in case. So now you're going to have to listen to it. I think there'll be a fair bit of surveillance on this one, but it could be dangerous, so don't underestimate what this case is going to be about. I know it's not a working day, but are you free tomorrow morning?'

He laughed. 'Of course. We got a date, Nan?'

'Kind of. We're going to Hathersage. Definitely the three of us, possibly Mouse also.'

'Mouse has a long conference call booked in for ten thirty tomorrow.'

'No problem.' Doris smiled. 'Let's go and get to know the family of the woman who killed Konrad Bialik.'

Kat frowned, then pulled her notes towards her. She read through them twice, while Doris sipped at her drink. 'Something wrong?' Doris asked.

'Nan,' Kat said. 'Do you want to tell us how you know he's called Konrad Bialik when all that has been said in here today is Bialik?'

5

Doris's hazy recollections of the man she had known as Konrad Bialik were definitely that – hazy. She typed in her Secret Service access code, and then his name. Half an hour of reading, and skipping around one or two other files left her in no doubt that Julie Clark had inadvertently done the world a great favour.

Drugs, people trafficking, money laundering, all of it had seemed to be second nature to him. Only once in all the time he was operating had he been brought in for questioning, and his alibis had never been broken. The loyalty of his cohorts had seen to that, and several had served time when the police knew it should have been him that was locked up.

The files were closed but not hidden following Bialik's death. It had rocked the criminal underworld, there was no doubt about that. He had been a charismatic man, a philanthropist when it came to donating to charities, happily married to Eva for many years when he was killed.

Doris disconnected, walked across to her door, and locked it, then picked up her mobile phone. 'It's me.'

'I know.' The man laughed. 'It says so on my screen. Yorkshire.'

'You know me as Yorkshire?'

'No, I know you as lovely Doris, but anybody stealing my phone would know you as Yorkshire which would be no help at all to them, because Yorkshire is a big place. You want something?'

'Not really. It's only to make you aware of something. Remember Bialik? Konrad Bialik?'

'Clearly.' The jocularity had disappeared.

'He's cropped up again.'

'As a vampire? He's dead.'

'Connection have accepted a case from the woman who killed him. I'm going to be doing some digging around in the files to make sure I'm fully cognisant of everything about him, and everything that was said at the time of his death. I know it will flag up, so I'm prewarning you.'

'Thank you, Doris. You need help?'

'No, I'm good thanks. It seems the man who organised Bialik's death has been let out on licence, but he's disappeared. There's a possibility, and it's a strong one, that he intends carrying out his threat of nineteen years ago and intends wiping out Julie Clark's family. She's the woman who actually fired the shot that killed Bialik. Paul Fraser got a life sentence, but the parole board have cocked up as they occasionally do, and have let him loose on the community. We've been asked to track him down. Apparently, I can't kill him. That would be the easiest, and the best, thing to do, but it's not allowed in this country.'

'You're not working alone on this?'

'No, we have a team. Don't worry. Thanks for listening, and if I need anything, I'll get back to you.'

'Anything and anytime, Yorkshire,' he said, and disconnected.

Doris stared at her screen for some time, letting her thoughts go back many years. This man had been her strongest ally, especially when it came to promoting her over Harry, her husband. Harry had always suspected there was an affair going on, but she had laughed at him, not knowing that Harry had become the expert in having an affair.

She knew if she needed help he would do whatever she asked; she had no intention of compromising his position by asking for anything, but it had been necessary to put him on the alert that Bialik was posthumously back on the scene.

She unlocked her door and went into the main reception area. Luke was out, and Mouse was sitting reading a book at his desk.

'You're busy then?' Doris said to her granddaughter.

'Pulled out with it.' Mouse smiled. 'You've been busy. Door locked and beavering away in that little office.'

'How did…? Oh, Luke's indicators.'

Luke had installed an electronic system that told him if any of the partners were unavailable for callers – if they locked their doors, it meant do not disturb, so he didn't.

'Everything okay, Nan?'

'It will be. Has Kat filled you in on the Julie Clark case?'

'She has. I can't be there tomorrow morning, but keep me notified, will you? If I'm needed at short notice, I'll know what's going on. Is there something going on that I should know about?'

'No. Listen to the recording, it will tell you as much as we know. I think Kat is beavering away at an action plan for the family, but I suspect we may have to get in touch with Mark Playter and discuss bringing in a security team. We can't be with them all the time, but if Greg Clark is prepared to stump up the cash until we find this evil man, then we should get at least four men into that house. Two working the days, two working the nights. I'll talk to them tomorrow and see how they feel about it. It is infringing on their privacy, but the operatives are as discreet as they can be, and it wouldn't be for ever.'

Mouse closed her book and stood. 'I'll get on to them and get a quote for various options. At least you'll have some figures to show the family when you get there tomorrow.'

'Thank you. I'll take over guard duty,' Doris added with a smile. 'Where is Luke?'

'Buxton. He said if you wanted him, call him and he'd come straight back. I think he wanted to catch Henry the Philanderer as he came out of work, get some photographs.'

'Henry the Philanderer indeed. One day we'll say that in front of him, and we'll all be mortified.'

'Or rolling about on the floor laughing.'

'You heard anything from Tessa and Hannah? I've got a gift each for them for Christmas.'

'They're calling in next week. They made various comments about going out for a Christmas meal but I think we've left it a bit late to book anywhere, so the discussion turned to a Chinese takeaway instead.'

'Tessa's got over Martin Robinson moving back to London, then?' DCI Tessa Marsden had been living with the pathologist for a couple of months when he was approached with a job offer he couldn't turn down. They parted amicably, and not a tear was shed; happy memories were stored.

Mouse laughed. 'Definitely. She's where she should have been a long time ago, and that's with Hannah. They live together anyway now, Tessa was telling me. As far as work is concerned, Hannah is Tessa's lodger, but I'm not convinced they're fooling anybody. They'll tell us all about it, I suppose, when we see them next week.'

'Wonder if they're on the team looking for this Fraser feller. I can't imagine they are, as they're on the Serious Crime Unit, but you never know. I'll ring Tessa tonight, tell her what we've signed up to do, and keep her in the loop.'

Luke lifted the binoculars and watched as the office staff exited the glass-fronted building. It was the usual Friday-night rush, everyone eager to get home so they could go out and hit the town. He could hear *see you later,* and *have a good night,* but then he saw him, Henry Little, walking a bit too close to the side of a blonde woman, who was laughing at something he was saying. They had clearly waited a couple of minutes after the general exodus.

Luke picked up the camera and took several pictures before laying it back down on the passenger seat. Henry flagged down a taxi, and he glanced around as if checking nobody was watching. He ushered the blonde woman into the cab, so Luke started his car, and edged out into the traffic, following two cars behind the taxi.

'Cheapskate,' Luke mumbled, as he followed the taxi into the car park of the Premier Inn. He grabbed hold of the camera again, and snapped pictures as they left the cab and headed towards reception.

He ran across to the building and followed them in, his phone in his hand. He couldn't risk his camera at this stage, but he could record conversations.

He edged closer to Henry and the woman, pretending to text on his phone. It began to record.

'Simon and Ann Jeavons,' Henry said to the smiling receptionist.

'Yes, sir,' she responded. 'It's good to see you again. Can you fill in your details as usual, please?' She handed him a form, and

Henry wrote. He eventually passed it across the desk, and the receptionist handed him a key card. 'Room 102, your usual one, Mr Jeavons. Enjoy your stay.'

Luke stopped recording and moved away from the reception desk. He lifted his phone slightly and snapped off several pictures, hoping he was aiming the lens in the right direction. He didn't want it to be obvious he was taking photographs.

He could sense the receptionist was watching him, so he walked over to her and said he would be back in a minute. 'I've left my wallet in the car,' he explained.

She smiled at the personable Luke, and watched as he went through the open plate-glass doors before turning to deal with another guest. She didn't see Luke drive away, and it wasn't until much later that she thought about him, and wondered what had happened to him.

It was DS Hannah Granger who answered the phone that night, and expressed her delight at hearing Doris's voice.

'We're coming to see you next week,' Hannah said. 'You'll need to stock up on biscuits.'

'We're always stocked up on biscuits,' Doris said with a laugh. 'Luke moans every time he has to go and get them, says he doesn't know how we don't all look like whales. We'll be really pleased to see you both. Is Tessa okay?'

'She's fine. She's in the bath. You want me to take the phone to her?'

'I only rang to see if you've anything to do with the missing feller who's out on licence and not reporting in to the police. I don't expect you to be involved, it's not exactly a major crime, but we didn't want to step on anybody's toes.'

'What's his name?'

'Paul Fraser.'

There was silence for a moment. 'Doesn't ring a bell. Want me to find anything out?'

'Don't risk getting into bother. We've been asked to trace him. I'll tell you the full story when we're sat eating our doughnuts and biscuits. So, you any plans for Christmas?'

'It'll be our first together, we're staying at home. We're going to tackle a Christmas dinner together. As you know, neither of us is expert at cooking, so it should be interesting.'

'You'd be welcome at Kat's with the rest of us. I hope you know that.'

'Thank you, Doris, but we're getting to know each other, the side of us that's not connected to work. If there's an invitation going for New Year's Eve, I think we could be persuaded...'

'Leave that with me. Nobody's mentioned it yet. You'll be top of the list for an invite. Give my love to Tessa, and we'll see you both next week.'

'Will do. Take care, Doris.'

Doris smiled as she replaced the receiver. If ever two women were meant for each other, it was DCI Tessa Marsden and DS Hannah Granger. She hoped the blossoming relationship wouldn't impact on their working lives.

6

Luke went into work early Saturday morning. By half past seven he'd already refereed a massive argument between Imogen and Rosie, his younger sisters, concerning who would be first up on Christmas morning to open their gifts, and it was a pleasure to get into his car and drive down into the village.

He still drove the Peugeot his mum had passed to him when he legally could ditch his learner plates, but with winter under way and a heater that only worked at random moments, he was seriously thinking about a newer one. He had been saving for some time with that intention in mind, but he also recognised that having a nondescript car allowed him to blend into the background when on surveillance.

He wanted the Peugeot to be the last nondescript car he ever had; his next car had to be smart, classy and good to look at. Exactly like Kat Heaton, smart, classy and good to look at. He grinned to himself as he reached the office still without any heat coming from the heater.

It was quiet once inside, and as they had retimed the heating to come on automatically at seven it was toasty warm. He entered his password, and brought up the file dedicated to

Henry the Philanderer. He entered details of all that had happened the previous afternoon, printed out copies of the photographs and placed them in a physical file. He had an appointment with Mrs Little for Monday morning, and he would be taking their invoice along with him. This case would be closed, he was certain. He guessed Mrs Little wouldn't be Mrs Little for much longer.

He pulled up the invoice file, filled in the details of hours he had worked, duplicating costs and other disbursements, then printed it off ready for checking by one of the partners.

He sat back, and took out his book. He guessed it would be a long morning, and reading a bit of Wallander might take his mind off Henry.

Luke, Doris and Kat travelled to Hathersage in Kat's car, Luke automatically watching for strange vehicles in the vicinity. He had once dismissed a tractor as not being relevant, to his cost, and had sworn it would never happen again. He also hadn't been impressed by the hilarity in the office when he had recounted his tale of woe.

There were no tractors in evidence on that crisp, clear morning; no motor bikes, cars sticking too closely to them, or vehicles parked near the Clark house.

They sat around the large dining table, Kat with a mound of paperwork in front of her. They had agreed that she would do the talking initially, then if anything involving technology cropped up it would pass over to Doris. Luke would round things up by emphasising everything Kat said, talking through his own part that he would be playing and making sure they were aware of his car.

Kat looked around at everyone and smiled. 'Welcome to our instructional meeting. I'm Kat Heaton, one of the Connection partners.'

'I'm Doris Lester, also a partner at Connection.'

'And I'm Luke Taylor, operative and surveillance at Connection.'

There was a momentary silence, broken by Greg.

'Greg Clark, I live here.'

'Julie Clark, and I live here too.'

'Oliver Clark, but please call me Ollie. I'm their son, for my sins,' he said with a smile.

'Saskia van Berkel. I kind of live here, but after much discussion this lovely family have insisted I live here full time until this issue is sorted. I've contacted the hospital where I work as a nurse and explained everything. I have a leave of absence until I can get back home safely. I normally live some of the time with my grandparents in the Netherlands as they are at the age where they need my help, but my sister is taking on more responsibility for them. I could have gone there out of the way, but...' She reached across and squeezed Ollie's hand.

Everyone smiled. They all knew exactly what she meant.

'And I'm Julie's full-time carer. My name is Tracy Worrall, and my daughter Kaya,' she patted her daughter on the head, 'and I live in the apartment in the back garden. We've been here for around ten years.'

'And that's everyone who lives here?' Kat asked.

'It is,' Greg confirmed. 'We have a gardener but I rang him yesterday and told him not to come in for a month. I figured it was safer for him, he's getting on for seventy, and I'm not sure he's capable of avoiding trouble. Nothing's growing at this time of year anyway, but he still enjoys coming and pottering, planting seeds and stuff for next year.'

Kat nodded. 'That was sensible. Kaya, the first thing is that I will be going to see your headteacher on Monday and explaining the situation. Until this is over I want you where you are safe, and that is with your mum and this family.'

Kaya looked at her mum and Tracy nodded. Then Kaya grinned and said, 'Yes!'

'Okay, none of you are going to like this, but I want you all on lockdown. If there's anything that needs anyone to be somewhere, it had better be a damn good reason. If it's to meet friends at the pub, then the answer is no. If it's a doctor's appointment you'd better make sure you're really ill, because we will be checking.' Kat's smile softened her words but nobody was fooled. 'Julie, do you have any medical appointments in the near future?'

'Not until January, and I sincerely hope it will all be over by then. It's going to be a strange sort of Christmas if it's not.'

'We'll do our best,' Doris said. 'It will also affect our Christmas too, but it depends on Paul Fraser surfacing.'

'And you really think he will?' Tracy asked, grasping her daughter's hand.

'Certain things point to it,' Kat continued, aware of the tension now she was starting to talk through the plan. 'When he shot Julie the intention was to kill her. I have no doubt of that. He never intended killing Greg and Ollie, it was always Julie who had to die because she could identify him. Greg and Ollie were the threat to get her to kill Bialik, and he needed her because his research confirmed she was an expert shot. The distance the bullet would have to travel meant it needed someone with proven ability, and a member of the Olympic team was definitely that. He clearly wasn't anywhere nearly good enough, because Julie survived. Logic tells me he wants to finish the job. He's coming for you, Julie.'

There was a collective gasp around the table.

'But...' Greg started to speak, but Kat held up a hand.

'Let me finish. The reason you're all going into lockdown is because he knows Julie will do anything to protect her family. She did. She shot a man in cold blood. He only needs to snatch one of you, and he has Julie.'

Julie's head dropped, and she brushed away a tear. 'I'm so sorry...'

'There's no reason to be sorry, Julie,' Kat said quietly. 'This man is evil, both for what he did to you initially, and what he is doing to your family now. Have the police done anything?'

'Not really. They don't have the manpower to station somebody here permanently, although they have increased patrols past the property. There's no proof he's coming here, of course, but he's definitely disappeared. That's how we know all this, the police had to warn us.' Greg's eyes fixed on Kat. 'We believe he will come. It's why we came to see you. I have money that hopefully will keep us safe. What I don't have is the knowledge of how to do it. You do, and whatever you advise, we'll follow it to the letter. Won't we?' He finished and looked all around the table. There were nods from everybody.

'Then we need to discuss security. I'm pleased to see you have the biggest Christmas tree in the forest in your bay window, so that in itself presents a barrier if he is still favouring rifles. It's not a physical barrier to stop a bullet, but it would inhibit his ability to aim properly at his target. Now, because we believe he is targeting Julie doesn't mean he wouldn't kill anyone here. He has nothing to lose. He was in prison for nineteen years so being caught will hold no fear for him. We have some more research to do on him and hopefully that will give us a lead as to his whereabouts, but in the meantime it's groceries delivered, cars unmoving for the foreseeable future, and luckily for you two, Greg and Ollie, you work from home anyway, as does Tracy.'

Kat sensed a lessening of the tension in the room, and knew

they were starting to accept the limits on their freedom at last. Now she could hit them with the security issue.

'Further to this, I want to have four operatives, specialised people, in this house. They will work twelve-hour shifts, in pairs. One will be inside, one outside. They will alternate, possibly every two hours as it's so cold, but you won't know. They will be on the periphery of your world, keeping you safe. Do you have a spare bedroom they can use for sleeping? If you don't they can travel home between shifts, but that creates an added danger.'

'We have several spare rooms,' Julie confirmed.

'Good. I have a quote for one week's employment of these four men which is eye-watering in itself, but we have to cover everything. Greg, is it okay?' She slid the paper across to him, and he pushed it back without looking at it.

'It's okay.'

'Thank you. I wouldn't suggest it if I didn't think it was important. We will employ them, and bill you at the end. It is a daily charge, so let's hope we find Fraser quickly. In addition, Luke will be on surveillance around and about here. You may see him, he may call in, and he will definitely be delivering your groceries because I want you to have them sent to Connection. That cuts out another risk level.'

'Kat, I can't thank you enough for this,' Greg said. 'It feels as though a weight has been lifted, and yes, it's going to be tough, especially with Christmas being so close, but hopefully he'll be back in custody soon, and there until he dies. I can't believe they released him, knowing what he did.'

'He probably played the system, Greg,' Doris said. 'I'll lay odds on that he became a Christian, went to church every Sunday, never got into fights, took innumerable courses to give him skills for when he eventually was released. It all adds up when he gets in front of that parole board and they can see in black and white what a good lad he's been, and how sorry he is for having caused Julie, his victim, so much pain and distress.'

Kat handed some pages around. 'This spells everything out in words of one syllable. Stay in, stay safe. You will meet your four protectors after lunch. They will have a password and it will be Nativity. That will change every two days, so make sure you're aware of it or they'll have you in a headlock before you can say don't hurt me.'

Tracy leaned back in her chair and ran her hand through her hair. 'Phew. I feel exhausted. And a little bit... scared. I don't know whether to make everybody a cup of tea or a large brandy.' She stood. 'Tea for everybody, is it?'

They laughed and she headed for the kitchen. The blind was down and she realised that this was their life for a short time. Luke had been in the kitchen and lowered it, and that was why Connection had been called in. The family wouldn't have even thought of it.

7

Kat moved into the library, a small room filled with hundreds of books, and four comfortable armchairs. It smelled of furniture polish and leather, and she drank in the scent, standing slightly inside the room. Finally, she settled herself comfortably in one of the antique leather chairs, rang Mark Playter, and they discussed the requirements of the family. Mark confirmed he would be part of the team, as this was a real threat to the lives of the entire family, and his team would be himself, Leila Palmer, Ian Downes, and Denny Evans. He confirmed that no one in his employ would be leaving the Clark premises for the duration; his operatives were used to that kind of set-up.

She added that the initial password was Nativity, and he laughed. 'Kat Heaton, Deacon of Eyam church, I think I could have guessed that. We'll sort them out with passwords as we go forward. My team will be there by one. I'll email the contract. Sign it and give it to me at some point. We'll no doubt see somebody from your place at the house?'

'You will. Probably Luke Taylor, but possibly Doris Lester

also. I'm pretty useless in comparison to them, so I'll man the barricades at the office.'

Again he laughed. 'Useless. Like hell you are. Kat, the reputation of the combined staff at Connection is somewhere up in the stratosphere. No wonder the Clarks approached you. You've spoken with them?'

'I have. Twice. There's Luke, Doris and myself here. Beth couldn't come because she had a conference call, but she's fully briefed on everything and no doubt will be here at odd times as well. However, we've been set on to find him, not to wait here like sitting ducks until he turns up. And that's where our secret weapon comes into play. We have Doris. When the Clarks came to see us and mentioned the name Bialik, her ears pricked up, and within half an hour we had a report on this man, a preliminary report she said. There'll be more to follow. She'll find Paul Fraser, I don't doubt, one way or another.'

'One way or another? How old is Doris?'

'It's not nice to ask a lady's age, Mark.'

'Go on. Tell me. It's the fact she's got an old name, but not an old face. Let me guess.' There was a momentary silence. 'Fifty-five tops.'

'That's near enough,' Kat said. 'I'll tell her your estimate. Don't be surprised if you get a big kiss when she sees you. See you later, Mark.'

She disconnected and her smile lit up her face. This snippet she had to pass on to Nan, she'd be proper chuffed.

The dining table was utilised once again when Mark's group arrived, and introductions were made. Mark explained his security business, and then they discussed sleeping arrangements. Two bedrooms were allocated to the team, with one of the bathrooms.

'There will, at all times, be two fully rested operatives, and the other two can awake at a moment's notice. There is one important issue we need to discuss. And this is pretty much directed at Kaya because she's a teenager and not used to listening to commands.' He smiled at the young girl, and she tried not to giggle. 'If any member of my team tells you to do something, you don't think about it, you do it. Immediately. Is that understood? The team won't tell you to do a damn thing unless your life is in danger, so rest assured if they say drop to the floor, they mean three seconds ago. And you do it.' Mark looked at everyone. 'The alternative is you may die.'

Everybody looked pale, but nodded.

Mark then softened his tone. 'I'm aware that the Connection staff have laid things on the line also, so I know you're probably feeling overwhelmed, but if I'd waited to say all of this until tomorrow, when you'd digested their comments, Fraser might have turned up here. And then it's possible you would have stopped being able to hear instructions ever again. So to round everything up. You can't go outside. For anything. Don't stand near windows. Keep blinds down and curtains closed. Follow instructions immediately. Any questions?'

'We wouldn't dare,' Kaya whispered.

For the first time they all laughed. Tracy turned and hugged her daughter. 'It's not for ever, sweetie. And I've moved us into that big bedroom at the back of the house until this is over. Greg thought we were a little exposed in our place, so we're all in one place now.'

Kat locked up the office and drove home with her mind reeling. She had had less fraught Saturday mornings than this one had proved to be, and she couldn't wait to get back to Carl. He would be home waiting for her...

He wasn't, and she switched on the answer machine. Delayed. Called into the office. Back as soon as possible. She felt a tear trickle down her cheek, but quickly brushed it away. Although he had only been away for two and a half days, it seemed an endless period of time since she had last seen Carl, and this, coupled with missing Martha, was the final knockout blow.

Kat wiped out his message, and ran upstairs to stand for a moment in Martha's room. She had tried to be a modern mum, and let grandparents share fully in her upbringing, but sometimes it was so damn hard. Her little one would be home on Monday, and that seemed a lifetime away.

She heard the familiar ting that prefaced an incoming phone call on the landline and she was halfway downstairs before it fully started.

'How's my favourite lady?'

'She's fine. She is, however, wishing her favourite man was home with her.'

'We've picked up a major case, a murder. I'll fill you in when I get home, but it's going to be a couple of hours. You want to go out to eat?'

'No, I want to cook us a simple meal, have cheese and biscuits for dessert, and then...'

Carl laughed. 'I'll be home in an hour and a half. Love you, Kat.'

One hour and twenty minutes later, Carl walked through the door. He pulled Kat into his arms and held her for a long time.

Carl and Kat decided to have cheese on toast for lunch, and it was while Kat was monitoring the toast that Carl settled at the kitchen table and they spoke of all they had done since they had last been together.

'So what was the problem this morning?' Kat began. 'I thought it was straight home and done for the weekend.'

'It was until the breakfast phone call. There's been a double murder.'

Kat lifted her head. 'Where? Locally?'

'Local enough. It's an elderly couple, live in Monyash.'

She waited. Sometimes he talked about his cases, sometimes he didn't, and she never pushed him for anything. 'They have a small bed and breakfast place, two letting rooms, but it had a brilliant reputation so they say. It's bad, Kat. A lot of blood. She had both her hands chopped off and it was pre-mortem according to the forensic people. The Super wanted me to cast an eye over the scene but I had to go straight there so they could move the bodies. The lady, a Mrs Olive Armitage, was much loved in the community. Her husband, Richard, known as Dick to everybody, loved working in his garden, and they took in ramblers and hikers, on a bed-and-breakfast basis. Been doing it for years, apparently. He was tied to a chair facing her. I suspect he was made to watch her hands being chopped off, but we don't know who did it, or what they wanted. There's a lot of digging to do with this one, I fear.'

Kat stared at him. 'How awful. I'm so sorry you had to go through that. Do they have family? It will be terrible for them at this time of year. It's bad enough any time, but at Christmas...'

'And you?' Carl wanted to change the subject. He couldn't get the images out of his mind of the blood, the hands on the table, the two bodies slightly leaning towards each other across the table, their duct tape bonds holding them in position, and the huge crater in Dick Armitage's head.

'We have a new case,' Kat said. 'Do you remember some years back a man called Konrad Bialik being shot by a woman?'

Carl frowned, trying to recall details of a distant memory.

'Wasn't the woman forced into it because some bloke threatened to kill her family?'

'That's right. Julie Clark. The man who threatened Greg, her husband, and Ollie, her son, was called Paul Fraser. He's been released on licence and he's disappeared. The family have contacted us to provide protection and to find him.'

'Shit, Kat! This is police stuff, surely!'

'Maybe it is, but the police haven't anything to go on. They're sending extra cars out to go past their house in Hathersage, but Fraser hasn't issued any threats, approached the family, nothing. They're scared. We had a big meeting at the house this morning, and while Connection is doing the head work, Mark Playter and three of his people will be doing the actual protection detail.'

She busied herself with turning over the bread and laying cheese on it. 'You don't need to worry, I'm not really going to be doing anything. This is my busiest time of the year at church for a start, so all I'll be doing is collating reports. Luke is on surveillance, and Doris will be doing what Doris does best. Mouse is fully up to speed on it, and will help whenever she can.'

Kat put the grill pan back under the grill, and picked up her cup of tea, before turning back to face him.

'You might say I don't need to worry, but bloody hell, Kat, this is major. Do you believe he's coming back to finish off what he threatened?'

'I do. I also believe Mark Playter and his merry band are more than capable of protecting all the family. And I think it's Julie who Fraser's targeting, because she didn't die the first time he tried to kill her.'

Kat pulled out the grill pan, and rotated the slices. 'Now stop it, Carl. You knew what my job was when we met, so don't come the "I worry about you" bit. This is what I do. This is what Connection does. We pick up the slack when the police won't help.'

'Ouch. That's not strictly true, Kat. If they were to receive any sort of threat we'd lock them down until it was sorted.'

'And what do you think we've done? Trust me, they are locked down, and Greg is paying a fortune for the privilege. We eating in here, or watching a match?'

'In here. I'm not in the mood for football. And it's not exactly true that I knew what job you did when I met you. I didn't know about all these dead bodies you find, the relationship with Tessa and Hannah, Doris and her killer kicks – I knew none of this, and I happened to fall in love with you. Instantly. And I have to keep you safe because I love you.'

She looked at his face, somewhat woebegone, and laughed. 'You're a proper numpty, Carl Heaton. I don't do anything to land me in harm's way. Stop worrying, and let's talk of other things. Like Christmas tree shopping.'

8

DCI Tessa Marsden pulled the crime scene photographs towards her and imprinted them on her brain. She would have preferred to have seen the scene as it was, but calling DI Heaton to deputise for her until she could get there had been good – now she had been allocated him as part of her team. And that, as far as she was concerned, was a smart move.

'Bad, aren't they,' DS Hannah Granger said. 'Why would anybody need to do that to people of their age? What did they know that the killer wanted to know?'

'No idea.' Tessa frowned. 'We need to keep an open mind on this, dig deep. You'll go with me for the next of kin visit. Do we have details yet?'

'We do. A Mrs Clark, lives at Hathersage, is the daughter. According to the neighbour she has no other siblings. Oh, and she's in a wheelchair.'

'Right, here's the plan. That's our priority. We'll head there now, we'll leave Forensics to do their forensic things and tomorrow morning I want the whole team in. This isn't some accidental death, this is torture and horrific murder, so I want everybody assembled by eight in the briefing room. By then we should have something to tell them.'

Hannah pulled the pictures across the desk. 'I'll set up the murder board. Give me five minutes and we can go.'

It was shortly before twelve when Tessa and Hannah pulled up outside the house at Hathersage, to find they were halted at the gate by a man who dwarfed the pair of them, and who checked their warrant cards with a degree of care unusual at any time. To have Luke suddenly spring up behind them was also a bit unnerving.

'DCI Marsden, DS Granger,' Luke said, and spoke to Denny Evans. 'I can vouch for them. I know them, senior police officers.'

Denny nodded and opened the gates. Hannah drove through, to be met by a woman who directed them around the side of the house to a parking area.

They sat for a moment before getting out. 'Why the hell is Luke here? And why do they need security on the gate? We're missing something.' Tessa stared through the windscreen. 'No doubt we're about to find out what it is.'

Julie's face was ashen. 'But... Mum and Dad would have been no threat to anybody. Why? Why would anybody want to kill them?' Her face crumpled and she sobbed silently, as if it was simply too much to make a sound. Tracy handed her a box of tissues and Greg wrapped his arm around her shoulders, holding her tightly.

'I suspect the answer to that lies with all the security you have surrounding you,' Tessa replied. 'I know we're running additional patrols past your house, but is there something you're not telling me?'

Greg spoke. 'We appreciate that, but it didn't give us a feeling of safety. We have set our own security in place until you get Paul Fraser, and we've done it through Connection, an investigation company based in Eyam.'

'We know Connection well,' Tessa said. 'But things have changed. I'd like to get you all away to secure accommodation, a safe house.'

'We can't and we won't,' Greg said. 'My wife has certain medical requirements, thanks to Paul Fraser, and this house is set up purely for her. This entire household works around and with the needs of Julie, and there's no way you can give us that. We have four operatives plus a Connection operative who I know is outside as we speak. We are safer here, in our own home, than you could ever make us, so we're going nowhere.' He looked around. 'Does anybody want to move to a police safe house?'

They all said no, or shook their heads. Kaya simply looked scared and leaned on Tracy.

'I'll keep you fully informed of how the case is progressing,' Tessa said as she stood. 'I am deeply sorry that you have lost your parents, Julie, and we can't begin to understand this man's mentality yet, if it is him who killed them. We have nothing that shows it is him, but whoever did it will have left something of themselves at the scene. We're going to need somebody to attend to identify the bodies, but I'll let you know when that can happen.'

'I'll see to that, Mum,' Ollie said.

Julie reached across and squeezed her son's hand. She didn't feel capable of speaking; she didn't want to speak.

'Are Connection aware of this?' Greg spoke quietly, still holding on to his wife.

'Possibly. DI Heaton, Kat's husband, covered the scene until I could get there. However, he didn't know at that point who the victims were other than their names, so it's possible that Kat only knows there has been a double death, not that it's your parents. Would you like me to tell her?'

Greg shook his head. 'No, I'll do it. I'd like her thoughts on whether we need even more protection.'

Tessa and Hannah left, waving to Luke as they passed his car. He waved back; they both knew things would change for Luke, because none of the three women would have him on surveillance if it was proved that Paul Fraser had murdered Julie's parents. He would be too vulnerable sitting in a car outside the house Fraser would be keen to infiltrate.

Hannah drove as they headed back towards their headquarters, leaving Tessa free to answer her mobile when it rang five minutes into their journey.

Forensics were ringing to confirm that fingerprints matching those of Paul Fraser had been found on the garden gate. Nothing inside the house, but a careless moment by a murderer as his thoughts were distracting him from being careful, placed him well and truly at the scene.

'We need to get his face out there, Tessa,' Hannah said, a frown on her face. 'He's one sick and twisted bastard if he could chop Olive Armitage's hands off without a second thought. And to either make her husband watch while he did it, or to make her watch while he bashed her husband's head in, is...' Hannah felt she couldn't finish the sentence. 'They were old, Tessa, old people who were enjoying their last years in peace. And they lost their lives because he wants revenge, bloody Fraser.'

'His picture will be all over the evening news.' Tessa's grim tone reflected exactly what Hannah thought of the callous killer. 'I'll make damn sure of it. That family won't be able to sleep until we find him.'

Kat and Carl arrived at the Clark house within quarter of an hour of Greg contacting Kat. Condolences were expressed, and Greg explained his wife had gone to bed. 'She's been under the weather the last few days, understandably. Out of sorts, not eating, that sort of thing, ever since we found out he'd been released. Then when they said he'd disappeared she withdrew into herself, it seemed. The doctor prescribed some tablets, but she wouldn't take them. She's had a couple now and gone to bed.'

'Greg, I'm so sorry,' Kat said. 'We can cancel everything that's been agreed if you want to be taken to a safe house.'

Greg shook his head. 'No, we can't do that. We have a lift, widened doors, lowered kitchen units – we have everything here for Julie's comfort. Even her bed is a special one. The safe house the police provide won't be able to cater for her needs. I've asked everybody else,' his arm swept around the room, 'and they've all agreed with me, that we stay here.'

'And do you feel comfortable with four security operatives?' This time it was Mark Playter who joined in the discussion.

'I think so. Ollie and I can help out on surveillance if needed.'

Mark frowned. 'I don't want any of you to leave this house, not for anything. I don't want any of my people compromised by anyone even going to the front door. No Amazon ordering, no ordering of any kind. I understand you're having groceries delivered to Connection? Whatever the previous arrangement was, it's cancelled. One of the four of us will pick anything up of that kind from Connection and bring it here. Connection personnel will have to stay away. We can FaceTime for any reports you need to make, Kat, but young Luke isn't trained to take a man, a killer, down, and from here on he is off surveillance.'

Kat nodded. 'Totally agree, and we would have reached that decision anyway. I sent him home as we pulled up outside. We'll have an early meeting on Monday to thrash out the situation from our point of view – don't forget we've actually been hired to track down this man. We'll speak to DCI Marsden, give her whatever we've managed to find out, and take it from there.'

Mark smiled. 'I love your optimism, Kat, but...'

'Don't even go there, Mark,' Kat said. 'Don't suggest we're not capable. I can guarantee we already have information that neither you nor Tessa Marsden possess, and I can't begin to guess what it will be, but I have something you don't have. I have Doris Lester. And this case didn't start with a man disappearing after he was released on licence, it started nearly twenty years ago with a man named Konrad Bialik. Paul Fraser forced Julie Clark to kill that man, so that's where we'll begin our search. And, I might add, I would back Doris Lester any day in a locked room against this pathetic little man who tortures elderly people in an effort to find out information. Luke isn't trained to kill – yet – but by God, Doris and Beth are. In other words, don't underestimate Connection.'

Carl remained silent. He'd never seen Kat in working mode in this way, and he knew if he said one word it wouldn't go down too well. She was fully in control, and he stood as his wife moved to pick up her bag.

'We're going now. Greg, if you need anything, you ring me. We're here for you at this difficult time twenty-four hours a day. One of us, probably me, will be checking in with you around six every day, and keep that Christmas tree lit. It looks wonderful, by the way,' she finished with a smile. 'Ollie, if you need one of us to accompany you to identify your grandparents, you only need to ask. Presumably, the police will escort you, but you may want somebody less... official with you.'

Ollie inclined his head. 'Thank you, Kat. I'll let you know as soon as they tell me when they want me to go.' Saskia reached out and touched his arm, and he smiled at her.

Carl's head felt as if it was on a swivel as he escorted his wife out to their car, and he inwardly cursed Paul Fraser for making them feel like this, under threat and vulnerable. Damn the man, the sooner he was found the better.

On the way back home Kat and Carl stopped off to get a Christmas tree. Kat wanted some normality, and a Christmas tree represented that. When Martha arrived home on Monday she would have eyes seemingly too big for her face when she saw the tree in the lounge, filling one of the alcoves.

The car stereo was playing Christmas music, and Kat shivered as she heard the familiar words of 'In the Bleak Midwinter', her favourite carol. She sang quietly along to it, and Carl smiled. How he loved his deacon, his Kat Heaton.

9

The tree looked wonderful. It filled the corner by the fireplace, and appeared to have fallen directly off a Victorian Christmas card. Kat and Carl were snuggled under fleece blankets on the sofa, blankets used for comfort rather than for warmth. The fire was glowing, and probably wouldn't need any more fuel before bedtime.

Christmas music played softly in the background, and they both held books. Carl placed his by his side. 'Another wine?'

'I'm good, thanks. I've got a bit of a headache, so I think I'm going up shortly.'

Carl kissed her gently. 'Fantastic idea. I can make your headache better...'

'You can? Best go now then.' She felt a huge rush of warmth deep inside herself, and leaned against him. 'I like your cures.' She placed a bookmark in her book and stood.

'Come on, let's make the most of the weekend, our bundle of trouble is home Monday evening, and this case is going to be a heavy one.'

'You think?'

'I do. I've got this sick feeling that he's not here only for Julie.

I think he would wipe out all of them in his quest to get to her. I hope I'm wrong. Did I go a bit over the top with the way I spoke to Mark this afternoon?'

'Nope.' Carl continued to fold the fleeces. 'You said it like it was. He was bordering on the edge of being patronising, and if he'd known you better he wouldn't have taken that route.'

'That's okay then. Come on, let's take some wine up with us, my head's feeling better by the minute.'

He grinned at her. 'I'll sort the fire and switch off the tree. You go up, I want to double check the locks.'

Kat paused on her way to the kitchen. 'You think we might have a problem?'

'I think Paul Fraser wanted some information from Julie's parents, and he didn't get it. If he was anywhere in the vicinity of Hathersage today, he could easily have seen us leave the Clark house. I'm taking no chances. There's a patrol car passing here at odd times throughout the night in addition, so we're covered. I want you to be on your guard. Grab that wine and get upstairs, wench. I'll be up in a minute, soothing your worries.'

Sunday morning arrived with a grey sky, a half promise of snow and a car ride instead of a walk down to the church.

Kat didn't argue when Carl said they would take the car; he tried to say it was because it was so cold and miserable, but she knew he was in protection mode and didn't want them exposed to a maniacal killer. *And understandable too*, she thought.

Kat took the service. The Christmas tree glowed, the congregation were in a good mood and they sang 'Once in Royal David's City' with some gusto. The children sang 'Away in a Manger' after weeks of tuition by their Sunday school teachers, and Kat's couple of hours devoted to her Lord brought a feeling of peace. Coffee and mince pies in the church hall after the service brought a further sense of well-being, and as she finally locked up the church for the day she smiled. All was good in her world.

Carl felt differently. He felt uneasy; if he'd had hairs on the back of his neck they would have been standing on end. It was as they were driving through the village on the way home that they saw Doris's car parked outside Connection.

'It's Sunday.' Kat sounded perplexed.

'You want to stop?'

'Yes. Let's make sure she's okay.'

Carl indicated and they pulled in behind the red Jeep, Doris's Christmas present to herself. He sat for a moment looking longingly at the car.

'Forget it,' Kat said with a laugh. 'We're not ready for a new car, and I need a new kitchen.'

'But look at it, Kat. It's a Grand Cherokee, and a seventy-year-old woman has bought it.'

'You being sexist and ageist, Carl Heaton?'

'Too bloody right I am. And I'd say it to her face, as you know. In fact,' he said, opening his driver's door, 'let's get inside and have this out with her.'

Kat laughed and climbed out of her side. 'I warn you now, Carl, you start whinging about her having a new car and you not having one, and she'll wipe the floor with you. I'd keep quiet, I think.'

She waved her card at the door and it clicked open.

The reception was empty, and the light indicator on Luke's desk showed Doris was in her own office, but it was locked.

Kat knocked gently on the door. 'Nan? You okay?'

'One minute, Kat.'

Kat and Carl waited, and eventually the door opened.

'Sorry.' Doris didn't look sorry. 'I've been on the phone, and working on my laptop...'

'It's Sunday.' Kat looked puzzled.

'I know it's Sunday, but there's danger. You know I'm not normally given to creepy feelings and suchlike, but there's something about this Paul Fraser case that's unnerving me. We need to know more about him, where he was born, lived, that sort of thing. He might go back there. Or use it as a base. And he's a killer, nothing to lose, especially now. We have to find him fast, before he kills anybody else.'

'You've bought a new car.' Instantly the tension lifted and Doris's face lit up with a huge smile.

'I know. It's extremely nice.'

'Certainly is. I can't have one.'

'Why not?'

'The wife says I can't.'

Kat was struggling to hold in the laughter. 'We were discussing Paul Fraser. Your case as much as ours, Carl.'

'I know. Nan's got a new car and if you need a new kitchen, I'll never get a Jeep.' He sighed. 'Okay, old lady, can I take it for a drive round the village? Please?'

Doris moved into her office and picked up a bunch of keys. 'Five minutes, that's all.' Her tone was threatening, and finally Kat's laughter exploded from her.

'You're a sucker, Doris Lester. And he'll never shut up about it now.'

. . .

They watched as Carl tentatively pulled away from the kerb, and then he disappeared.

'That's it,' Kat said. 'Forget your five minutes. And I'll never hear the end of it. So, to get back to Fraser. Am I permitted to ask what you've unearthed?'

'He lived in Hope for the first fifteen years of his life, then moved to Sheffield. His father was killed in a motorcycle accident, so his mother upped sticks and moved to the city. When he was sentenced for what he did to Bialik and Julie he said he was living on the streets, but he has an older half-brother, also living in Sheffield, and I suspect he lived with him. They were only a year apart in age, and it seems were close. His brother is called Todd, Todd Fraser. Same mother, different fathers. I'm putting together a file with everything I've found. I'm happy to pass it on to Tessa and Carl, as long as no questions are asked. Because of Bialik, a lot of stuff has been locked away, and I don't want my sources to get into bother.'

'Bialik? So we are going to have to go back. I lost my temper a bit yesterday about this, said it probably went back to Bialik, but I didn't really believe what I was saying.'

'Kat Heaton! Lost your temper!'

'Even Carl was shocked, I think. Connection was being patronised, I felt, and it couldn't carry on, so I bigged you up into superwoman, and let Mark Playter have it with both barrels. I took Luke off surveillance, by the way. I sent him home.'

'I know. I've had him on the phone. He picked his mum up from church, and saw my car. Wanted to know if I needed him to come in. We got a proper gem with him, didn't we? I said no, I was only doing research, but part of it consisted of phone calls and I thought it best if he wasn't here.'

'And he accepted that?'

'He did.'

'You want a coffee?'

'I'll do it. I actually need to move, I've been seated for so long.'

Doris headed for the tiny kitchen, and Kat sat at the reception desk. She pulled a magazine towards her, and flicked through it. She looked up with a start; the old-fashioned doorbell pinged as the door opened.

'Luke? You okay?'

'I saw Nan's car heading out of the village, so I thought I'd come and see what's going on. It wasn't Nan driving it...'

'You saw it was Carl, didn't you? Go on, admit it, and you thought you might be missing out on something.'

He held up his hands in surrender, then laughed. 'I'm bored, and you lot seem to be working or something.'

The office door opened once more and Mouse walked into the reception. 'I could see you lot in here, and thought I'd see what you're doing,' she explained. They had connected a CCTV camera to the flat upstairs, Mouse's home she shared with Joel, and it appeared the camera worked as she had spotted unusual Sunday activity.

Doris returned carrying two mugs of coffee and looked shocked at the sudden influx of people. She breathed a silent sigh of relief that she had quickly closed down her laptop when Kat first arrived. 'I'll get two more coffees then,' she said.

'Make that three,' Kat said. 'Jealous Jimmy is back with your car. I'll never hear the end of this now. Thanks, Nan.'

Luke and Doris were the last to leave, and Luke walked her to the Jeep. 'Nan,' he said, 'I'm not happy you were in there on your own today. This feller we're looking for, he's dangerous.'

Doris touched Luke's arm. 'I can handle myself, Luke.'

'I'd bet against Tyson if you were fighting him, but this man doesn't fight, he shoots, and you can't dodge a bullet. All I'm saying is that if you feel a need to do what you've done today ever again, you ring me. I can always bring a book with me, or even work if it comes to that, but I don't think any of us should be on our own. Not till Tessa's got him back behind bars anyway. Promise me, Nan.'

'Okay, I promise. I'm heading home now, and I'll give you a ring when I get there. Will that satisfy you?'

'I could follow you, make sure you're okay...'

'No. I won't let this thug interfere with our lives. Go home, Luke, and I'll see you tomorrow. Don't forget we have an eight o'clock meeting to discuss what happens next with this. Who'd have thought it would escalate at this speed when we saw Greg and Julie that day?'

'My point exactly. It has escalated, and it's a scary situation. I'm glad Kat has Carl and probably half the local force driving past at all hours, and Mouse is safe here with all the security we have on the shop and her flat, but you live on your own, and I find that worrying. You'll set your alarm when you go to bed, won't you?'

'Stop fussing. I'm security conscious as you know. I'll be fine.' She started the car, and Luke watched as she headed out of the village.

Smart car, he thought as he watched the brief flash of her brake lights, *wonder if my savings will stretch to even buying one of its tyres.*

He climbed into his little Peugeot, and drove home. Two more months to the car needing its MOT, and he had no doubt in his mind that it would fail. Maybe he'd have to settle for something a little less smart than a Jeep.

10

Luke was a mere two minutes away from home when he became aware of how close the headlights of the car behind him actually were. He dropped to a lower gear and put his foot down, accelerating away.

The car followed, keeping pace with him, and as he rounded the bend at the top end of Eyam village he felt the thud as the other car hit him. The Peugeot spun wildly out of control and flipped over before beginning to roll.

By the time the tumbling back down the incline had ended, Luke was unconscious and in urgent need of medical assistance.

Naomi Taylor, Luke's mum, wasn't aware of the tears rolling down her cheeks. The knock at the door informing her of the accident had catapulted her into action, and she had run the short distance from their home to get to the upside-down car.

Luke was trapped inside, and paramedics were surveying the scene and treating him through the window. In the distance she could hear the cacophony of the approaching fire brigade.

She made herself known to the ambulance crew, and then

stood to one side as they battled to save her son's life. 'Don't give in, Luke, don't give in,' she begged, and the tears continued to flow. She had never felt so helpless.

A combination force of fire and medical people eventually placed Luke on a stretcher, and they hid their concern from Naomi. His pulse was weak and he was unconscious.

'Are you coming, Luke's mum?'

Naomi nodded, unable to speak, and waited patiently at the back of the ambulance while they strapped her son on to the narrow bunk. She turned to see two police officers on the road outside the ambulance's back doors.

'Tell me it's not Luke,' Tessa said to the ambulance driver.

'It is, ma'am, Luke Taylor. You know him?'

'I do. Extremely well. Is that lady his mum?' Tessa stepped inside the ambulance and knelt by the side of Naomi, strapped into a side seat. 'Hi, I'm DCI Tessa Marsden. We'll find who did this, I promise you. Your son is a wonderful young man, and fortunately healthy.'

Naomi stared at Tessa. 'Luke has spoken of you many times. What do you mean, you'll find who did it?'

'We have a witness... Luke was deliberately rear-ended, and the car catapulted off the kerb and rolled. The car that hit him carried on. An elderly couple were out walking their dog and saw it all, so my sergeant is talking to them now. I'll leave you alone, they need to get this ambulance on its way, but I will call around and see you.' She leaned across towards the bunk, and lightly touched the stretcher. 'Stay strong, Luke,' she whispered, then climbed back out of the vehicle.

. . .

Hannah was speaking to the elderly couple who had called the emergency services within seconds of the incident, and she was making notes. She looked up as Tessa approached. 'Ma'am, this is Mr and Mrs Earnshaw, Freda and Bob. I think we should let them go home for now, it's really cold. I've got a description of the car, no reg plate but we'll check if anybody has CCTV in this locality.'

Tessa smiled at the elderly couple and at the shivering little dog in Bob's arms. 'Please, go home. I'm sure DS Granger has taken your address. We will have to speak to you again, but that's enough for tonight.'

The Earnshaws thanked Tessa and headed off up the hill, still carrying the cold little dog. 'Marmaduke,' Hannah said. 'Promise me, Tess, if we ever get an animal it will have a sensible name like Jack or Buster.'

'Hannah,' Tessa said quietly, 'did you recognise the car?'

Hannah turned around, and looked at the chopped-up car, its roof squashed down. Slowly the colour drained from her face. 'It's a clapped-out Peugeot. Please tell me...'

'I can't because it is. It's Luke. And it's serious. They had to cut him out. His mum's gone with the ambulance, so when we've done here we'll go and tell his nan what's happening. I'm going to ring Kat.'

Kat and Mouse drove to Little Mouse Cottage; the tension in the car was palpable. Following Tessa's report of what had happened to Luke, Kat hadn't cried, numbness took over. Carl had held her, had made her a cup of tea, and then she had rung Mouse.

She could hardly speak for the sobbing that engulfed her, and by mutual consent they decided to go see Doris, this wasn't news to despatch over the phone. Mouse arrived within minutes, and they drove over to Bradwell.

Doris looked through the spyhole and smiled, but as she went to release the locks on the door dread hit her. Why? Why were they here? She had a phone – why were they here? Her fingers wouldn't behave as she fumbled to release both bolts, and then she was face to face with them. Neither of them smiled.

The water in the glass in Doris's hand moved like a wave pool as she tried desperately to corral her thoughts. 'Should we go? To the hospital?'

'Not yet. Naomi is with him. We have to let the Clark family know, because I think we all realise this is connected. I'd place a bet on it being Paul Fraser who was driving the car that rear-ended Luke's. Let's hope he's picked up somewhere on CCTV. We're meeting Tessa and Hannah tomorrow at nine to discuss what comes next,' Kat said, wiping yet another tear from her face. 'Obviously, we have to be a lot more careful, and I suspect he knew Luke from having seen him outside the Clark home. He would have recognised the car, and he's possibly taking out anybody who has any connection at all to the Clarks. He's nothing to lose, has he, since he killed Julie's parents.'

'Nan, you'll come back with me?' Mouse said.

'Or me? I've got my own personal protection detail.' Kat reached across and grasped Doris's hand. 'We can't leave you here.'

Doris gave a deep sigh. 'I'll go and pack. Can you get food and cat litter for Belle, please, while I'm upstairs? I am taking my own car though.'

'That's fine,' Mouse said. 'You lead, we'll follow.'

'But I'm not happy with that.' Doris frowned as she looked at Mouse. 'You and Kat could be the next ones he tries to rear-end. How do you think I'd feel about that?'

'That's the way it's going to be, elderly relative,' Mouse said firmly. 'And don't think for one minute we're travelling in that order to safeguard you, because we're not. It's to protect the Jeep. Luke and Carl would never forgive us if that Jeep ever got so much as a scratch on it.'

Doris smiled for the first time since the girls had arrived at her home, and she headed up the stairs.

Belle slept in her cat carrier throughout the entire journey, then settled into Mouse's kitchen as if she had lived there for ever. Her owner, however, didn't settle so easily.

Luke. What had he done wrong to upset Paul Fraser? And now he was in hospital unconscious, according to Tessa. Doris wouldn't settle until she had more information; she needed that meeting at nine, and desperately hoped nothing would happen to delay it.

Joel made her a hot chocolate and she settled in the armchair to try to read, but she had to keep pressing the back button; nothing was staying in her brain.

She stood, having given up on reading. 'I'm going to my room.'

'You want anything, Nan?' Joel asked.

'No, I'm fine. I need to use my laptop.'

'Nan,' Mouse said. 'You can't find anything out tonight. Leave it until tomorrow when everybody will know more.'

Doris smiled at her granddaughter. 'Watch me. Watch what I can find out inside my extremely smart bedroom in your extremely smart flat. It looks lovely, by the way.' Doris was referring to the bedroom Mouse and Joel had created for her, when it was obvious she needed support after losing Wendy, her best friend, in the summer.

Mouse shook her head. She knew it was pointless arguing. 'I give in. Shout out if you need a drink or anything, and don't forget to go to sleep.'

Naomi settled by her son's bedside, and stared at the mass of tubes leading into his battered body. His left arm was supported; it required surgery to put the bones back together, but for tonight it was held firmly in place. They said he had taken a massive blow to his head, and it was still touch and go, but they had to keep him sedated to allow him to heal.

She didn't care what they did as long as he did heal.

Tessa and Hannah's visit to Luke's home was heartbreaking. His sisters had been distraught, inconsolable, and it was clear his nan was struggling to cope.

'Who would want to hurt our Luke?' Geraldine kept saying, while cuddling the two young girls.

The older girl, Imogen, had appeared to be a bit more savvy than her younger sister, Rosie, and had asked Tessa if it was one of the bad guys Luke had come across in his work who had hurt him.

'We don't know yet,' was Tessa's response, and she smiled at the two girls. 'But we like your brother a lot, and I promise you we will find who did this to him. We have to focus on sending Luke nice thoughts to help him get better, don't we?'

Tessa's phone buzzed, and she excused herself to go out and take the call. The other car had been found, dumped on a side road in Hathersage. 'You're sure it's the right car?'

'Positive, ma'am. The left front is damaged where he hit the

Peugeot, and we can see the paint scrapings from the young lad's car. Forensics will prove it, we can only see it. We're waiting for the recovery vehicle now.'

'Thank you for letting me know. Out of interest, can you check with headquarters and see if we've had any reports of stolen cars tonight in the vicinity of where that car has been dumped. If he's dumped it, he needs transport to get away from it. Ring me back when you've checked.'

'Will do, ma'am.'

Tessa walked back into the lounge and saw that Rosie was almost asleep. 'We'll go,' Tessa said quietly. 'This is my card if you need anything.'

Hannah was subdued on the way home, and Tessa reached across and held her hand. 'I know it looked bad, but he had medical help quickly, and they know what they're doing at the hospital.'

'I'm thinking more about the Connection people – they'll be devastated by this. At least we can tell them we've got the car, and that will confirm, I'm sure, that it was Paul Fraser who was driving it. He has no fear, does he? He's the worst type of person for us to be looking for, because he doesn't care. And where the hell is he? He disappeared. We had nothing back from getting his face out there, and we've only been drawn to his car because he dumped it and left the driver's door wide open. A nosy neighbour saw him park it up, and simply stroll away from it. He's taunting us, Tess, bloody taunting us.'

11

K at quickly contacted Mark Playter, telling him all the details of Luke's attack. Mark immediately reassured her there would be two extra operatives on duty within the hour, and that he would assemble the family and pass her information on to them.

'Please,' she finished, 'tell them that if they need to contact me at any time, to ring. I don't think I'll sleep much anyway.'

'I will. Kat... are the three of you protected?'

'Yes, I've more equipment here than Durham jail, following the Leon period in my life, and we've moved Doris in with Beth until Fraser has been caught. I obviously have Carl with me, and he's organised drive pasts by the night shift at intermittent intervals throughout the night. Beth is pretty secure – the door next to the office is her access door, and then at the top of the stairs is another locked door before you can get into her flat. She also has CCTV covering both her door and the shop, cameras inside the office, and it's all linked to monitors in her flat. Her security is second to none, it's why we persuaded Doris and her cat to move in, until this is all over.'

Kat replaced the receiver and stood staring at the phone. She knew there was one more call she had to make.

'Mum... it's me.'

'I know, sweetheart, it says so on my screen.'

Kat could hear the smile in her mother's voice. 'Sorry, I'm a bit distracted. Is Martha okay?'

'She is. She's absolutely loved it. Our concerns that she might still be a bit young for a Father Christmas trip were unfounded, I'm telling you. She adored him. We've taken loads of pictures to show you what she's been up to... Kat, there's something wrong, isn't there?'

Kat felt her eyes fill with tears yet again. 'There is, Mum.'

Half an hour later, after having spoken in detail with both of her parents, they had agreed that Martha wouldn't come home until it was safe.

Kat went to bed hoping she had done enough to protect Martha, alongside her parents; Carl held Kat close until she drifted off into an uneasy and disturbed sleep.

Doris worked through the night. She needed to know every last little detail about Paul Fraser, about his connection to Bialik, to Julie Clark. Why had Fraser chosen her? He hadn't spoken a word during his trial, they only had Julie's testimony to go on, and he had simply said to her that he had watched her as she practised at the shooting range, knew she was a contender for the Olympic team, but more importantly knew she was happily married with a small child. Leverage.

And if he had been a better shot himself, he would

potentially have got away with it. He recognised he wasn't good enough to kill Bialik... Doris paused in her thoughts. Wasn't good enough, or was there some other reason he couldn't kill Bialik? A familial reason? A lover's reason? A health reason? Could he possibly have some medical issue such as an eye problem that prevented him being able to focus accurately?

Her brain buzzed with theories and she knew that everything boiled down to why he had had to kidnap Julie Clark so that she could carry out his plan to execute Konrad Bialik.

Everything led back to Bialik.

Doris thought long and hard about her next action, and she hit the new mail button. Her first email to him in many, many years. For the safety and security of her family, this had to be done and sometimes it had to be with the help of someone on a higher level. She began to type.

Saskia stared at Ollie, whose face was expressionless. She needed him to reach out, even if it were only to take her hand. With the attempt to kill Luke, the game had changed. She suspected he was angry; they all felt helpless, and even more so following Mark's relating of the evening's events.

'And have we heard how Luke is?' Saskia asked.

Mark shook his head. 'Nothing yet. It seems he'd called into the Connection office because as he drove past he spotted Mrs Lester was in. He stopped to see if she needed help with anything, and also to check on her because of this current situation. They eventually closed, Mrs Lester drove home, and so did Luke. He didn't get there. Nice lad, didn't deserve this.'

· · ·

Greg looked around the table. 'This makes it all the more imperative we don't move from the shelter of these walls.' He watched as all the heads nodded. 'Kaya, you're clear on that?'

Kaya lifted her head and nodded once more. She felt unhappy. She had enjoyed a few minutes of chatting with Luke when he attended the first visit to the house, and she had liked him. A lot. And she thought he had liked her. Now he was in a hospital bed with serious injuries and Greg was asking her if she understood the gravity of the situation. Too bloody right, she did. She felt her mother take her hand and squeeze it, and she turned to her. 'I do understand, Mum, I really do.'

'I know. We all do,' Tracy responded. 'Greg's not getting at you, he's worried. About everybody.' She looked around. 'Have we finished? Because if we have, I think Kaya and I will go and watch TV in our room. Julie, is there anything you need?'

Julie felt sick. All this trouble was on her head, and she could tell there was a feeling of panic creeping into the household. She forced a smile. 'No, I've had my medication, and Greg will help me into bed. Go, Tracy, I think Kaya needs you more than I do tonight. And, Kaya, don't worry. You're safe here.'

They watched as mum and daughter left the room, and then Mark turned to the remaining members of the family. 'Please don't leave by any doors that will lead to the outside. If you do, I cannot guarantee your safety. This man clearly doesn't care what he's doing, and hasn't really cared since the day he abducted you, Julie. He never said anything about where he lived, or where he was going?'

Julie shook her head. 'I thought he was going to rape me, so I stayed silent in case it sparked anything off. He said little while we were in the car, apart from giving me directions to Bialik's house. I had to believe he would let me go after I'd killed this man, who I was ultimately told was the kingpin for most of the drugs being brought into the country, akin to the head of the Mafia in Italy. I didn't know that at the time, and maybe if I had it would have been easier to pull that trigger...'

Julie looked at Greg. 'I'd like to go to bed now.'

Greg stood, and after Julie had wished everyone goodnight he followed his wife to their room.

Saskia left the table and moved to sit on the sofa, staring morosely at the Christmas tree. She hoped with everything she had that all this stuff would be over and done with by Christmas; nothing was more guaranteed to put Ollie off proposing to her than a mad gunman stalking them, especially one who intended killing each of them. And she so wanted that proposal.

Ollie moved to sit by her side and slipped his arm around her shoulders. 'You okay?'

She nodded. 'I am. I'll be glad when this is over, I need to go Christmas shopping, and we can't even order from Amazon.'

He took his arm from her shoulder. 'This isn't anything of our doing, you know. This is some crazy man who is full of revenge because he didn't kill Mum first time he had a go, and I'm sure the police will sort it.'

She realised she'd slipped up. She sensed his withdrawal, and she took his hand in hers. Turning to face him, she gave a gentle smile. 'I'm sorry. I'm feeling stressed, and it's making me selfish. And then there's Luke – I really hope he recovers, he seemed a genuinely nice person.'

'And that,' he said, squeezing her hand gently, 'is why we have to follow the rules. If we don't get Christmas shopping done, it's not the end of the world. We'll wait until Easter. Problem solved.'

She sighed. 'I know. And we can still use our phones, so I can ring Nan and Granddad and Petra.'

'Oh God! Petra! If this isn't over quickly, and it drags on beyond Christmas, she'll not be able to come.' Ollie pulled Saskia close.

'I know, let's hope they find him soon. She was really looking forward to coming here. I'm going to explain everything to her next time I ring. I know she'll understand, but it won't stop her being disappointed.'

The long night drew to a close. Naomi Taylor didn't sleep. They worked on Luke until he eventually arrived in intensive care, and she was called through to see him. He had tubes everywhere, his nurse explaining they were to keep him sedated. He needed time with his brain closed down.

Doris compiled a detailed file on Bialik. He had been the virtual drug overlord for everywhere south of Manchester, and had ruled his empire by force and threats. He had done a brief stint in prison for grievous bodily harm but it seemed the police could never pin anything heftier than that on him, and he had protection around him at all times. That protection didn't save him from a skilled marksman like Julie Clark, it seemed. There was a list of people who had worked for him that the police knew about, and there was a secondary list of people who had gone missing while being part of his entourage – occasionally the same name was mentioned on both listings.

It seemed the police had known of his penchant for killing people, but knowing and proving had been worlds apart; several of his workforce had served prison terms for crimes in which they hadn't really played much of a role, but she guessed they would have been financially rewarded, and their families cushioned.

She found the link between Bialik and Fraser around four in the morning. Fraser had suddenly appeared on the list of Bialik employees. Her eyes were itching, and she closed down her computer, climbed into bed and after sending healing thoughts and her love to Luke, dropped quickly into sleep.

In a large house in London a man got up. It was early. He dressed in joggers and left the house shortly after six to go for a run. By seven he was home and showered and heading into his office while he waited for Ursula to make his boiled eggs and toast. He switched on his computer as he routinely did at the same time every day, and picked up his newspaper, hoping the crossword would be a bit more difficult than the previous day's effort.

He heard the all-too-familiar pings as his computer registered incoming emails, usually from his staff who knew what time he was awake every day, and gave no concession to the fact that it was a Monday morning, and the start of another stressful week.

The door opened and Ursula entered carrying a tray of food and his hand-delivered mail.

'Good morning, sir. Not so much mail today.'

'Good morning, Ursula. I won't require a meal tonight, so take the day off when you've finished whatever you need to do. I'll see you in the morning.'

'Oh, that's nice.' She smiled. 'I'll catch the train up to Ware and have a couple of hours with Victoria and the baby. It'll give her a break, I know she's finding it hard being on her own.'

'Then give her my best wishes.' He took out his wallet and

removed two twenty-pound notes and a ten-pound one. 'Tell her this is for something for the baby.'

Ursula thanked him and left him to enjoy his breakfast, blessing the day she had arrived for her interview all those years ago.

Ursula closed the door quietly and took out her phone. Her daughter would be happy at this unexpected treat, and she intended making the most of every minute with this precious grandchild.

He placed his tray outside the door and returned to his desk. He pulled up his emails and saw he already had five work-related ones. And one from Doris Lester. His heart accelerated and he took deep breaths. Doris Lester.

12

The carving on the tree had announced to the world that Doris loved Alistair. He smiled as the picture memory flashed across his mind. Then, of course, she hadn't been Doris Lester, she had been Doris Freeman. And Doris Freeman had loved Alistair Glentham. Alistair Glentham had also loved Doris Freeman.

But their worlds had separated, and he had been sent by the Foreign Office to various parts of the globe. When he eventually came back home for a brief three months' respite to recover from a serious bout of pneumonia, she had become Doris Lester. He had lost her to that bloody waste of space, Harry Lester, who always wanted to be as bright, as intelligent, as smart as his wife, but never managed it.

Once Alistair's recovery was complete, he headed to Saudi Arabia and tried to forget Doris, but there had been nobody since who he wanted to be with every minute of every day. Oh, there had been dalliances, and he had considered that maybe Francesca Kray could be in the running to be the future Mrs Glentham at a time in his forties when he was having a midlife crisis, but he knew he would have been settling for second best.

What was more to the point, Francesca had also known she was second best.

A couple of times he and Doris had come across each other, either in reports or group emails as part of their work, but they had been strictly job-related. And now, one month before his seventieth birthday and his retirement from the Foreign Office, there was an email. He hesitated then worked through the five that had now become six that applied to his work. All were requests for his approval of different actions, and he had no hesitation in agreeing to them.

He clicked on Doris's email and swiftly read through it. It was a long missive, she had put a lot of thought into the words, and he reached the end and rubbed his forehead. 'Oh, Doris,' he murmured, and went back to the beginning to reread it.

He sent off a quick *I'll be in touch* and closed down his emails. Another screen opened at the touch of a key, and he entered in the name Konrad Bialik.

Tessa Marsden and Hannah Granger arrived at the Connection office before nine, having struggled with the early morning sun in their eyes for most of the journey. It was bitterly cold, and both were wrapped up in winter coats and scarves. Kat took them from them, and showed the two police officers into her office. Doris and Mouse were already waiting, coffees poured and biscuits in the middle of the table.

'Oh, you're absolute stars,' Tessa said. 'We didn't have time for anything at headquarters, it's bloody chaos there. They're chasing their tails off trying to find Fraser, but a man who doesn't care isn't going to be easy to track down.'

'We'd reached that conclusion,' Kat said. 'Come on, sit down and have a drink before we start, and tell us how you are. You settled in together at last?'

'We have. We're still a secret, of course, at work, but away from work we're happy.' Tessa turned and smiled at Hannah. 'Aren't we?'

'Sometimes,' Hannah said, trying to show a serious face. 'She doesn't like Henderson's Relish on everything, but I'll get over that. If I have to.'

Tessa reached across and picked up a biscuit. 'You got any Henderson's, ladies?' she said, and winked at them.

Hannah grinned. It was so obvious to the others, and had been for some time, that these two women were made for each other, but being open about it created problems at work, and everyone understood their reticence to speak of their new relationship.

'So, our Luke,' Tessa began. 'I understand he's stable. Bit of a worry at one point during the night, but his mum's with him. His nan is taking care of the two girls. I've asked to be updated if there's any change.'

'Any change?' Mouse looked aghast.

'Any change either way, Mouse,' Tessa said gently. 'He's in a really bad way, but he's young, he's fit, and we know he never gives in to anything without a fight. And with Reverend Kat and her boss on his side, he'll make it. I imagine you've talked to Him all night, haven't you, Kat?'

'I certainly have. We have a prayer meeting this evening, and we'll be holding him before God then, at that time. I know Naomi will have been doing the same, while she's been holding Luke's hand. Does he have police protection while he's in hospital?'

'He does. We have an officer outside his ward constantly, and we've said nobody can go in unless the officer knows who they are. We'll keep him safe, don't worry about that.'

'So,' Doris said, 'this man is a major problem. The car he used to take Luke off the road was stolen?'

'I'm not going to ask how you knew that, but yes it was.' Tessa opened her folder. 'It was stolen from Hathersage. And he took it back there, dumped it with its driver's door left open and disappeared. We believe he left his own car in the same area, and simply went back and picked it up. However, nothing is showing on CCTV from that locality, so it may even be that he is living in Hathersage.'

'That would make sense,' Mouse said. 'He would want to be close to his intended victims. He obviously knows where they live, so what was the information he wanted from Julie's parents, if that was the reason for targeting them?'

Tessa shrugged. 'Who knows. We do believe he used violence to get something from them, but when it wasn't forthcoming he killed them anyway. I don't think it was to intimidate or frighten the Clark family, that doesn't make sense. The whole team think he needed some information and he didn't reckon on family love. We can only use supposition, but if he thought there was a different way into the house say, he would reckon the parents would know about it. Or maybe he wanted the alarm code. If that was it, they didn't have it anyway. The Clarks change the settings on the first of every month, so they tell both sets of parents if they actually need to know at any time, rather than updating them every time they revise it. Greg's parents live in Spain anyway, so it never matters to them what the code is, and Julie's parents hadn't been told it for about three months. Even if they had been prepared to give it, they didn't know it.'

'An evil man,' Doris said quietly.

'So you're stopping your commission to find him?' Tessa looked troubled.

'No, of course not,' Kat said. 'We've taken on the job, and having Luke injured makes it even more imperative Fraser's found.'

'Kat, he's dangerous. I reckon he only went after Luke to give everybody the warning. He'll get to the Clarks' by hook or by crook. If he is resident in Hathersage then he'll have seen Luke's Peugeot on guard outside the Clark home, and he's probably rear-ended the car simply because he could, and because he recognised it.'

'And presumably you've no idea what he drives?'

'No, none.' Tessa stared at Doris. 'Doris... what do you know?'

'Nothing yet, but I promise you if I do find anything, you'll be the second to know.'

'The first, Doris, the first.'

'We're working for Greg and Julie. They're the ones who are paying us. But you will know quickly, I promise.'

'Doris Lester,' Hannah interrupted, 'you're sounding far too confident you'll find him. You do know something, don't you?'

'Precious little, but open your minds. This isn't about this crime that's happening now, it's about Konrad Bialik, the man Fraser had killed. That's where my concentration is at the moment.'

Kat stood and refilled the coffee cups, then sat down again. 'So,' she said, 'do you have anything to tell us?'

'Huh,' Tessa snorted, 'nothing that you didn't find out three days ago.'

Tessa and Hannah left half an hour later, amidst promises of calling in to the office during the week. Kat and Mouse both turned at the same time and stared at Doris.

'Okay, time to talk, Nan. You have found something, haven't you?'

'Not yet, not something that would stand up in court, but I'm waiting for the response to an email I sent about four this morning.'

'You were awake at four?'

'I was asleep by half past four.' Doris sounded defensive.

'So who did you email who could possibly know anything about Paul Fraser?'

Doris laughed. 'I do love you two girls, love your optimism that I would answer that question. Let's get back to work, and when I have something to tell you, I will.'

Luke was too still. Naomi kept stroking his hand and talking to him, careful to avoid touching his broken arm. The doctor had explained they would need to operate to set it, but they wanted to see signs of life first as it would have to be done under general anaesthetic. She talked to him all the time, but there was nothing. No response of any sort.

Her son, her rock. He had stepped up to become the man of the house when his father had walked out on them, and he had taught himself the intricacies of electrics, of minor repairs that needed doing around the place, even a little gardening. He couldn't die. She wouldn't let him die.

She picked up a newspaper one of the nurses had left for her, and read parts of it to Luke. She told him about the Brexit negotiations that were ongoing, reminded him of their family unified chant of 'Liar, liar, pants on fire' every time they saw Boris Johnson on television; she even read out the clues in the crossword, and smiled as the nurse in attendance answered one of the questions. But still there was no movement from the bed.

She couldn't feel his presence. That was the hardest part to bear. He always had a ready joke, or a response to everything that happened in the family unit, and now there was nothing.

The police had told her they believed they knew the person

responsible, but they hadn't managed to locate him. She hadn't asked why they thought that, hadn't asked anything really except 'will my son live?'

She was gently stroking his hand and telling him about a rogue lorry that had run away down a hill without its driver, and there had miraculously been no injuries. 'That's wonderful, Luke, isn't it? God's hand was at work there.'

The machine connected to Luke emitted a warning beep that didn't stop, and a flat line was showing on the monitor. Naomi screamed, and the nurse dropped the chart she was annotating to get to Luke's side. She hit the alarm button, and the door crashed open.

Naomi was ushered outside and the policeman on duty stood to let her sit on his chair. She was shaking.

'Trust the doctors, love, trust the doctors,' the policeman young enough to be her son said, as he put his arm around her to comfort her.

13

S lowly, the memories of Konrad Bialik and the events of twenty years earlier hit chords in Alistair Glentham and he loaded files from his computer onto a memory stick. Bialik had been a worthless piece of shit at the top of the tree as far as importation of drugs, of girls, of anything that could be sold on to make a profit. Particularly specialising in high value works of art, he had personally trained an elite team of people to steal the paintings before shipping them to the United Kingdom, and he had put his trust in a further team in the UK with the remit to place the pictures, and occasionally sculptures, with people prepared to pay a premium for works they could never display, other than in a hidden room.

All the information was downloaded; if this wealth of knowledge kept Doris alive, that was all the justification Alistair needed, and he would take full responsibility for what he was doing. He recognised she would have access to most of it, there were a few odd bits that had been made for his eyes only, and now they were for Doris's eyes. She had requested, he would provide. He spent the full day collating the information, such was the vast amount they had not only on Bialik but on the man who had arranged his execution, Paul Fraser.

He followed the link from Paul to Todd Fraser; there was nothing to say who Paul's father was, but Todd had been fathered by a man who had held Christy Fraser captive for several days, then simply walked away. She had only known him as Judd, and although she had reported it to the police because she had needed to be hospitalised following the brutal rapes over a six-day period, he had never been caught. A pregnancy had followed, and Todd had been born.

Alistair didn't finish until nine, and went out for a late meal to think over the work he had done during the day. There was no way he could send it by email, it would have to be delivered in person and again his heart rate accelerated a little at the thought of seeing Doris for the first time in a long, long time.

He knew she had lost Harry, and also their daughter Claire, but she seemed to be working now with her granddaughter Bethan. It appeared that seventy-year-olds didn't retire, they worked as long as they wanted to work.

Out of curiosity, and as a break from reading about Bialik and Fraser, Alistair had checked on Connection. He wasn't in any way surprised by what he read. There were simple reviews, yet all of them stressed reliability, speedy conclusions, reasonable rates.

He tried to picture how she would look now; they were the same age, and he had remained reasonably trim despite not following any sort of diet regime, his hair was silver grey, and he acknowledged to himself that he had more than a couple of lines on his face. He desperately hoped she wouldn't look at him and think *My God, you're an old man! When did that happen?*

His blue eyes closed briefly as he recalled her face the last time he had seen her, and he knew he would still see the same

Doris no matter how many years had passed. It was worth travelling to Eyam for one day, he knew it was. He could swan off to the South of France in March with no regrets then, waving a fond farewell to England.

The thought of his second home being prepared for full retirement reminded him he needed to check in with his builders, and he left money on the table to settle his bill. Marco gave a thumbs up that he had seen it, and Alistair strolled back to his home, keen to ring France and speak to Michel about his idea for an office space in the loft. He wanted a huge window; the views over the Mediterranean from St Raphael would be spectacular.

He poured himself a brandy and settled into his library to make the call. Conversing in French gave him a great deal of satisfaction, and as Michel had only limited English, they used the beautiful language for quarter of an hour, Michel making notes of Alistair's thoughts. He promised to get back to him the following day after doing some measuring in the loft space.

Michel reassured Alistair that all would be finished by the end of March, and he could look forward to a long hot summer on the French Riviera.

Alistair disconnected, picked up his brandy and stared into the glass, letting his thoughts go back to Doris. An exceptionally gifted woman, he knew she would have gone so much further in the Service if she hadn't been forced into looking after her granddaughter following her daughter and son-in-law's deaths. Her consultant status would always remain with her, as would her access codes, and he blessed the fact that his were higher than hers, and she had had to contact him.

He couldn't wait for his journey to Eyam – he reckoned he could be on his way by ten the following morning, and in Eyam by two at the latest, depending on traffic. He wouldn't use a driver; he rarely got the pleasure of driving his Bentley, and tomorrow he would take himself off for a couple of days.

He would send her an email to say he had some information for her, but omit to tell her it would be hand-delivered. He took out his phone, sent the briefest of emails, and switched it off. Perversely, he switched it back on. She might respond...

I'm coming to see you once more, Doris, he thought, *before I leave the country*. He took a final sip of his brandy to empty the glass, topped it up with water and took the tablets his doctor insisted he take, before climbing the stairs to bed. He placed his phone on the bedside table, and plugged it into the charger. No flat batteries required, not when he thought he might receive an email.

Doris heard the ping of an incoming email and picked up her phone. She smiled.

```
Collating information for you. It will be
with you tomorrow. Xxx
```

Three kisses. He had given her three quick kisses as he had left for the airport fifty years earlier, on his way to his first overseas posting. These were the only kisses she had received from him since that awful day when, despite his words, she had known he wouldn't be back and it was over between them.

She took a quick screen shot of the message, not trusting herself with the delete button; she was liable to delete and then regret.

She returned to her Kindle, snuggled lower in bed and read. Her thoughts kept wandering to Luke and away from the book she was trying to follow, so she switched it off, sent her thoughts to Luke, and closed her eyes.

. . .

It was a long hour and a half before Naomi was reunited with her son. The doctors wouldn't give in, wouldn't let him die; they finally stabilised him, and eventually led Naomi back to his side. Her eyes were raw and itchy, so many tears had been shed. The police officer, whose name turned out to also be Luke, had been so gentle, so understanding, and he had let her cry.

She reached his side, a complete wreck emotionally. The doctor explained Luke's body had tried to give in, but they had worked hard to stabilise him. He wouldn't be allowed to surface anytime soon, but eventually he would, and then they would know what damage, if any, had been done.

Alistair had left London in bright sunshine, cold and crisp. Once he'd left the extremities of the capital he relaxed, and the beautiful Bentley ate up the miles with ease.

He thought of Ursula's face when he had said she could take whatever time off she wanted, he anticipated being away two or three days and he would ring when he knew when he was coming home. He had discussed his retirement plans with her and knew she was retiring to live nearer her daughter; at first she had been shocked. Then she thought he was ill and not telling her the full story. She took some convincing that he had actually decided it was time to move to warmer climes, and where better than the South of France.

Now they spoke freely of their retirement years, with both of them relishing the idea of freedom from the workday life.

And then along came Doris once more, doing the unthinkable and stirring everything up inside him. He indicated to come off the motorway, deciding a coffee was needed, and by the time he re-entered the northbound traffic of the M1 he felt refreshed, and aware that the sun had disappeared. He shivered as he climbed back into the Bentley, and turned up the heating a notch.

Eyam is a pretty village, steeped in the history of The Plague. The cottages where the residents had lived and died during that terrible year were preserved, and the whole village was immortalised by death. He would ask Doris to show him the historical sites before he returned to London, Alistair decided.

He pulled into the side of the road and glanced around, checking he wasn't violating parking restrictions. He guessed there would be a few dotted around the village for when summer visitors turned up here en masse. He had made good time, even allowing for his brief stop for coffee, and it was only one fifteen. Would she be at work given the pressure Connection was currently experiencing, or would she be doing the sensible thing and sheltering away from the world? He smiled. She would be in work.

He realised after sitting there for ten minutes that he was putting it off. What if she froze him out? Took the information he had brought, and said 'Thank you, I'll take it from here'?

Time to find out. He switched on the engine, indicated to pull out and felt the car begin to gently accelerate down the hill. He saw the shop and rolled slowly past it before stopping.

You have reached your destination.

'Thank you, Clarissa,' Alistair said automatically, and stopped the engine. For a moment it felt as though the silence engulfed him. He pulled down the mirror and checked his hair looked okay, then opened the driver's door. Whatever he had faced during his long career was as nothing to how he felt getting out of that car and preparing to walk to a shop.

He tugged on his jacket, clicked his key fob to lock the car, and turned. He took a deep breath, and headed towards Connection, noting the shutters were up so there had to be somebody in the shop.

'Please let it be Doris,' he whispered.

14

Doris noticed the Bentley, travelling slowly, as it passed the large office window, and she stopped what she was doing. Sitting at Luke's desk gave her a much wider view of the world outside the office, and being on edge for anything suspicious didn't help at all. A Bentley was pretty unusual, and she stiffened as she saw the car door open.

The man was tall, with silver-grey hair that matched her own. Not Paul Fraser then, and she relaxed slightly until the point when he turned.

He hadn't had silver-grey hair when she had last seen him, but he had had that face. 'Oh my God,' she said, almost inaudibly. Panic rose in her, and she took deep breaths as she watched the same confident walk come towards her that she remembered from first knowing him.

Almost in a dream, she moved towards the office door and released the security lock. 'Alistair.'

'Doris.'

'You haven't changed a bit,' they both said, then laughed.

'I had grey hair in my twenties, did I?' Doris said.

'Yes. Amazingly, like I did. Can I come in, or do I need to be searched first?'

'I'll vouch for you.' As she moved aside for him to get into the reception area, Kat's office door opened.

'Everything okay?'

'It's fine, Kat.' Doris smiled. 'This is a friend of mine from many years ago. Honestly, there's nothing to concern you. I'm going to make a drink. Do you want one?'

Kat shook her head. 'No, but I'll take over reception for a bit. Use your office while you feed chocolate digestives to your friend.' She held out her hand. 'Kat Heaton.'

'Alistair Glentham,' he said, and shook the proffered hand. 'Good to meet you, Kat. And I promise Doris is in no danger, ever, from me.'

Beth's door opened. 'Okay?'

Alistair laughed. 'Are these two lovely ladies your bodyguards?'

Kat spluttered. 'Are you kidding? She's our bodyguard. Mouse, this appears to be Nan's friend who we know nothing about. Alistair, this is Beth Walters, Doris's granddaughter. We're all equal partners in Connection.'

Doris's cheeks were turning a delicate shade of pink. If she'd known of Alistair's arrival she could have prepared, could have told them he was coming, that he was a colleague from her working days, but no, she was left flustered, uncomfortable and slightly amused at how quickly the girls had jumped to her defence. Paul Fraser had a lot to answer for.

Doris took control. 'Alistair, would you like to follow me. This is my office,' and she opened her door. He smiled at Kat and Mouse, and left them with open mouths, looking at each other and shrugging in unison.

. . .

Kat moved towards Luke's desk, and sat, surveying outside and spotting the Bentley. 'Crikey,' she said under her breath, 'who is this feller?'

She pulled the desk diary towards her, feeling a little guilty she hadn't checked it earlier. She was so used to Luke saying she had appointments, and as she opened the book she said a little prayer that she hadn't missed anything.

She hadn't, but Luke had. He had an appointment to see Henry the Philanderer's wife at two. She glanced at her watch, saw she had five minutes left, and picked up the phone.

'Mrs Little? Hi, my name is Kat Heaton of Connection. I'm sorry, but Luke won't be able to meet with you today...'

'It's good to see you,' Doris said quietly, 'even if it's a little unexpected. A lot unexpected.' She placed their coffees on the desk.

'If I had said I was coming, what would you have said?'

She hesitated for a moment, thinking. 'I would have assumed that whatever you have found for me, is better not being sent by any means other than personal delivery.'

He smiled. 'And not only are you as beautiful as ever, you're as smart as ever.'

He reached into his pocket and took out a flash drive. 'When you've taken off everything you can use, please wipe it.'

'Of course, and thank you so much.'

'You explained a lot in your email – first of all, how is Luke?'

'In a coma. It seems they need to close him down to let his brain recover. His mum rang this morning to say she thought she'd lost him during the night, but the staff battled and brought him back. It's pretty serious, Alistair, and we're confident it's all down to Paul Fraser.'

'The police have locked down the Clark family?'

'We have. The Clarks are paying for protection which we've provided, and after last night it's been upped by a further two operatives. Talk to me about Fraser, Alistair. We're being paid to find him. The police will apprehend him, obviously, but our remit is to find him. Apparently, I'm not allowed to kill him for what he's done to Luke, but I hope I'm in the room when we do find him.'

'You keep up with your karate, then?' He laughed.

'How did you...?'

'How did I know? If you think for one minute I haven't followed your life, you're mistaken, Doris Lester. I couldn't contact you, not even when Harry died, because I figured I wasn't wanted in your life after disappearing for all those years with the job, but that didn't mean I couldn't keep an eye on you. And to get that email yesterday, had me riding to Derbyshire on my white charger.'

'It's a black Bentley.'

The lines at the corners of his eyes crinkled when she smiled. 'You saw it? Nice car.'

'Not as nice as mine.'

'Yours is the red Jeep?'

'It is. Had two men in this office virtually fighting over it yesterday. How did you guess that car was mine? Kat's and Mouse's cars are outside also.'

'It fits you. The car fits you.'

She nodded. She knew what he meant. 'So, Paul Fraser.'

'Put in the flash drive.' Alistair stood, picked up his chair and moved around the desk to sit beside her. She tingled. Never in a million years would she have guessed she would be this close to Alistair Glentham again.

He reached across the desk and pulled his coffee towards him. The information appeared on screen, and he leaned forward.

'I believe I've found everything we have on him. He's evil, Doris. Totally uncaring about what he does, who he hurts. We have no idea who his father was, and his mother died about a year ago, while he was in prison. His brother visited him regularly, and this is where I think your search has to start. Todd Fraser has dropped off the radar over the past six months. He's the older brother, and from what we know he protected Paul during their childhood. They both dealt drugs, and while Paul was a user, Todd wasn't. Todd had epilepsy, and his episodes increased with the use of even marijuana, so he steered clear of any drug that wasn't related to his illness.'

'And you've no idea where Todd is? You think he's harbouring Paul?'

'I think it's highly likely. It seems the epicentre of this is Hathersage. I've never been there so I can't really picture it. I checked it out on Google Earth, but I think we need to go there. I also want the tour of Eyam. Fascinating place.'

Doris stared at him. 'You're here overnight?'

'Two. Maybe three nights. I need to find a pub or a hotel or something, so I'm hoping you can suggest a nice place. Are you at Bradwell still? There's a place there, The Bowling Green, that does bed and breakfast.'

'How could you possibly know I live at Bradwell?'

'I shamelessly check on you occasionally, and to be honest, everything that is updated on our operatives passes through my hands eventually. It stands out when I see your name.'

'You're right, I do live in Bradwell, but I'm currently staying upstairs here. Mouse owns this building, along with the flat upstairs. I have a room there whenever I need it, and she and Kat have insisted I stay there until we sort this out. The security on my cottage isn't as good as our security here.'

'So is there someone in Eyam who does bed and breakfast?'

'There is.' With a couple of keystrokes she brought up the

Cambridge B&B, and he copied down the number. Within seconds he was booked in for two nights, but mentioned he might need it for three.

Doris's head was in a whirl. She was no more sure now than she was when she sent Alistair the email asking for any information he could glean on Fraser; had she done the right thing?

Alistair left to go and book in at his 'home' for a couple of nights, promising to be back as soon as he had done so.

As soon as the Bentley pulled away from the kerb, Kat knocked on Mouse's door, and they waltzed into Doris's office.

'Okay, elderly lady, where did that rather attractive gentleman appear from, and how come you're blushing?' Kat grinned as she spoke.

'Nan?' Mouse said.

'He was my boss for a number of years, but we haven't met up for many years. I've known him since I was twenty-two.'

'Twenty-two? That's a lifetime.'

'Were you lovers?' Mouse was nothing if not blunt.

Doris's face was starting to resemble a beetroot. 'That's for me to know and you to wonder about.'

'You were then. Was he before you met Granddad?'

'Stop asking questions, Mouse.'

'Huh. Fat chance. You split up?'

'Yes, if you must know. He was sent abroad. We worked together, which was how we met, and he showed exceptional promise so was sent to several different foreign embassies. They said it would broaden his horizons. By the time he came back I had married Harry. Since then we've been in contact a couple of times, but it's always been strictly business. As this is. Now, instead of jabbering on about my non-existent love life, has anybody been in touch with the Clarks?'

'I have,' Mouse said. 'They're fine, lying low, and behaving themselves. They asked about Luke so I told them as much as we know. I spoke to Mark also. He's suggested we run a check on the people who aren't family members, so that's Tracy and Kaya Worrall, Saskia van Berkel and the gardener. I can't remember his name for the moment, but he's not currently there anyway, as you know, Greg told him to take some time off.'

'Then let's check out the other three. I also want a check running on Todd Fraser, he seems to be off the radar. We need to know where he's living. We need bank details for him, then we can follow cash withdrawal trails. He might be in hiding and sheltering his brother, but he still needs money.'

'Is Alistair eating with us tonight?' Mouse asked.

'You've changed the subject.'

'Is he?'

'As long as you promise not to question him about what may or may not have gone on in the past, I think he'll welcome that. But I'm warning you, Mouse...'

'Nan, stop it. You terrify me.' Mouse laughed.

'I'll disinherit you.'

'Then I'll put you in an old people's home, elderly lady. I can fight back, you know.'

All three dissolved into laughter.

'Do you really want to know why Alistair is here? And it's the only reason...'

'We do,' was the chorus.

'He hand-delivered this,' and she held up the flash drive. 'He brought it himself because he wanted no evidence of its existence. Okay?'

'Okay,' they said solemnly. 'We believe you. Not many would, of course, but if that's your instruction, we'll believe every word you say.'

'Do not,' Doris repeated firmly, 'interrogate this man tonight or any other night. Is that understood?'

'Any other night?' Kat and Mouse looked at each other. 'He's here for a bit then?'

Doris ushered them out of her office. 'Go and play, girls. Get out of my room. And stop asking questions!'

15

In the cold and rain, night arrived early. By four o'clock it was dark, and it was silent. Inside the house it was also quiet; Kaya was in the room she was currently sharing with her mother, and Tracy was downstairs attending to Julie, helping her have a shower and take her medication.

Greg was on a conference call in his office, and Saskia and Ollie had retired to the kitchen to prepare the evening meal ready for when everyone began saying they were hungry. Monday night was always easy – chips and cold meat left from the Sunday roast, with lots of fresh bread and an assortment of pickles. It was always followed by a defrosted dessert for anyone still feeling the need for more.

Saskia was peeling potatoes when she heard, and felt, the thud. She looked at Ollie, who had heard nothing because his earphones were in as he listened to *Kamikaze*, Eminem's newest offering that Ollie had decided was the best thing he'd heard in a long time. He was tapping a beat out on the kitchen table with the carving knife he was supposed to be using to slice the cold joint.

'Ollie,' Saskia said, staring at the kitchen window, the blind obscuring everything outside. 'Did you hear that?'

There was no answer. 'Ollie!' Saskia shouted, and he pulled out one of the ear buds. 'Yes? You want me?'

'Did you hear that thump from outside?'

He glanced towards the window, then took hold of Saskia's hand and pulled her into the hallway. 'Don't move from here,' he said. 'Nobody can get to you in the hall.' He hit the newly installed alarm button that would notify Mark they had a problem.

Immediately Mark rang. 'Get everybody in the hall. Are you all safe?'

Ollie confirmed they were, and still carrying the carving knife, he walked towards his mother's treatment room and knocked.

'Come in,' Tracy called.

'Tracy, is it convenient to leave Mum?'

'Yes, we were only chatting. Why?'

'Saskia heard a thump from outside. I'm not taking chances. Go up to Kaya and bring her into the hall. Mum, I'm wheeling you into there as well. It's the safest spot, with all the doors closed.' Tracy grabbed the wheelchair and moved her patient quickly, then ran upstairs to Kaya. Saskia positioned the wheelchair to one side and Ollie went to his father's office.

Greg had finished his call seconds before and was mulling over some changes he would need to implement. He stood as Ollie explained. 'You've hit the button?'

'I have and I've confirmed we're all safe. They'll be checking now. What if it's nothing?'

'How can a thud be nothing? It's something even if it's a bird flying into the back door or the kitchen window. Come on, let's go to the hallway and check everybody's okay. They'll be scared anyway.'

. . .

Tracy had her arm around Kaya, who looked bleary-eyed. She had fallen asleep during *Countdown*, and Tracy had had to wake her.

'Any news?' Julie asked.

'Nothing from Mark yet. He'll contact us when it's safe. I don't want to ring him in case it would alert this Fraser bloke to his presence. It might be nothing, but let's stay here until we know we're free to move around.'

The three chairs were taken by Kaya and Tracy sharing one, Saskia and Ollie sharing another and Greg facing the front door. Five minutes passed, and there was a ping on Ollie's phone. He looked at the text message and then at the others. 'Mark's coming in through the front door in two minutes.'

Ollie and Greg stood as the key went into the front door lock, and they visibly relaxed as they saw Mark.

'Everything okay?' Greg asked.

'No. Denny was covering the back area. He's been shot.'

Greg stood, alarm showing.

'It's okay, it hit him in the calf. He's down and it's painful, but not life threatening. An ambulance is on its way, and everybody is out there covering him. I'm going to bring him through the back door into the kitchen, but I need all of you to stay in the hall. The ambulance will drive around to the back of the house, so keep the front door locked and bolted, and I'll stay with Denny. Police are in attendance also. There's no need for panic, we have it covered. Ollie, can you notify Connection, please?'

. . .

The call to Connection came through as Alistair returned, having checked in at his bed and breakfast. Doris was speaking to Ollie as Alistair came through the door, and he saw the expression on her face.

'Okay, Ollie,' she was saying. 'Thank you for letting us know, and please tell Mark I'm so sorry Denny's hurt, he's one of my favourites. I take it Mark believes it was Fraser? And armed police are in attendance? Is DCI Marsden there? Or DS Granger? If they are, or they turn up, tell them I'm staying with Beth so we're available at the office if either wants to see us.' She disconnected.

'Problems?' Alistair asked.

She explained what had happened, and frowned. 'I have to go through this file, Alistair, I have to find him. And he clearly didn't shoot to kill Denny – was it simply a warning?'

'Probably not. Why do you think he needed somebody who could shoot to kill Bialik? Look, on that stick are a lot of the answers to all your why questions. Let's make a start. And can I take you out to dinner later, or even a takeaway if you don't feel safe outside?'

'Oh... I forgot to mention. We're eating with Beth and Joel if that's okay. Joel's a pretty smart guy, so maybe we can throw ideas around while we eat. Are you happy with that?'

Happy? I'm bloody over the moon, woman.

'Yes, that would be lovely. But I need to talk to you in complete privacy. And I'll be telling you stuff that's been locked down, but I did the locking down. I know you signed the Official Secrets Act, and that signature's never been more important. You will have to choose what to tell your partners carefully.'

'Then let's go into my office. We can finish for the day anyway. Kat's gone home, and I'll send Mouse up to her flat.'

. . .

Doris locked the office door and brought down the shutter. Connection was closed.

She made them coffees, and they sat side by side, documents open on both her laptop and her second monitor.

'As you've probably realised, because I know how you think, everything that's happening now with Julie Clark is because of Konrad Bialik. In 1999 a young man was pulled over by traffic police, and because he was a gibbering wreck in their estimation, they searched his car. They'd actually only stopped him for a rear light not working. They found a bag of heroin under the spare wheel. He was arrested, and there began a real merry-go-round of a story.'

Alistair clicked on an image and a photo appeared on screen. 'This is that man. His name is irrelevant because we ended up putting him into witness protection and helped him leave the country. He's nothing to do with the current situation because he died two years ago, heart failure.'

Doris waited. Alistair was clearly putting things into order in his mind. 'When the police questioned him about the heroin, he fell apart. He said he worked for Bialik and he was terrified. He had witnessed Bialik himself use a small electric jigsaw to cut off a man's toes on one foot, then drip acid into that man's left eye. He said the man's name was Paul Fraser, and they had made his brother Todd watch while they did it, sending a highly effective message to Todd and an even more effective one to Paul. Paul Fraser's crime was that he had withheld two grand after a drug delivery for Bialik.'

Alistair took a sip of his coffee and picked up a biscuit. 'Don't let me have any more of these,' he said, waving the offending chocolate digestive around. 'The chap we picked up, let's call him Arthur, had done exactly the same thing and he was terrified, because he'd watched it all at the same time. The heroin we found in his car he was taking to sell on to get the money he was short, but he'd stolen it from Bialik's stash anyway. They'd have blinded him in both eyes and cut both feet off. The upshot was he talked. He gave us names, locations, Paul and Todd Fraser's address, he sold Bialik out. We then "found" Arthur's body in the Thames, had a funeral for him and hid him away in a little flat in Yorkshire, near Huddersfield. He spent time changing his appearance – when we first met him he had long dark hair in a ponytail – but he had it cut and turned it blond and he deliberately put on some weight. He was really skinny the first time I saw him. He also came off the drugs completely. I tell you, Doris, I've never met anybody before or since who was so scared. He talked constantly about the gag around Paul Fraser's mouth, and the screams that couldn't escape fully because of that red gag as Bialik jigsawed his toes off. He said Bialik smiled all the way through it. Todd was sick in a corner, and then when they got the acid out, Todd tried to go outside but they forced him to watch. They held one eye open and used an eye dropper to blind him. They left Todd there to sort out his brother.'

'Dear gods,' Doris said quietly. 'So it was revenge. And I'm assuming being blinded in one eye is the reason he needed someone else to shoot Bialik, because he wasn't able to aim straight from a distance. He knew he would never get up close and survive it.'

'Yes. He didn't aim straight with Julie Clark, his intention was to kill her. But there's even more to the story with regard to Bialik. He did us no favours by killing him. Once Arthur had told us everything he knew, we put together a comprehensive case against him. You worked on that, probably without knowing why, and you really dug deep to find out every last little thing about the man.'

Doris nodded. 'I know, I've already reread that document. It didn't particularly help, but I knew it was part of something much bigger, which was why I had to contact you.'

Alistair turned to her. 'I can't begin to tell you how I felt when I saw your name in my inbox. When this is over, I don't want to lose contact again. I retire shortly, and you won't be able to get in touch with me anymore on that email address so I'm giving you my personal one.'

Doris touched her cheeks. Suddenly they felt as if a fire was raging inside her. 'Thank you. I'd like that. But this is urgent – let's find Fraser.'

He clicked on another picture. 'This is Bialik, taken about a week before he was killed. When we had got everything we could possibly get from Arthur, and we put our experts onto him to drag every last morsel out of him, we then built a case against Bialik. We did it quickly, because we didn't want him getting any insider knowledge and going after his missing Arthur for the money he owed, and two of us went to bring him in for questioning.'

He nursed his coffee mug, studiously ignoring the biscuits. 'That day was the beginning of the end for many of the drug barons all over the country.'

16

'You arrested him? I heard nothing about that if you did.'

Alistair laughed. 'No, not exactly. He was quiet, polite, offered us coffee – a bit like coming here really,' he said with a grin.

'You expected trouble?'

'We did. We'd gone in with microphones on and three police cars full of coppers outside. He sent out his bodyguard or whatever he was, and we told him we wanted him to accompany us to the station. He said he had an appointment at the hospital for 12.15 for chemotherapy, and would it be okay if he came to the station the following day. I tell you, Doris, we stared at him. It was the old cliché of the rug being pulled from under us, only this time it was a carpet. I asked for proof, and he showed me the letter. It was his first session of chemo and he had bowel cancer. Incurable bowel cancer.'

'Go on, be honest, Alistair. Did a small part of you think what goes around comes around? He'd killed so many people, tortured, sold drugs...'

'I did, but the man in front of me seemed to have come to terms with it. Don't get me wrong, we didn't get any confessions out of him, but he came over to the side of the angels in a way. He realised we'd got enough on him after Arthur's help, and I don't suppose he fancied spending the rest of what he had left in a prison cell, because if we'd interviewed him at the station that day, we would have charged him. We were fully prepared when we went to pick him up. He wouldn't have got bail, not with the stuff we had on him, he'd have gone down for the rest of his life. As proof that he had things to tell us he gave us a name, a name we knew, and he gave us an account sheet of sorts which showed how much cocaine was finding its way to Middlesbrough. We ended up cutting a deal with him for information supplied, knowing he only had about eighteen months of life left anyway, and we took down loads of villains. Operation Sweep-up, we called it, because that's what we did. Todd and Paul Fraser had disappeared by this time, and then suddenly, about a year later, Paul resurfaces, takes Julie Clark and forces her to shoot Bialik. He was at the end, was Konrad, when he was killed. The autopsy showed he couldn't have lasted much longer than a month. Julie's survival and DNA evidence, which we didn't reveal was semen, put Fraser where he belonged, in prison, but Todd was never charged with anything. At the time of his death we were working with Bialik, we had an undercover officer in with him who he knew about but nobody in contact with him did. I don't believe anybody ever found out how much he had helped us, and I actually grew to appreciate his fine brain and ability to plan, but in all fairness that was how he'd built his drug and trafficking empire, that cleverness and his planning skills.'

Doris leaned back in her chair. 'That's awful. Julie's been in a wheelchair for all this time unnecessarily. So, now I understand the situation, does this help in any way towards finding these two brothers? Has Todd managed to keep out of prison all these years?'

'He has. We know precious little about him really. He's

always visited Paul and, believe it or not, Paul has never been in any bother inside. Maybe there's some kudos in the criminal fraternity if you manage to kill someone of the stature of Konrad Bialik. He's been left alone, he's found God, and he managed to con the parole board into releasing him. He's played a long game, played it extremely well, and he's after Julie Clark to finish everything off. Possibly Greg and Oliver also, as that was the original threat to get Julie to do his bidding.'

'Do either of the brothers have any connection to property in this part of the world?'

'I couldn't find anything. I checked last night while I was downloading files for you. They're probably using false names.'

Doris's brain was churning. She had a couple of friends who were connected to estate agencies and could contact them, but she certainly didn't have the broadness to cover the entire Peak District. She sent off two emails as the start of their search for a property that was currently housing two middle-aged men, and was about to set up a search expedition on her laptop when the telephone rang.

'Doris? It's Naomi.'

Doris felt sick. 'Naomi? How... how is Luke?'

'He's opened his eyes! I had to tell you. He's closed them again now, but he opened them and closed them straight away. I told the nurse who sent for a doctor, and as the doctor bent over him, Luke opened them again. Luke said "Mum". Doris, he said "Mum". It seems he started to wake up on his own, so they've reduced his sedation to let him surface naturally. The doctor said it may take some time, and we'll have to be patient, but the signs are looking good. Oh, Doris...' and Naomi cried.

'Naomi, you have to go home and get some sleep. Leave Luke to rest until he wakes on his own, you know the signs are positive now. You'll be no good to him if you're wrecked. Have you got transport? I can come and get you if not.'

'No, I'm fine, honestly. I only wanted you to know. I'll stay another hour or so, and then I'll grab a taxi. You can come and see him once he wakes up.'

Doris laughed. 'I'll be waiting outside his door. Give him my love, Naomi, and tell him I'll be there soon.'

Doris replaced the receiver and smiled at Alistair. 'He opened his eyes and knew his mum was there.'

'Wonderful. He's a nice lad?'

'Oh God, he's the best. We advertised for an office junior, and got Hercule Poirot. He's taken to this business and never once complained. We've had some real laughs when we've been out on surveillance despite the age difference of over fifty years. He takes every course I organise for him and he attends the dojo with me, doing really good there also. A proper smart chap is our Luke. He has his own cases now, and I merely sign his invoices off at the end.'

'A good find then, a bit like my Ursula.'

Doris stiffened. 'You have a partner?'

Alistair laughed. 'Not a partner in that sense, no. Ursula is my housekeeper. She's been with me for a long time – her daughter was part of the package at first, but Victoria has moved to Ware and has a newborn baby, so we're both going to retire at the same time, and Ursula is going to live near Victoria. I, on the other hand, will be retiring to the South of France, to live in what is currently my holiday home but is being refurbished to make it a little more luxurious as it's going to be my full-time home.'

'You'll be selling up in London?'

'It's going on the market after Christmas. My initial thoughts were to rent it out, but I really don't want the hassle of being a landlord, especially a long-distance one, so I've decided to sever all links and sell it. You're happy here?'

'I am. I have a lovely cottage in a beautiful village in the heart of the Peak District. Mouse is settled with Joel, and although Kat is no relation genetically, I think of her as my granddaughter, and she is happily married to a police officer and has a little girl, so I have a good life. And maybe over the next couple of days I'll tell you about my extended family who live in Hucknall, but not today. Today we have to track the Fraser brothers. You think they're definitely together?'

'I do,' Alistair said, emphasising his words with a nod. 'Since their mother died Todd has been missing. Paul had every reason to feel optimistic that he would be let out on licence, he's been a model prisoner. How can anybody keep up nineteen years of good behaviour? He was the right-hand man for the prison chaplain, never missed a service, even played the piano for the services. It seems he was a natural musician, and had begun to have piano tuition when he was younger. He carried it on once they got him banged up.'

'Good job Bialik cut off his toes and not his fingers then,' Doris said drily and Alistair laughed.

'Not lost your sense of humour then. All of this sweetness and light and remorse was leading up to that parole board. He was warned when he went inside that his sentence would most likely mean whole-life because of the nature of the crime, coercing somebody else to take a life then shooting the coerced person himself. He figured he wanted out, and the only way to do it was to behave himself. It seems it was all about revenge. I reckon, if Julie Clark had died that night there's a hell of a possibility we would never have known who killed Bialik, there were too many suspects. He'd managed to upset a lot of people, Fraser included. Fraser was a minor player, and I don't think he would ever have come to our attention. We'd have looked at the likes of the people he was giving up to us, the big noises in the underworld, not the nondescripts. But Julie lived, and could identify him. We also confirmed that ID with the DNA he left after he raped her.'

'You are aware that Greg Clark doesn't know his wife was raped?'

'Yes, I did know. She asked us not to reveal it if it was possible. Was there a reason she didn't tell him?'

'Fraser gave her an STD, and I think she felt ashamed. She asked the doctors who treated her not to say anything, which they wouldn't have done anyway, and she kept it to herself until she met us. She sent Greg to the car to get her inhaler and while he was out she told us. She wanted us to have all the facts.'

'They're a nice family?'

'They're lovely. Oliver is their only child, and he's got a girlfriend, Saskia van Berkel, who is at the house with them, although I'm not convinced that's a permanent arrangement. She was supposed to be there anyway over Christmas, and her twin sister was to join them, but that depends on finding the Frasers.'

'Is she Dutch?'

'She is. Pretty, although a little clingy, I feel. There's also a lady called Tracy Worrall and her daughter Kaya. Kaya is still at school, she's fifteen, but I've been in touch with the school and explained the situation. Tracy, her mum, is Julie's live-in carer, been there since Kaya was little, so a long time now. And that's it. Normally Tracy and Kaya live in a granny annexe in the back garden, but they're currently sharing a room in the house. The police wanted to move them all out to a place of safety, but Julie has complex medical needs, and their own home is set up specifically for her, so they said they couldn't leave.'

'Can I meet them?'

'I'll ring them and take you tomorrow. I believe Ollie is going at nine to identify his grandparents, so if we go in the afternoon he'll be back. He's another fine young man, like Luke. This bloody Fraser has a lot to answer for. Let's close down and put it on hold till tomorrow, when I want to do a bit of ferreting to find where they could be staying. I know it's somewhere close, I can sense it. Come on, we'll head up to the flat, and enjoy this meal. Mouse will be getting desperate to question you by now.' Doris laughed. 'Ignore her, she'll soon get the message.'

They stood and he kissed her lightly on the cheek. 'Thank you for this, Doris. I'm sure I'll enjoy Mouse's company, and I'm looking forward to meeting Joel.'

Doris's cheeks glowed once again, and she gently touched the spot where he had kissed her.

17

The Christmas carol playing quietly in the background was 'God Rest ye Merry Gentlemen', and Todd Fraser sang along to it, misremembering half the words. He hadn't bothered putting up a tree, figured one way or another they'd be out of the house by Christmas anyway, leaving it empty until next time they wanted a bolthole.

He was worried about Paul. They'd discussed his plans for getting to Julie Clark so many times over the years, but if Todd was brutally honest with himself, he thought they were all flights of imagination; he never thought for a minute they would let Paul back out into the community.

For the first week Paul had behaved himself, checking in with the police, his social worker, and any bugger else who wanted to check on him, but then he'd walked away from all that, and the two of them had come to the house their mother had lived in for the last three years of her life.

He felt on edge. The house was traceable. Christy owned it. What the police possibly didn't know was that she had married Lonnie Brown three years earlier, but then Lonnie had gone to meet his maker unspectacularly, sitting by the river, fishing rod by his side and a float bobbing up and down with a fish attached to the hook. The house had automatically gone to Christy as his wife, and then on to Todd in her will when she followed Lonnie a year later. She too had never imagined her younger son would ever get out of prison.

Todd had never lived in it. He had explained to Paul why he had got it, and Paul hadn't seemed bothered. It was only when Todd had briefly mentioned selling it that Paul became agitated and asked him to keep it, it might come in handy he had said, when he got out.

And it had. So here they both were, him singing along to Christmas music, drinking lager at breakfast time and Paul zonked out in bed after getting bladdered the previous night.

Paul had been out in the car during the afternoon and before he'd started drinking, which meant he'd been out with the gun. Todd hoped to God he hadn't been taking pot shots at rats or rabbits – he could have hit anything, his eyesight was so bad.

Todd felt thankful that talk of getting even with Julie Clark for sending him down seemed to have dried up; now they only had to deal with the police looking for him because he wasn't reporting to anybody.

The carol changed to 'Away in a Manger', and he knew most of the words to that one. He slurped the lager, and stood to put some toast in the toaster. He seemed to be living on toast.

'The little Lord Jesus lay down his small head,' he sang, almost getting the words correct as he struggled to remember what came next.

He put marmalade onto the toast and sat at the kitchen table, wondering what to do about Paul. The blood on his clothes from a few days earlier had been a bit of a worry. He said he'd been in a fight, but there were no bruises or marks on him, only blood. At first he thought he'd stuck to his plan and killed that woman who seemed to possess him all the time, but there'd been nothing in the papers about somebody called Julie, only a couple of pensioners who'd been murdered. He couldn't imagine Paul would know them, so that ruled them out for the blood.

Todd walked to the window, still nibbling on his toast, and having given up on 'Away in a Manger'. He watched as his neighbour, Nosy Edna as she was in his mind, crossed the road towards the bus stop. At least he'd be able to go outside without her accosting him. Still, the scones she'd handed over the other day had been welcome.

The radio station had moved on, playing more upbeat Christmas songs. 'Rockin' Around the Christmas Tree' came through the airwaves, and he danced, toast in one hand and can of lager in the other. All this music was really putting him in the festive mood, and he wondered about going up in the attic. He reckoned his mother would have a tree up there, along with some decorations.

He went upstairs, pulling down the loft ladder with some difficulty. The loft was bigger than he expected, and he surveyed the area before carefully traversing over to the right. Three boxes, all with 'Christmas' written on them.

It seemed to take forever to get them down to the kitchen, and he could hear Paul snoring all the time he was doing it. Muttering, 'Thanks for your help,' he latched the loft ladder back into place, and turned to go downstairs.

'Ey up, bro,' Paul said, rubbing his hands through his hair and yawning, 'lot of clattering going on. Want a hand?'

They decorated the tree, still listening to the radio, with Paul drinking lager although not enthusiastically. After the second one he decided to switch to coffee.

Todd was placing the baubles carefully, and handed two of

them over to Paul. 'Here, you can put these on. Looks like Mum did love us after all,' he joked. The baubles were in royal blue and had the Sheffield Wednesday logo on them. On the opposite side were their names, Paul and Todd.

Paul grinned, feeling a sense of happiness he wasn't used to feeling. 'Good job she didn't call us Christopher and Alexander, she'd never have fitted our names on!' He stood and walked to the tree, carrying the baubles carefully. He placed them near the top, stood back and surveyed them. 'I like them,' he announced, then went back to sitting in the armchair and watching his brother work.

By lunchtime, the tree was looking good. It had two sets of lights on it, but only one lot worked; they had draped tinsel around mirrors and pictures, and stood up two Christmas cards which had arrived addressed to Christy, one from an Ella and one from a Bren. Todd briefly wondered if they should look for an address book in his mother's stuff, which he had taken to the third bedroom. She clearly had friends who didn't know she was dead.

The one o'clock news temporarily stopped the Christmas music, and Todd went to put some more bread into the toaster. He turned to wave a slice of bread at Paul, about to say *want some?* when he saw the colour drain from his brother's face.

'What's up?'

Paul waved a hand. 'Sssh, I'm listening.'

The announcer spoke of the man who had been shot at a house in Hathersage, Derbyshire. He had been employed as security for the family who lived there, who had come under threat of attack from an escaped prisoner.

'Shit,' Paul said. 'I thought I'd fucking missed him.'

Todd sat down with a thud. 'You? You shot somebody?'

'Target practice, really. I wanted to see how much I could aim properly. I'm better than I thought.'

'Paul, for fuck's sake, they're saying you're an escaped prisoner.'

Todd groaned. He knew it would all go tits up, he knew he should have run a mile rather than get involved on the outside with Paul.

'Paul, we're ten minutes away from Hathersage. They're going to come for you, and soon.'

'I'll have to kill her quick then, won't I?'

Although Todd Fraser didn't know it, it didn't take long for the Christy Fraser name change to Christy Brown to flag up, and it soon became apparent that Christy Brown owned a house in Bamford. Fifteen minutes' walking distance of Hathersage. Two minutes by car. Remarkably close to the Clark family home, Dovewater, much too close.

Doris turned to Alistair. 'Thank you for making this quicker for me.'

'Doris,' he said with a gentle smile, 'I probably took five minutes off the length of time you would have needed to track it down.'

She shrugged. 'Maybe. I'm going to ring the Clark household and pass this on to them. Then I'll tell DCI Marsden.'

'Is that the right order?'

'It is. We've been employed by the Clarks to locate Paul Fraser. If he is at this house, we've completed our mission. If he isn't, Tessa will soon let us know, and we'll continue, but our first port of call is Greg and Julie Clark.'

Alistair gave a brief nod, and waited while she rang Greg. The conversation was brief, and she stressed it didn't mean they had definitely found him, it only meant they had found a residence that they could link to him and his brother.

'I'm going to ring DCI Marsden now,' she said, 'and no doubt they will contact both you and Connection if he's there. The same goes for if he isn't.'

'Thank you, Doris,' Greg said. 'Fingers crossed they find him. Since Denny was shot yesterday, we're all keeping as much in the hall as possible. It's a strange way to live.'

Doris sympathised. 'Hopefully it will be at an end quickly. I'll ring you later, whichever way this goes.'

Greg replaced the receiver and threw his hands in the air. 'Can everybody hear me? It seems Doris has located a house in Bamford that belongs to Todd Fraser. She's notifying the police as we speak, so it should soon be over.'

Everybody clapped and shouted, and he smiled. That's what he liked, a happy family once again. Bugger this being on full alert all the time, and everybody miserable as sin. Christmas was coming!

They arrived quietly. Tessa had found it to be the most stressful time, waiting for the armed response unit to arrive, and when they did they took over.

Finally in position, the two lead officers approached the front door with caution, suddenly standing and levelling their weapons towards the door as it opened.

'Armed response! Armed response! On the floor now!'

Todd stood in the doorway, his coat on and his key in his hand. 'What the...?'

'On the floor, sir. Now. Hands on your head.'

Todd dropped to his knees and raised his arms, locking his

fingers together on his woolly hat. He looked around helplessly. 'Who are you? What do you want?'

'You are?'

'Todd Fraser.' Fear was written all over his face. 'What are you doing? I haven't done anything.'

'Is your brother inside the house?'

'My brother? Paul? No, of course he isn't. He's in Lincoln in some halfway house place, so I believe.'

Tessa looked towards the DS in charge of the armed response unit, and tipped her head towards Fraser. He acknowledged her action and inclined his head. She walked down the path, careful to keep behind the two men with their guns trained on the hapless man kneeling on his garden path.

'Mr Fraser? Todd Fraser?'

'Yeah, that's me. Can I stand up now?'

'Very slowly, and you will be searched. Do not move or give us cause to think you are going for a weapon, because you will be shot.'

The fear returned to his face. 'I don't have a weapon, not a gun, not a knife, not so much as a fucking teaspoon. Can you tell me what's going on here?'

'We have reason to believe your brother is in the area. I am going to send these men in, with one exception. He will remain with a gun trained on you while you sit in the back of a police car. We're going to search your home for your brother and if we find him, it could be some time before you see your home again.'

18

Todd Fraser was sitting downstairs in an interview room, and Tessa didn't really know why. There had been no physical evidence inside the house at Bamford that Paul had ever been in it, although she had sent in a forensics team to fingerprint everything. It was a three-bedroomed property; one was clearly being used by Todd, a small bedroom was full of what Todd said were his mother's belongings that he didn't know what to do with, and the other had little in it apart from a futon.

Todd seemed bewildered by it all, repeating constantly that his brother had contacted him once, to say he was at the halfway house, and Todd had no idea that he had disappeared.

'Why are you bothering me?' he had said, while being searched on his garden path. No weapons had been found on his person. 'It's you that's lost him, and he's not contacted me.'

'Shall we go down and get this formal statement from him?' Hannah said, aware of Tessa's disappointment.

Tessa sighed. 'Yes, and as soon as Forensics are finished, we can let him go. I could hear the deflation in Doris's voice when I told her there was only Todd at the house, and there was a silence when I rang the Clarks that spoke volumes.'

Hannah stared out of the window. 'So we think it's a coincidence that Paul Fraser is in the neighbourhood, his brother has a house close to the Clark house, and Todd Fraser has visited him constantly over the years he's been in prison, but suddenly he's not there for him? Something's not sitting right.'

'No, it's not, and that's what I keep coming back to, because there's no way anybody in that house saw our cars and van pull up. And if they had, they couldn't have got rid of evidence, not in the minute's notice they possibly had.'

'He doesn't have a car?'

'Todd? No, and DVLA confirm that. We've also had confirmation that Paul doesn't even have a licence, never mind a car, because of his eyesight.'

Hannah gave a short laugh. 'Driving a car isn't dependent on having a licence. Paul stole one to run Luke off the road. Although I don't accept he stole it specifically for that purpose, I think spotting Luke's car while he was driving through Eyam in his stolen car brought out the devil in him, and he rear-ended Luke's car with devastating results. He soon got rid of it, didn't he?'

'You think Todd could possibly have organised some other accommodation for Paul? Somewhere fairly local? And I bet next month's salary that Todd has been the one finding out where the Clarks live, because Paul wouldn't have been able to do it, not easily anyway.' Tessa was thinking aloud, not really expecting answers. 'Is this feller downstairs acting? Is he trying to fool us into thinking he's not too bright, and he wouldn't have any idea where brother Paul is? They've been planning this for years, haven't they? All Paul had to do was keep his nose clean, and wait out his time.'

'He left a fingerprint at the Armitages' home. You think that could have been deliberate? Paul Fraser seems so... cocky. As though he couldn't care less, he's going to kill Julie Clark no matter what we do. God, that makes me so angry.' Hannah walked away from the window, where she had been watching snow falling softly, turning the scene outside the police station into a breathtakingly beautiful winter wonderland. 'Let's go and give the little bastard some hassle.'

The little bastard in question was quickly released when Forensics confirmed no fingerprints belonging to Paul Fraser had been found in the house.

'If he gets in touch, Todd, I want you to ring me.' Tessa handed him her card.

He looked at it for a moment, and then handed it back. 'You forced me onto my knees, held a gun to my head, put me in the back of a police car with another gun to my head, searched and probably trashed my home, kept me in an interview room for...' he looked at his watch, 'four hours, and you think I'll contact you if Paul gets in touch with me? On your bike, DCI Marsden. Find him yourself.'

He turned away from her and walked out of the main doors.

Costa Coffee was busy, and Todd ordered lattes before finding a table for two. A minute later Paul joined him and grinned.

'They didn't lock you up then, bro?'

Todd laughed. 'They wanted to, but they found no fingerprints to tie you to the place. I've never cleaned so fast. Good job we'd practised. Thing is, now they've done this, I don't reckon they'll be back. To be on the safe side though, carry on keeping your toothbrush and stuff all in that bag so you can grab it and go, and leave your clothes in the holdall. If

I'd had to start getting rid of stuff like that, I wouldn't have been able to wipe everything down. I wouldn't have had time, so we'll have to live carefully until everything's over, then we'll go.'

'You reckon I can come back tonight?'

Todd shook his head. 'No. Book into a Travelodge or something. You look nowt like that picture they've put on the telly, so you should be okay. Give it a couple of nights then we'll see what's what. I feel wiped out. There's nowt like having a gun held to your head to make you a bit wobbly, mate, I'm telling you.'

'At least you knew it was coming.' Paul's grin lit up his face. 'Thank God for text messages.'

The snow was lying heavily, and Doris clung on to Alistair's arm as they walked through the village. Christmas trees lit up most windows, and many of the Eyam villagers had woven fairy lights through front garden trees, creating a magical wonderland as they strolled along. Every so often they would stop to admire a garden full of reindeer, or a huge inflatable snowman, and Alistair felt as if this, this walk, was so right.

'Tessa was pretty pissed off, wasn't she?'

Alistair nodded in acknowledgement. 'She certainly was. And I get the feeling she doesn't believe the forensics. She's as sure as hell Paul Fraser has been there, because it would have been the logical thing for him to do. She knows he's not the brightest fairy on the Christmas tree, but his brother is no dumbo. Whatever's going on in Paul Fraser's life, whatever his feelings surrounding Julie, Greg and Oliver Clark, it has to be Todd who's masterminded everything, because while Paul has been the good little lad with the carefully conceived plan for eventually getting out, Todd has similarly worked hard at keeping out of trouble, and being a model citizen. None of that sits comfortably with me.'

'Me neither. Seen too much, haven't we? Cynical old dodderers, the pair of us.'

Alistair laughed, and pulled her closer. 'Not so much of the old dodderers. Cynical maybe, but old, never. Fancy a tot of whisky in that smart-looking pub?' He nodded towards the fairy-light bedecked building higher up the main road.

'That would be lovely. We're heading towards that anyway, because I need to show you the plague cottages. This is where you'll lose any cynicism, and become in awe of what these people did by locking themselves away, knowing it meant certain death for them but life for people beyond this village. The Black Death spread no further.'

Standing in front of the cottages, waiting while Alistair brushed away the snow from the plaques so that he could read this history of the village and the people who had given up everything so selflessly, Doris knew this night would be a memory to hold for ever.

When Alistair was back in London, and then further afield in St Raphael, they would keep in touch; but this magical night, snow-filled and aglow with lights to entice them onwards would be a part of her life for the rest of her life.

Paul gazed down at the girl in bed with him, fast asleep with her long blonde hair all over the pillow, wondering what she would do if she found out who he was. Scream? Lock herself in the bathroom?

He'd had a good night after Todd had gone back home. Checked into a hotel, walked back downstairs to the bar and the beautiful Olga had been on bar duty. It had been a quiet night, snow falling heavily outside, and they had chatted. He had bought her several drinks and had told her his room number. Success.

His first sex for many, many years and he hadn't lost his touch. When she'd queried his lack of toes, he'd explained he'd been in a car accident. He neither knew nor cared if that sounded plausible, he had other parts of his body in full working order and ready to go.

And he wanted to sleep but to sleep alone. He raised himself up and straddled her body. *Nice tits*, he thought, and then put his hands around her neck and squeezed.

She didn't struggle much and it was over quickly. He carried her to the bath, dropped her in it, had a wee and returned to bed. The cleaners wouldn't be in until about eleven, he reckoned, and he'd be long gone by then. He wouldn't be able to have a shower, but there wasn't much he could do about that. He'd have one in the next hotel, but maybe not kill the bar staff in that one.

Todd was uneasy. He'd sensed a difference in Paul, a flippancy he wasn't sure was good for him. To pull this Julie Clark thing off they had to be focused, and he had a feeling that Paul was changing his.

Paul was seeing the changes in the world from when he had last been part of it, the mobile phones that could control every aspect of your life, the iPads he had become obsessed with, the big cars that he craved; the car he had hired for two hundred quid wouldn't satisfy him for long. It was doing its job. It was nondescript. It ran fairly smoothly. It was taxed, tested and insured and it was ten years old. The garage said it was their runabout, but they could hire it for a few days while they did their research and decided which new one to go for.

Todd rang Paul but he didn't answer, so texted him to say he would see him the following day. Still no reply, and he hoped fervently that Paul wasn't drunk somewhere talking about things he shouldn't be talking about.

Most people didn't sleep a dreamless one that Monday night; the Clark family members, particularly Ollie who had had to identify his grandparents officially, were on edge.

Kat's overactive mind remembered the file covering Henry the Philanderer and knew it had to be dealt with and got out of the way and Mouse was bubbling over with happiness and unable to sleep because Joel had talked of marriage, tentatively and obviously unsure how she would react.

The security people at the Clark house slept; the ones on duty didn't, aware of the silence of the night, magnified by the deep snow. It made them all uneasy.

Doris felt her mind was in overdrive, and wouldn't close down. What had they missed? Where was Paul Fraser? What was he doing if he wasn't with his brother?

Alistair smoked a late-night cigar standing outside the bed and breakfast hotel, and thought about Doris. He had been such a fool to let her get away from him all those years earlier, and he guessed at their ages it was much too late to do anything about it now. He put out the cigar, and headed back inside. The owner handed him the cup of hot chocolate he had requested, and Alistair headed upstairs, his mind not settled, and unable to see what his future could possibly hold.

. . .

Tessa and Hannah lay in each other's arms, and said goodnight. At three o'clock they both got up and made cups of Horlicks, sleep having evaded them.

'Bloody thick snow again,' Tessa grumbled as she looked through the bedroom window. 'There's always a death connected to this job when there's thick snow. I hope it's not Julie Clark.'

19

It was a tight squeeze in the hotel bathroom; Tessa and Hannah stood looking down into the bath at the naked woman, her eyes staring and her lips tinged with blue.

'Her name is Olga Kovak, twenty-six. She works here and was on duty last night in the bar. The chap who was in this room registered as Neil Underwood. We have him on CCTV, sort of. He had a woolly hat on so we don't really know what he looks like, but I have a feeling...' Hannah shivered.

'You think it's Paul Fraser?'

'I do. The manager said he limped. I think Forensics will definitely find his fingerprints here.'

'Shit. Maybe we're wrong about Todd Fraser then. Maybe he doesn't know where his brother is. If he's here he's not with Todd. What time did he check out?'

'Shortly after eight. Paid cash for everything, then the cleaners moved into this room about half ten. You can imagine the state they're in. One of them is only eighteen, bless her, she's fallen apart. The other one is an older lady who was training the younger one. She got them out of the room straight away and locked it, then told the manager. He sent for us. The older cleaner's a lady called Yvonne Staniforth, sensible, a little shaken but handling it okay. She's currently comforting the younger one.'

Tessa nodded. She felt a sense of relief she could despatch Hannah to a scene and know when she arrived all the information would be waiting for her. Her meeting with Superintendent Yarwood had seemed interminable, and the call from the hotel had come in as Tessa was about to head to his office. Her instructions to Hannah to 'sort it' had been met fully.

Tessa hadn't considered it might be Paul Fraser who had surfaced at the Travelodge, she thought it was yet another murder to add to their books and hoped it would soon be cleared up. Driving to the hotel after her meeting had finished, she was actually working out in her head who to delegate the case to, but Hannah's words showed it wasn't going anywhere.

'Come on, let's get out of here. Pretty girl, isn't she? Does she live local?'

'She does. Despite her name, she's British, her mother is Polish. No father, she lives with her mother in Chesterfield. She stays in the hotel when she does a late shift followed by an early, but when she works a normal day she goes home. Olga was due to start today at eleven, so she was in that period where nobody wondered where she was. Her mother would have thought she'd stayed over here, and the manager wasn't expecting her until eleven.'

Hannah and Tessa edged their way out of the bathroom and allowed the forensic duo to get in. She didn't envy them their job; space was extremely limited.

'We'll go to Chesterfield and break the news. You have the full address?'

'Of course,' Hannah said. 'This is me, you know, Little Miss Organised.'

Tessa smiled and wanted to kiss her. 'I know. It's automatic for me to check. Ignore me, it was a long meeting and he pushed for a result on the Fraser case. I had no idea this one was connected, so he's going to be even more pissed when I tell him that.'

'Shall we get a coffee from the hotel before we head off? It's freezing out, and that snow's going nowhere fast.'

'We will. I want a quick word with the receptionist who checked him out this morning. I'll not hassle the cleaners today, they've been through enough. We have their details...'

Hannah looked at her boss before she finished the sentence.

Tessa smiled and held up a hand. 'Okay. I know. We have the details.'

She asked the receptionist if they could have two lattes and a bit of a chat, and Laurel, according to her name badge, turned to the machine. 'I'll bring the coffees over and take five minutes,' the tall, dark-haired woman said. Tessa thanked her by name.

It transpired that Laurel had little to add. He had been nondescript. A dark-blue woolly hat completely covered his head so she had no idea of hair colour, and brown eyes but she felt there was something wrong with them. His clothing was unremarkable, and he had carried a black holdall. He hadn't registered a car with them, and he had ordered a snack from the bar during the previous evening, paying for it instead of running a tab. He had paid for his and Olga's drinks as they had them.

In other words, Tessa thought, he was leaving nothing of himself. Except probably semen and his fingerprints all over the room. Again he seemed to be taunting them. And how do you get around dealing with someone for whom prison holds no fear? Or even death, because if they did ever trap him, the armed response unit would play a major part in his capture, or otherwise. And where the hell did Todd Fraser fit into all of this?

Laurel left them after apologising for not being able to help them further, and they finished their coffees before venturing outside and round to Tessa's car. Their journey to the late Olga's home took hardly any time, and they exchanged few words, each lost in thoughts of what to do next.

Luke stared at his mother. 'Mum?'

Naomi opened her eyes; she had had to rest them. Lack of sleep was making her dizzy, and she didn't want to be at home, she wanted to be with Luke. And suddenly it seemed she was.

'Oh God, Luke, you're awake?'

'Mum?' he repeated.

Naomi and his nurse helped him sit up slightly, and all his vital signs were checked before Naomi was allowed to grasp his hand.

'What...?' Luke began.

'You're in hospital. Can you remember anything?'

He paused and it was clear he was trying to force thoughts. 'Car. My car.'

'Yes, you were in an accident.'

'No!' His voice was getting stronger. 'Not accident, Mum. Another car... drove into me.'

'Okay, sweetheart. Don't get upset. Is it okay if I send Doris a quick text to let her know you've surfaced?'

He smiled. 'Ring her.'

Naomi looked at the nurse, who nodded. She pressed Doris's number, and held the phone to Luke's ear.

'Nan,' Luke said when the call connected, 'you got home safe?'

Doris sobbed after disconnecting. Half a dozen words and she was in bits. It felt natural to let Alistair hold her, and he did so willingly. He let her cry it all out, then said, 'Let's go for a cup of tea.'

They had stayed in Eyam, deciding to not risk venturing further afield in the snow for no reason other than sightseeing. Besides, there was plenty she still had to show him in and around the village.

Alistair led the way to a café, and ordered drinks and scones for them. Doris took out her phone and rang Kat and Mouse, telling them the good news that she had spoken to Luke and although he wasn't better, he was getting there.

Her heart felt lighter, and she smiled constantly. She spread the jam and cream on her scone, and bit into it. Clotted cream formed a moustache across her top lip, and she licked it.

'This is so good,' she said. 'I'm sorry I cried, you must think I'm a proper numpty.'

Alistair laughed, and leaned forward to wipe off a small amount of cream her tongue had missed. 'Not at all, I wanted to cry myself. Even over this couple of days I've been fully aware of how much you care for Luke. You cry all you want, I'll mop up the tears.'

They had a second pot of tea, watching as the snow fell again.

'Alistair, when are you going home?' Doris asked.

'You're trying to get rid of me?'

'Not at all. I asked because Derbyshire villages tend to get cut off from civilisation when the snow falls as heavily as this lot is falling, and it's coming down on top of the six inches or so we've already got.'

'Oh, that's good news,' he said and winked at her.

Paul Fraser booked into a bed and breakfast in Holmewood, on the outskirts of Chesterfield, and took himself off to bed for the afternoon. His car, non-existent as far as the B&B owners were aware, was parked on a side road; a walking tour, he had told them, no, I don't have a car. He slept until five, then went out to find food. He was back in time for the evening news, and saw the results of his night of passion with the lovely Olga. Her mum was distraught, asking people to come forward if they knew anything. The police officer with her, a DS Granger, asked for information concerning a man they wished to interview, last seen wearing a navy-blue woolly hat, a black jacket and walking with a limp.

Yet another thing to hate Bialik for, that bloody limp. Paul felt his temper begin to rise and he switched off the small television set and took out his phone, one of a pair Todd had purchased for them to use. Todd didn't want his swish iPhone showing any calls from a strange number.

'What?'

'Ey up, grumpy.'

'Grumpy? What the fuck are you playing at, Paul? Have you killed that bird, 'cos it sounds like it's you.'

'Don't have a go at me. It was an accident. It got a bit rough, that's all.'

'So they'll know by now it's you. DNA and stuff, fingerprints all over that room. Where the hell are you?'

'I've booked into a bed and breakfast. They think I'm a walker, staying here for one night, then setting off tomorrow morning.'

'For fuck's sake try not to kill anybody tonight.'

'Can I come back to yours tomorrow? I need to get in that house and finish bloody Julie off.'

'No. It's not safe. What if that DCI comes back? She wasn't convinced you'd not been here. Book in somewhere else tomorrow, and we'll think about it for the day after. And wear a different bloody hat. That blue one is all over the news.'

'I'll get a red one.'

'Where's the gun?'

'In the boot.'

'Jesus, Paul.' Todd hesitated, unsure what to say next. When Paul had told him of his plan for revenge all those years earlier, he'd never imagined it would get to the stage it was now at. 'Look, I've changed my mind, you'd better come here tomorrow night if you can. The roads are covered, no buses, precious little else getting through. Don't blow it all by taking chances.'

'Yeah, it's bad here. I'll see you tomorrow all being well, then.'

They disconnected, and Todd sat down with a thud on the sofa. He laid his head back, pulled a cushion onto his knee in an odd attempt at seeking comfort and closed his eyes; despair washed over him. He'd genuinely thought he could talk Paul out of it, but it seemed the things Bialik had done to him had warped his mind. In Paul's mind, Julie Clark and her family, not Bialik, were to blame for the loss of his toes, his blurry vision in his one remaining eye, and his incarceration. If Julie had died when she was supposed to...

20

Kat sat alone on the front pew having a few personal words with God. The midweek early morning prayer service was normally well attended but today only five people had made it through the snow. It had been peaceful, and she had prayed individually with each person, something it wasn't always possible to do if the attendance was high. Now she had her own moment of peace. She switched off from the sounds of the two ladies who had stayed to do a quick clean, and dropped her head in prayer.

Luke was at the front, back and centre of her prayers. She doubted they would even be able to get to see him until some help in the form of gritters and snowploughs arrived. She held the Clark family before her Lord, and again asked for help, her thoughts wandering to the woman who had suffered so much, losing the best years of her life because of this invisible adversary.

Kat stood and waved across towards where she could hear laughter, shouted bye and left the church. The snow had stopped falling and she was thankful. It was deep and she was careful to keep to the path as she walked across to the Connection office.

Mouse was sitting at the reception desk, and she smiled. 'Good service?'

'Wonderful. Only five of us, and private prayer as a result. Has Joel gone to work?'

'No, it's a snow day for him. He can't get there. Manchester may as well be on a different planet when it snows. We're going sledging later.'

'No!' Fear enveloped Kat. 'You can't take risks like that. Tessa's no idea where Fraser is, and he obviously knows we're involved. He was quick enough to target Luke. And we know he's carrying a gun; he shot Denny. Please, Mouse, don't do it. It would kill Nan if anything happened to you. For somebody who's such an intelligent, smart woman who's tackling world domination, you can be a bit thick.'

'Say it like it is, Kat.' Mouse laughed. 'Okay. The going sledging was something we jumped at to get out of painting the bathroom. The bathroom it is then.'

Kat exhaled. She felt as if she'd been holding her breath.

'Where's Nan?'

'In her office. She's determined to track down a location for Fraser. Tessa rang earlier and confirmed the girl who was killed at the Travelodge was with Fraser all night. There's his fingerprints everywhere and they're waiting for semen DNA. So far he's got two attempted murders with Luke and Denny, and the three murders of the Armitages and Olga Kovak, and Tessa is being asked for answers as you can imagine. She asked to speak to Nan, so I put her through. It seems she said to Nan that if Nan came up with any little thing, she wouldn't ask how she knew. Tessa and Hannah are coming over to the side of the angels!'

Kat laughed. 'So that's what Nan is working on?'

'She was already on it way before Tessa rang. This man shouldn't have targeted our Luke. Now he's got Nan to deal with. She'll leave no stone unturned to get to him.'

'And Alistair?'

Mouse shrugged. 'Not here. It is only half past nine, you know. I know it feels like the middle of the day, but it really isn't. I think he was supposed to be going home today, but something tells me that might not happen, and it's not because of the snow.' She gave an exaggerated wink, and Kat laughed.

'Are you serious?'

'Have you seen the way he looks at her? And she's certainly got a big smile these days. But... I'm saying nothing further.'

The object of their discussion opened her office door. 'Coffee, please. Hot and creamy.' The door closed as Doris disappeared back inside.

Doris waited until Kat delivered her coffee and biscuits, then picked up the phone. 'Tessa? Can you talk?'

'To you, anytime. To my Super, not at the moment. I'm avoiding him.'

'Okay. None of this makes sense.'

'Tell me about it. We've been awake most of the night going over and over everything. I've asked the prison for behavioural reports, he can't be as squeaky clean as they're making out, and I want to know everybody he was pally with, everybody he might have shared a cell with at some point, I want the lot. Somebody is helping him.'

'It's the coincidences. The house in Bamford keeps coming to the forefront. I know he wasn't in it when you got there, but it's so close to Hathersage. They couldn't have a better base without it actually being in Hathersage itself.'

'They?'

'Definitely they. I think Todd Fraser has been in on the plan from the beginning. They're only a year apart in age, he's visited him constantly in prison, and I'm convinced Todd is the organiser. He's a smart cookie, is Todd. I don't know why Paul wasn't there when you raided the house, and I don't know why there were no fingerprints, but I'm dead certain it's their base. If I put myself inside Todd's head, I think he'll be telling Paul to stay away for a couple of days until everything calms down and there's been no return visit from you, and he'll tell Paul to come back. Tell me about that house.'

Tessa stared out of the window, bringing the Bamford place to the forefront of her mind. 'Okay, you go in the front door and ahead of you is a long hallway, with the stairs facing away from you. You walk past the stairs to go up them. To the left is the lounge, then at the end is the door to the kitchen, which is an open-plan diner kitchen. I think at one time it was two separate small rooms, if that helps you visualise it. In the kitchen is a back door that leads outside to a garden. There's hardstanding for a car there. He doesn't have a car, he says, and that's been confirmed. When you go upstairs there are three bedrooms and a bathroom. The main bedroom where Todd sleeps overlooks the front garden, which is tiny, and the second bedroom, which is much smaller, also overlooks the front. That's where he's stashed everything of his mother's while he decides what to do with it.'

Tessa paused and picked up her drink. 'You with me so far?'

'I am. Diagrams everywhere. I'll ask questions when you've finished.'

'The third bedroom and the bathroom overlook the back garden. In the third bedroom is a futon and nothing else. The bathroom held men's toiletries, but only one toothbrush, one toothpaste. You get the picture?'

'I do. Clearly. It's portraying a picture of a house where only one person lives, only one person sleeps. A futon isn't a long-term ideal sleeping spot, but it's still a darn sight more comfortable than a bed in a prison cell.'

'You think that's Paul's room?'

'I'm sure it is. And I bet when you catch up with him he's got a sleeping bag in his holdall. He took it leaving a totally clean room, his holdall still containing his clothes inside it because it's safer to live out of that holdall until they can both leave having completed their mission. Let's figure out the lack of fingerprints. The fingerprints that were taken from that back room... there were only Todd's?'

'There weren't any.'

'None at all? But his mother only died a year ago. Hers would still have been there. And surely his would have. He must have been in it, because I bet some of his mother's stuff that he's moved into the front bedroom was in there originally. That room has been wiped clear of fingerprints, hasn't it?'

'But as you say, none of this makes sense. Where was he if he's living there? They didn't know we were coming...'

There was silence from both ends of the line.

Todd watched the police car pull up outside his home, and swiftly sent a text telling Paul to stay away. He switched off the phone, knowing Paul wasn't the brightest button in the box and might ring him to ask why. He walked into the hall and waited for the knock on the door.

It didn't come. He headed back into the lounge and peered through the window. The car was still there, but DCI Marsden and DS Granger appeared to have vanished.

· · ·

Tessa and Hannah accepted the offer of a drink, and Todd Fraser's neighbour confirmed her name was Edna Davis.

Gently, Tessa led the elderly lady towards talking about her neighbour.

'Oh, she was lovely, was Christy. Lonnie lived here for years, and then he married Christy. She helped me a lot, it was so sad the way they both went within a year of each other.'

'And did Todd live with her and Lonnie?'

'No, he turned up after she died, and said he'd been left it in her will. I never see him, not like I used to see his mum. He never speaks really, not even when he spent a week doing that car space in the back garden. I like my plants, so I'm out there a lot, but I think he only spoke twice all that week, even though we were only over the fence. I baked him some scones, to try to make friends, but he didn't speak apart from "thanks".'

'He has a car?'

'No, but there's been one there on and off, so I think he must borrow one sometimes. It's a red Astra. A fairly old one. About ten, maybe twelve years old. Don't ask me the registration, I can only remember the last three letters, ECV.'

Tessa and Hannah looked at each other.

'You recognised the make?'

'Of course I did. My husband and I owned a car sales business until he died. I've always been interested in cars, but I had to give up my licence last year, my eyes aren't so good now.'

'How old are you, Mrs Davis, if you don't mind my asking?' Hannah smiled at Edna.

'I don't mind at all, dear. I'm eighty-nine next month.'

'And you've been driving for a long time?'

'About sixty years, give or take a month.'

'Mrs Davis,' Tessa said, sipping at her tea and picking up another biscuit, 'you've absolutely made my day.'

'Good. Is he in trouble?'

'Could be. If that car comes back, please don't approach anybody from next door, but ring me.' Tessa handed over her card.

'Oh this is so exciting at my time of life. Of course I'll ring you, dear.'

'And promise me you won't go near Todd. I don't want you in any danger.'

'I won't. As I said, I don't really speak at all, I don't like him. He's got that sort of face, shifty. No, you can stop worrying. It's been missing a couple of days now, that car. I didn't see it go, because I wasn't here when you came the other day, and it was there when I went out but not when I came back. He disappeared then, the other feller?'

Tessa cursed herself. That should have been the first question, if she hadn't allowed the old lady to take over her investigation. *Is there someone else living next door apart from Todd Fraser?* 'Yes, he's disappeared. Do you know him?'

'No, seen him a couple of times. He's been in and out with the car, but doesn't seem to walk anywhere.'

'Mrs Davis, you've been really helpful.' Tessa put down her cup, and they both stood.

Edna smiled at them. 'Oh do call me Edna, dear. It's been lovely having you pop round. Anytime you fancy a cup of tea, please pop in. I'm sorry I can't remember the first two letters of the registration, but the year's come to me. It's a 58 plate, which means it was first registered in the second half of 2008. Does that help?'

'Edna Davis, you're a marvel. You've been more help to this investigation than anything else. Thank you. We'll be back for a cuppa, I promise.'

'They put the Christmas tree up that day, you know. It wasn't there when I went out because I saw Todd stood in the window, but it was lit when I came home. Although I don't suppose that's in any way helpful. Take care driving, you two,' she finished.

Edna waited until they drove away before closing and firmly locking her door.

21

'They put up the Christmas tree.' Hannah scribbled the fact down in her notebook while Tess negotiated the snow-packed roads.

'I know. I'm sending Forensics back to fingerprint every one of those shiny little balls. Todd Fraser might have been able to wipe every surface clean of prints, but I'll bet anything he didn't clean the baubles. Let's hope his brother got off his backside and helped him with the festive chores.'

Todd watched in disbelief as the two men in white coveralls carefully took his Christmas tree apart. They took prints from almost every one of the baubles, including the well-handled ones with the Sheffield Wednesday logos.

'Ma'am?' The disembodied voice at the other end of the phone had a rasp to it that suggested a sore throat.

'DCI Marsden, yes.'

'Sorry, ma'am. It's Cliff, in Forensics. We're detecting a signal that's been used from the house we're watching, but it's not the iPhone we know is there. It's another one, and it's now switched off. Thought you should know.'

'Thank you, Cliff.' She disconnected, and sat back in her chair. So Todd Fraser had a second phone, probably a burner whose only calls and texts went to a burner that Paul Fraser was toting around with him. She sighed. This time Hannah could drive.

'I can't believe it's only a couple of hours since we got back from this place,' Hannah grumbled. 'It's a good job there was a four-by-four in for us to take, these roads are like glass. Why can't people commit crimes only in the summer?'

'There's a novel thought, Hannah. I've not got an answer for you, but it's still a novel thought.'

'The Chatsworth murders took a lot out of us, and that was a snowy one. It makes it twice as hard, and I don't mean only getting around. I mean the brain freeze it causes when it's too cold to think, and the need to get by an open fire with a glass of wine in your hand.'

Tessa laughed. 'You rarely drank before...'

Hannah turned and smiled at her partner. 'I know. It's you. You've corrupted me.'

'Happy to oblige.'

The car slid, and Hannah quickly corrected it. 'What are we going to do about us?'

'About us? Carry on carrying on. If you mean with regard to work, at some point we're going to have to bite the bullet and be open about our relationship.'

Hannah concentrated hard as they negotiated a bend. 'I can't wait for the day. However, it might mean I have to move stations. You know what they're like.'

'I know.' A frown furrowed Tessa's brow. 'Let's get a good resolution to this, and we'll make the relationship known to Superintendent Yarwood. We'll have to take his guidance as gospel, I suppose, but if we *do* get a good result maybe he'll smile favourably on us and say we can both stay.'

'Or I could pack in work and we could have a baby.' The words were said quietly, the car carried on in a straight line, and the world didn't implode.

'A baby?'

'Yes, you know – tiny wriggling things, human, bald and toothless, wear nappies.'

'I know what a baby is. Do we want one?'

'Do you?' Hannah turned her head to look at Tessa.

There was a long period of silence, then Tessa reached across and touched her hand.

'I think we might.'

'It's taken me two weeks to bring up that subject.' Hannah's face was wreathed in smiles. 'I'm not sleeping with a man, though. Artificial job or nothing.'

'We'll talk further about this when we get home. Now concentrate, or we won't be going home. This series of bends is a killer in the summer, so take it steady.'

'I know.' Hannah gripped the wheel even tighter as they began the descent into Bamford.

Todd reactivated his burner phone to see three messages from Paul.

What's going on bro
You okay bro
FFS TODD ANSWER ME

Todd rang the irate sounding Paul, and held it away from his ear as Paul's tirade began; he eventually calmed down, and Todd laughed.

'Look, dickhead, I forgot to switch it back on. That DCI and her sidekick were around this morning, and I thought they were coming here. They went to dozy Edna next door, so that's okay 'cos she don't know what day of the week it is, so she'll tell them nowt. So what's a matter then?'

'I'm on my way back.'

'Here?'

'Yep. They know I'm not in that house, so I reckon it's the safest place.'

'For fuck's sake, Paul. It's not safe at all. I've had Forensics here today checking for fingerprints on the bloody Christmas tree. You can't come here.'

'I can't go anywhere else. It's like driving a bloody dodgem car in this weather. I don't ever want an Astra again. Right, here's what I'll do. I'll put this in the pub car park and sit and watch. I can put my sleeping bag round me to keep warm. If nobody's turned up by nine tonight, I'm sleeping in that house. If somebody does turn up, I'll scarper. Okay?'

Todd thought it through. 'Okay. But we need to sort this tomorrow. We need to find somewhere safe for you to stay. You've got to forget this mad idea of killing Julie Clark and make sure you don't go back inside. That means us going abroad.'

There was a silence from Paul that stretched and stretched. Eventually Todd heard a sigh. 'I'm going nowhere till that cow is dead.'

Todd felt sick. Everything was out of control, especially Paul. He wasn't listening to common sense, and Todd guessed that within a couple of years, Paul's eyesight would have gone altogether. He was out there driving in really bad conditions, as blind as a bloody bat, more than slightly loopy in the head, and with a killer fixation. Two near misses, and three definite, and he still hadn't got to Julie Clark.

Todd switched off the Christmas tree lights so that he could see better outside, and remained standing in the window, watching for Paul's arrival in the car park immediately opposite the house. He still had on the Christmas music, and he felt under different circumstances he would have been happy with this little house, the approach of Christmas and the snow presently keeping everybody prisoner. Except Paul.

The red Astra crept down the hill and he saw Paul turn into the car park without any sort of indication. He watched as it circled the parking area until Paul was in a position where he could sit in the car and see what was happening at the house.

Christmas tree lights shone out of windows, and many of the houses had trees in the garden festooned with outdoor lights, made all the brighter by the darkness of the hour. He checked his watch. Ten past six. Paul would be freezing by nine o'clock.

Todd saw his brother's driver's door open, and then nothing. At the same time, in his peripheral vision, he saw the police four-by-four approaching the row of houses which included his own, and his immediate thought was that the fingerprints on the baubles had given them a positive for Paul's prints.

'Shit, shit, shit,' he muttered, and reached for his phone to ring Paul.

Paul got out of the driver's door, and edged his way carefully round to the boot of the car. It was icily cold. He had decided there was no way he could sit in the car without some sort of cover, and his sleeping bag was in his holdall, in the boot.

He lifted the boot lid, then glanced across the road towards the house. The four-by-four was pulling up.

'Shit, shit, shit,' he muttered, and reached for his phone to ring Todd.

Hannah slowed the car and let it glide to a stop, then turned to Tessa with a smile. 'Told you I'd get you here safely. Now, what's the plan. What do we do next?'

'Let's look around. It was good of Cliff to work late and get that fingerprint match. Now we know Paul Fraser was here, which gives us a starting point and we can lean a little heavier on Todd. But I don't want us blundering in there; we know Paul's got a gun and he's free and easy with using it. I'm going to ring Edna and see if that car is parked up round the back. If it is, we get a firearms team out here, and we drive across to that pub and wait till they arrive. That sound like a plan?'

Hannah nodded. 'It does. You want me to drive over there before you ring Edna?'

'No, I'll do it now.'

Edna was surprised to hear Tessa's voice. 'Hello, DCI Marsden. How can I help?'

'Edna, I need you to go into your kitchen without putting on your light, and look out to see if that red Astra is parked in next door's back garden. If it is, I need to know, but I also need to know you're safe. If it is there I want you to go upstairs and barricade yourself in your bedroom, or the bathroom if it has a lock on it. If the car's not there, I think it means you're safe to stay downstairs. Do you understand?'

'I do. I'll go and look now.'

There was silence for a minute and then Edna spoke again.

'No, it's not here.'

'Thank you, Edna. Make sure all doors and windows are locked, will you? I'll ring you when I know everything's safe.'

'The car's not there. I'm calling it that we go to the front door, although there's a possibility Todd Fraser isn't there because the tree lights aren't on. Let's see what we can stir up.'

'Okay, you're the boss,' Hannah grinned, 'and as we're officially off duty, is it okay to tell you I love you?'

'Certainly is. Love you too. Let's get on with this so we can go home and talk about this baby.'

Paul stood hidden by his boot lid, the sleeping bag forgotten, his rifle in his hand. He dropped down, and scuttled across the short distance to the drystone wall surrounding the car park, resting the barrel of the rifle on top.

He watched as both doors opened on the four-by-four, and he lined up with the target by using the one eye with limited vision.

'Target practice,' he said to himself, ignoring the ringing telephone lying in the car boot.

Tessa was still talking as they exited the car, and Hannah was smiling as she stood with her back to the pub, pressing the key fob to lock the car.

The crack of the rifle was loud and Tessa and Hannah immediately dropped to the ground.

22

To Todd it seemed as if time became frozen. Fucking Paul. Idiot. If Todd had heard the crack of the rifle clearly, other people would have also. He could see Marsden on the floor, immobile apart from her arm trying to reach the car door handle.

He heard the roar of an engine and looked across to the car park; the Astra was moving, manoeuvring to leave without skidding into one of the drystone walls that surrounded it.

Marsden had levered herself semi-upright, and was tugging on the handle now she was in a better position to exert some leverage.

The Astra finally barrelled out of the bottom gap in the car park wall and disappeared with a screech down the road.

Todd stood, rigid, not knowing what to do.

Tessa reached the handle and tugged. Nothing. 'Hannah,' she whispered, 'unlock the car. Then slide round to this side, we're safer here. I think he shot from the car park across. Hannah?'

There was no response. Had he hit Hannah? Was she remaining quiet so he wouldn't try again? Tessa realised she wasn't going to be able to get into the car to use the police transmitter, so slid her phone out of her jacket pocket.

'Officers under gunfire attack. Armed response unit required at Bamford, we are at location given earlier. I am okay, I'm going to check on Hannah, who is on the other side of our car. Wait...'

Tessa lifted her head at the sound of the roar of a car, and saw the Astra disappear from the car park.

'I believe the suspect has left the scene driving a red Astra. The registration you'll find on the computer in the case notes. Get somebody here and it's possible we'll require an ambulance. Send one anyway. I'm signing off now to go to Hannah.'

She slipped her phone back in her pocket hoping her message wasn't as garbled to the recipient as it had sounded to her, but at the forefront of her mind was that there had been no sound from Hannah.

Tessa didn't stand. Okay, the Astra had disappeared, which presumably meant Paul had, but she also had to assume Todd was in on the whole thing. She slid, wormlike, around the back of the four-by-four; she reached the driver side and saw Hannah.

So much red. Hannah's head was torn apart, and blood and brains dripped slowly down the side of the car. Tessa made no sound. Not then. She simply pulled Hannah towards her, sat with her back to the vehicle side and cradled her love in her arms.

She didn't feel the cold, didn't notice when the snow started once more. Didn't feel Edna's arms around her, nor the blanket that the old woman covered her with. She didn't relinquish her hold on Hannah, not even when the pathologist touched Hannah's throat to officially pronounce life extinct.

They eventually produced a body bag and Tessa watched as

they gently placed Hannah inside it. Tessa couldn't move. Her limbs felt frozen, stuck to the ground, and she felt Edna's arms around her, urging her to stand, to lean on her.

'Please come into my home and warm yourself,' Edna whispered. 'Let these people deal with your partner, your friend. You can't help her now, but they can.'

Todd watched everything happen in a mindless state of pent-up fury. Fucking Paul, blind-in-one-eye Paul, had finally found out how to shoot with his eye with minimal sight, and had chosen to kill a fucking police officer. Fucking mental Paul.

Todd had tried ringing him, but there was no response. He didn't move from the window until he saw two officers moving towards his front door.

'I don't know where he is or what he's fucking playing at,' he said. 'He's my fucking brother and I'm not him. I don't shoot people.'

'Todd Fraser, we're arresting you on suspicion of harbouring a criminal, namely Paul Fraser. You do not have to say anything, but it may harm your defence if you do not mention when questioned, something which you later rely on in court. Anything you do say may be given in evidence. Mr Fraser, do you understand the caution?'

'Yes.' Handcuffs were produced and Todd held out his arms.

'Behind your back, Mr Fraser.'

The officer was polite, this had to be by the book, but the cuffs were tightened a little too much, and he could have left Fraser's hands around the front.

Tessa found herself in Edna's lounge without really knowing how she got there. Edna pressed a small glass into her hand.

'Drink this, sweetheart, it's brandy, and I'll make you a cup of tea. Let's get you warm.' She tucked a fresh blanket around Tessa's legs, and placed a smaller one around her shoulders. The wet one from outside, with blood on it, Edna threw into the washer as she went into the kitchen to make the hot drinks.

Tessa felt numb. It wasn't only a physical thing, the numbness associated with extreme cold, it was a mental thing. She couldn't conceive of not having Hannah to cuddle with at night, to laugh with, to sing their special song they'd learnt from Rod Stewart: *If loving you is wrong, I don't want to be right...*

Tessa sipped at the brandy, welcoming the warmth as it slid down her throat, and pulled the blanket tighter around her shoulders. She felt wet; the newly-falling snow had escalated but she hadn't taken it in that it had been settling on her. The forensic team had worked swiftly to put up a tent over Hannah, her Hannah.

Tessa wanted to close her eyes and let everything drift away. She didn't want to wake to a world without Hannah, she wanted to go back two hours, to normality, to two police officers doing their jobs. And to a life where she would spend the rest of it with the woman who had given her the biggest surprise of her life, herself.

Edna took drinks outside for the people still working there, relieved to see that the ambulance had departed, ferrying DS Granger to the morgue. She placed the tray of mugs on her garden wall, told one of the officers and headed back inside to Tessa. She needed to get her warm again; the pallor of her face was frightening and her eyes were dead.

She sat by Tessa's side and handed her a mug of tea. 'Open

your eyes, lovey, and drink this cup of tea. And don't moan because it's got sugar, it's what you need right now.'

Tessa turned her head to look at Edna. 'Thank you.' She took the mug and sipped carefully. It was scalding hot and sweet, and she immediately felt the warming benefits. 'Hannah...?'

'The ambulance has gone. It's the people in white overalls and one or two officers out there now.'

There was a gentle knock at the door, and Edna squeezed Tessa's hand as she went to answer it.

Tessa could hear a conversation, and a tall man followed the diminutive woman into the lounge.

Tessa tried to stand, but couldn't. The blankets acted like a straitjacket.

'Stay where you are, Tessa,' Superintendent Yarwood said. 'And it's Eric while we're here. Edna, could I trouble you for a cup of tea, please?'

Yarwood replaced Edna by Tessa's side, and grasped her hand. 'I've been aware of your special relationship with DS Granger, Hannah, for some time, and I was ignoring it until you felt it was the right time to tell me. I'm so sorry, Tessa. I'm going to take you home when you're ready and when the lovely Edna has warmed you up, and you stay at home until you're ready to come back to work. We'll arrange the counselling as we would for any officer caught up in something like this, but for you it will be mandatory.'

Tessa's head shot up. 'But...'

'No buts. We have others we can swap around and who can take over this case. You go home, and we'll talk at the end of January. At the earliest.'

Edna rejoined them carrying a mug of tea. 'I don't think I've ever run out of mugs before, but I have now. Can I offer you something to eat?'

Tessa shook her head. 'No thank you, Edna. I thought I told you to lock yourself in.'

'I must have misheard you. I thought you said keep a lookout for any trouble and come and help if we need it.'

'There'll be an officer outside all night, Edna,' Yarwood said. 'If Paul Fraser tries to come back home he won't find it so easy.' He sipped at his tea. 'Tell me what you saw, Tessa.'

'Nothing really. Hannah was driving, we pulled up outside here, had a bit of a chat then got out of the car. We were here to see Todd Fraser because a signal had been detected being used from here that wasn't the iPhone we believed Todd to have. On the way here we received confirmation that Paul's fingerprints had been found on the Christmas tree baubles, so Todd had some explaining to do.'

She hesitated as the evening's events threatened to overwhelm her.

'Take your time,' Yarwood said, watching her face carefully.

'We got out of the car, still chatting. Hannah must have managed to lock it, because when I tried to open my passenger door to use the police transmitter, I couldn't open it. As I say, we were still chatting, and the crack of the shot was loud. I dropped to the floor and assumed Hannah did the same. I knew she would be still, and getting her bearings, because the shot had come from her side, not mine. I waited a short amount of time, and as I say, tried to get into the car but couldn't. I whispered to her to unlock it, but there was no response. I called for assistance using my phone, and then slid around the car to see...' and the tears came.

Heartbreaking tears, that rolled and rolled and rolled down her cheeks, unchecked.

'Here, darling,' Edna said, and passed her a box of tissues. 'You let those tears flow, for as long as you want.' She looked at Yarwood, who stood.

'Thank you for my drink, Edna. It was welcome. Tessa, I'm going out to my car and I'll wait there for you, for however long you want.'

Tessa gave a brief nod of acknowledgement, waited until he had left the house then took out her mobile phone.

'Doris? Are you still with Mouse?'

'I am, Tessa. Do you need me for something?'

'I need all of you. Can you get Kat there?'

'I can.'

'Good. I'll be there in about twenty minutes.'

'What's wrong? I can hear something in your voice.'

'I'll explain when I get there. We have work to do. Our team needs to be on full alert with this one, and I need your extracurricular skills.'

'Then in that case I'll ring Alistair. I'm sure he'll enjoy the walk across the village. You're not drunk, are you?'

Tessa gave a short bark of laughter. 'I wish. But no, blazing mad, and ready to kill.'

'Then we do need Alistair. And, Tessa – don't ask questions that we can't answer.'

'Doris, since the day I met you I've not been able to ask questions because you can't answer them. See you shortly.'

Tessa disconnected and slowly unpeeled the blankets from around her. 'Thank you so much, Edna. I'm going to let Superintendent Yarwood drop me off in Eyam, I need friends tonight. You've been an absolute star, and I won't forget you.'

'You go and catch that Paul Fraser, Tessa. You make him pay.'

'Haven't you heard, Edna?' Tessa gave a small smile. 'Superintendent Yarwood took me off the case.'

'Yeah, right,' Edna responded. 'You get him, Tessa, and give me a call to let me know. Good luck, lovey.'

23

Paul Fraser drove a mile away from Bamford, and parked on a small industrial estate to think through his problems.

'Fucking snow,' he grumbled, as he watched it settle on his windscreen wipers the second he switched them off. Within five minutes his vision was obscured and he laughed as he realised it was an everyday occurrence with him, vision obscurity. And on the one day he managed to control it, he brought down a copper. Good job he managed to get away quick, he'd ring Todd later and find out what was going on. He guessed he wouldn't be back at the house tonight, but he couldn't let an opportunity like that piece of target practice go to waste. He reckoned he'd hit her in the leg, the way she dropped straight to the floor. Pity he couldn't stay around long enough to get her mate. He'd always wanted to kill a copper.

So, what to do? He pulled the sleeping bag around his legs and immediately felt warmer. He didn't fancy sleeping here though, they probably had a couple of police patrols checking things during the night, so he had to go somewhere else. He daren't risk a hotel, not now they'd started showing his picture around.

He thought for some time, then remembered a small campsite in the Hope Valley, off the beaten track. It was sheltered, and he guessed on a night like this there'd be nobody checking it out. He needed to sort tonight, and then tomorrow Todd would be able to pull his finger out and get him a place to stay that was safe until everything had died down.

Paul tucked the sleeping bag a bit tighter around him, turned on the ignition and cleared the windscreen. He was surprised to see how much snow had fallen since he'd parked up, and he eased his way carefully off the industrial estate and down towards the main road.

He spotted the police car behind him getting closer and closer, and intuitively knew they'd recognised his number plate. He put his foot down and felt the car surge forward then lose traction. He wrestled with the steering wheel, tried to put the wiper blades on a faster speed, and felt the car begin to turn sideways before hitting a van parked on the side of the road. The momentum pushed the Astra towards the middle of the road and the gritting lorry coming up the other side couldn't stop in time.

The flames were initially small, and his shock evaporated as he realised the danger in front of his eyes. He tried to open his door but it was rigidly attached to the front of the lorry. He could see two men getting down from the truck, and he took off his seat belt and tried to get to the passenger side of the Astra, and then out through the door that wasn't jammed closed. His sleeping bag was wrapped around his legs and before he could untangle himself, the car gave a terrific whoosh.

Flames engulfed it and Paul Fraser died without knowing he'd killed a copper.

• • •

'You're sure you're going to be okay?' Eric Yarwood asked, as Tessa opened his passenger door.

She hesitated. 'For tonight I will be. I don't think I'll ever be okay again, in all honesty, but tonight I'm with friends.'

'Then I'll be in touch in a couple of days, Tessa.'

She watched as he drove carefully out of Eyam, then she walked towards the side door leading to Mouse's flat.

Inside were the people she needed: Kat and Carl Heaton, Mouse and Joel, Doris and the man she had referred to as Alistair, and Belle. No Luke, no Martha.

She looked around at all the faces so dear to her and burst out crying.

They listened carefully to everything she had to say, not knowing how to think, how to react to the awful news she had spent a mere couple of minutes conveying to them. Doris had immediately stood and hugged her, followed by Kat and Mouse.

'We're all here for you,' Doris whispered. 'You know that. You'll stay here tonight?'

'Thank you. You have enough room, Mouse?'

'Of course. If you don't mind the sofa bed in the lounge. Stay as long as you want. And cry as much as you want.'

Tessa nodded, mouthed a 'thank you', and accepted a brandy Kat handed her.

'So, how can we help you find this piece of shit?' Mouse was nothing if not blunt.

'The first thing you have to know,' Tessa explained, 'is I am off the case. Off work, in fact, not only the case. All bets are off, all restrictions lifted, I am free to do what the hell I want, and I want to see Paul Fraser squirm with a gun held to his head.

Doris, the gun that you used to blow Leon Rowe's hand off, I want it.'

Doris sat down with a thud. Alistair looked at her and openly laughed.

'Doris Lester! You didn't?'

Doris looked at the others for support and could see they were all holding back the threatened laughter, despite the sombre ambience that had been there a few seconds earlier.

'Can you really imagine me shooting off somebody's hand? Now come on, I was sixty-nine, I think, when Leon left Kat. Not a teenager with a trigger-happy finger. As if I would.'

'You'll get it for me, then?' Tessa asked.

'I'll have to go to the cottage,' Doris said, 'so it could be a couple of days. Bradwell is probably closed off. There must be a few in the village who don't pay their council tax, because we rarely see a gritter. But surely it doesn't have to be as drastic as that. He'll be in prison for the rest of his life when they catch him. And you'll be the one who'll put him there, because you were there when he shot Hannah. You'll be in court to smile when he's sent down for an all-life term.'

'Where's the damn gun, Doris?'

Doris heard Kat whisper, 'Oh my God,' before turning to look at Mouse, who was losing the battle with laughter.

'Can I take the fifth amendment?' Doris said.

'Doris, are you in trouble?' Alistair asked. 'Tell me what I need to do.'

Tessa stared at the good-looking man who was clearly infatuated by Doris. 'Alistair,' she said. 'I'm not sure who you are, but Doris isn't in trouble. It didn't take much working out why Leon Rowe only had one hand with all its fingers, but as he was dead I decided it wasn't worth pursuing. However, I filed it away for future reference in case I ever needed a gun under the radar. For some reason they don't let our police carry guns. And I don't really want to be meeting One-armed Freddy under some damn canal bridge at midnight to get one from him.'

'FYI, Tessa, Doris is licensed to carry. So, Doris do you want to tell the lovely police lady where the gun is?'

'It's up a chicken's bum in my freezer.'

There was silence for a moment.

'Oh, Hannah, my lovely, are you hearing this? All this time we've wondered what happened to that gun.' Tessa raised her eyes heavenwards.

Mouse handed Tessa a box of tissues, and once again the tears fell. Tessa tried to apologise and they simply hugged her.

'You talk to Hannah all you like, Tessa, then she'll never leave us. You want another brandy or something hot?'

Tessa blew her nose and wiped the tears from her cheeks. 'I'd love a cup of tea, no sugar, please.'

They all gave their orders and Kat and Mouse moved to the kitchen area to begin preparing the assorted drinks. Tessa's phone pealed out the Rod Stewart song that had become so important to her and Hannah. She looked at the screen and saw SupYar on it.

'Superintendent?'

He spoke for a couple of minutes, and then Tessa sighed.

'Thank you for letting me know. So it's over?'

She disconnected and turned to face everyone.

'He's dead. Doris, I don't need your gun, it can stay up your chicken's bum. It seems he was being followed by one of our cars that recognised the number plate and he panicked. His Astra went into a skid, bounced off a transit van and hit a gritter on the other side of the road. The Astra burst into flames.'

There was silence while everyone digested the information. It impacted on them all, and they processed the information.

'We have to tell the Clarks. They can release Mark and his

colleagues, and sleep easily in their beds tonight.' Kat looked around at the others. 'Do we tell them tonight or tomorrow?'

Doris was clearly troubled. 'Let's tell them tomorrow. I don't want to ease anything off yet because something has been bothering me for some time, and until that's sorted, I'm not convinced they're safe. Let me think this through overnight, and we'll have a meeting tomorrow morning, but I'd like to call Mark into that meeting. And you also, Alistair, if you're free. It'll be another brain going into the mix.'

Yarwood told Todd himself.

He was brought from his cell to the interview room shortly after ten, thinking that maybe it was a little late for them to start interviewing him, and maybe they had a night shift who did the interviews.

He was left sitting at the table for around fifteen minutes, the young police officer standing to one side totally uncommunicative. Finally the door opened, and although Todd didn't know who he was, he knew he wasn't PC Plod.

'Mr Fraser, I'm Superintendent Yarwood. We're not going to be recording this interview, because it isn't one. You'll probably have questions, but for tonight, we won't.'

'What d'you mean?'

'I thought I was pretty clear. I'm sorry, Mr Fraser, but I have some bad news for you. Paul, your brother, died tonight. He was involved in a road accident caused by him skidding in the snow. He died at the scene. I'm sorry for your loss, Todd.'

Todd stared at the tall man in front of him. 'He's dead?'

Yarwood nodded. 'The Astra crashed head first into a gritter truck after it had bounced off a stationary transit van. It burst into flames and your brother was unable to get out of the vehicle. The men from the gritter couldn't get close enough to the car to pull him out.'

There was a stunned silence while Todd let the news sink in. 'It's over? I can stop worrying what the loony is going to do next?'

Yarwood had seen some dreadful reactions over the years to news of deaths, but rarely this level of relief.

'You can. Any charges levelled against you, if they're proven, will still stand of course, but unfortunately your brother won't face the charges he should be facing, that of murdering a colleague in cold blood.'

Yarwood stood and made to leave the room.

'Of course,' Todd said, 'it might not all be over yet. I'll see DCI Marsden in the morning, will I?'

24

Tessa didn't really sleep, her mind kept going to the horrific scene that faced her as she crawled around the back of the patrol car, and the way her mind had immediately known Hannah was gone. There had been no sense of hope at any point. Only loss and intense overwhelming love.

Tessa got up shortly after four, knowing that the deliberations inside her head needed to be put down on paper before they drifted away; she heard the creak as Doris's door opened.

'I've got a page full of thoughts,' Doris whispered, echoing Tessa's own ideas, and keen not to wake anyone else. 'I can't sleep for thinking through everything that's happened from day one. We've shared some convoluted and twisted cases, Tessa, but this has been so much deeper and darker than anything that's gone before. How can a parole board be so gullible? He didn't turn into a psychopath on release day, surely he exhibited symptoms prior to that.'

'It seems not,' Tessa responded, keeping her voice low. 'But that's the thing about psychosis, the psychopaths make an art form out of keeping it hidden. Brady and Hindley, the Yorkshire Ripper, the Wests, all classic examples of how nice they could be, prior to taking a life. All psychopaths. Fraser set himself a task when he was sent down, and that was to get out again. If he had become involved in anything while inside, he'd never have got out, so he was squeaky clean. It seems he had two aims: to kill Julie Clark and finish that job off, and to then go into hiding and stay there for the rest of his life. But in all of this he needed his brother's help.'

'And he went along with it.'

'To an extent. I suspect originally Todd was humouring Paul's fantasies, because he never believed for a minute that Paul would get out. When it started to look as though he might, Todd had to start to plan. I think, when Christy Brown died and Todd got the house, it was like a sign to them. They had an escape.'

Doris sighed. 'What an absolute cock-up this has all turned out to be. I reckon Paul not only fooled the authorities, he also fooled Todd. He used Todd to get him close to Julie. But there's something we're missing, which is why I don't want to call off protection for the Clark family, not yet. We'll explain the whole situation to them tomorrow, and it will ultimately be their choice, but I'm hoping they listen carefully to me. It's why I want Mark Playter at that meeting tomorrow morning, he'll be able to back up what I'm saying if I can convince him I'm right.'

Tessa stood. 'I'm going to make a hot chocolate. You want one?'

'Yes, please. Maybe it will drug us to sleep.'

Tessa poured some milk into the pan, and placed it on the stove. 'I have to go about half seven tomorrow. I need to be at the nursing home at Bakewell shortly after breakfast time. I rang them while Yarwood was bringing me here, to see what time Hannah's mum gets up, and they said she has breakfast about seven, so I'm going to try to time it for when she's eaten. I've told them why I'm going, and they've promised to make sure she's back in her own room ready for when I get there. After I've told her, I'm going to stay with her for a bit, she'll need to talk about Hannah. We both will. I'll be back here for the meeting at ten. Is that okay?'

'Tessa, you do what you have to do. She has MS, doesn't she, Hannah's mother?'

'She does. A couple of months ago they warned Hannah that it seemed to be escalating, and I'd give the world not to be telling Joan Sharpe this news. She is a feisty lady, but this will likely be the end of her. They were really close, and even more so after Hannah's stepdad died.'

Taking their hot chocolates with them, they went to their bedrooms, and Doris managed to sleep until her alarm woke her at half past eight. Mouse knocked on her door, and once she heard her nan say she was up, she opened the door slightly. 'Stay in bed for ten minutes and come round. I know you were up with Tessa in the early hours, so I've made you a cup of tea.'

'Thank you, sweetheart,' Doris said, and shuffled up the bed. And suddenly she knew what was bothering her, the thing that had been on the edge of her consciousness. She grabbed her notepad and wrote.

'You writing a book?' Mouse asked, as she carried the tray with tea and toast through, placing it on the bedside table. 'It's nice I can do this for you, usually you're up first. Notes for the meeting?'

'They are. It's something that's occurred to me, that I don't want to let slip. We can't miss anything on this, Mouse. Losing Hannah is unthinkable, and Tessa is currently in denial, but once this case is out the way, she's going to implode. We can take care of her, but we have to sort this first, and sort it fast.'

Mouse sat on the edge of the bed. 'Want to talk about it now?'

Doris shook her head. 'No, I need to mull it over first. And while I've got you here, captive as it were, shall we discuss a certain gun in my freezer?'

'It was Kat.'

'What was Kat?'

'Who dobbed you in.'

'No, it was both of you.'

Mouse grinned. 'I can't get over the fact that Tessa knew anyway.'

'Smart cookie, that woman. On Leon's autopsy report, it concentrates on his death and basically which bullet killed him. The hand is an aside, although it is mentioned. It says something like "wound to left hand, approx. six to twelve months".'

'Does Kat know you've seen his autopsy report?'

'No.' Doris smiled. 'And neither do you. I'll deny it if it ever comes up in conversation.'

'Nan,' Mouse said as she stood, 'you live a strange life. Maybe it's time to consider leaving the working life behind, and settling down.'

'Certainly not. Why on earth would I want to do that?'

'Alistair Glentham,' Mouse said, and gently closed Doris's door.

Yarwood called Carl in early, and explained he'd taken Tessa off the case and told her not to consider coming into work until the end of January. 'So, I'm making you acting DCI, and I want you to do your sideways shuffle from Fraud and head up this case until we've crossed every T.'

'Been in it from the beginning, sir,' Carl said. 'It's partly a

Connection case, and I married the lovely Kat. Will you be talking to the team this morning?'

'I will. It's hard to take in, you know, when somebody like Hannah Granger is killed. I had a chat with Tessa last night, told her I'd guessed about her and Hannah but was ignoring it until they were ready to tell me. I'm guessing you know?'

'Known for months, sir, but it's not my place to say anything. DCI Marsden outranks me. Off the record, though – they were made for each other. Can I say something else? This case is virtually at an end, following the killer's death last night. I don't think anybody on Tessa's team would be happy taking on the DS role at this time, so can we leave it at the ranks that are there, and when Tessa comes back we'll sort something then? DC Ainsworth will have taken her sergeant's exams by then, so it won't be difficult stepping up to the rank. We have to be careful, sir. I'd like a chat with Fiona, explain the situation and see how she feels about being my acting-up sergeant, without it being general knowledge.'

Yarwood inclined his head. 'That's fine, Carl. Don't mention anything to Tessa, we'll tell her the plans when it's time for her to return to work. So we're winding this down, now? We have a case to prepare against Todd Fraser, and you need to get out to the Clarks' home and fill them in on what's happened.'

Carl felt a little uncomfortable. 'Can we have a conversation later today, sir? I'm going to a meeting at Connection at ten, but I know Kat was up half the night, and the notes on the dining table indicate we're being a bit premature in assuming this one's closed.'

Yarwood sighed. 'These bloody women. Can't we employ them, and keep them quiet?'

'We could, but they'd want positions considerably higher than yours, sir. I believe Doris already is.'

'What?' Yarwood looked puzzled.

'I know little, but certain things came out in the summer that showed Doris wasn't the little old granny we'd believed her to be. And she currently has a guest, staying in the village. Even I recognised his name. Alistair Glentham?'

'Alistair Glentham of–'

Carl held up his hand and cut him off. 'I'm saying nothing more, but that's why I don't think this is over yet. You're still happy to have me in Tessa's position? I'm assuming she'll be at the meeting this morning, because she'll not grieve properly for Hannah until this whole thing is closed to her satisfaction. I'll keep an eye on her, we don't want her seeking revenge for what happened to Hannah.' He had a brief flashback to the hilarity following the disclosure of the gun up the chicken's bum, and worked hard at stopping the smile.

'Of course. Look, keep me informed, and don't let those three women run rings around you, even if you are married to one of them.'

'Four women, sir,' Carl said quietly. 'You've kindly sent Tessa over to the side of the angels by taking her off this case. If there's one thing I know about Tessa Marsden, she'll not stop until this is finalised to her satisfaction. And now she's privy to everything Connection have on the case. Remember, they started on this before we did.'

Carl was the last to arrive. He walked into the office, and Kat locked the door and lit up the closed sign. He kissed her cheek, and walked through to the extended room; it was the first time they had used the folding room divider, and now Kat and Mouse's room housed the large gathering.

He spotted Tessa, standing looking out of the window at the unblemished snow around the back of the building, and tapped her on the shoulder. She turned, and he pulled her into his arms. 'I don't need to say much,' he whispered, 'but we're here for you, for anything you might want, twenty-four hours a day.'

Tessa nodded, and dried the tears that had been in her eyes on his jacket. The others were starting to sit down, and Carl gave a brief acknowledgement of Mark Playter's presence, then saw to his surprise that Greg Clark was there. They must feel confident, up at the house, that the problem had gone away with the death of the man they believed wanted to kill them, and anyone else in their circle. Both Mark and Greg looked relaxed; Carl hoped they would still look like that at the end of the meeting, but he doubted it.

Everyone had a hot drink, and Kat placed three jugs of water and glasses down the centre of the table formed by joining both desks together.

Kat, Mouse, Doris, Carl, Alistair, Joel, Tessa, Mark and Greg settled, and Doris, Kat, Mouse and Tessa placed their scribbled notes in front of them.

Joel felt nervous. He was used to attending formal meetings, most days he was at one or another, but this was different. This was his first one with Mouse's business at the forefront, not his own, but given the danger that had been present for all of them, and the fact he couldn't get to Manchester because of the snow, she had suggested he maybe should be there.

And he knew exactly how angry Nan, Mouse, Kat and Tessa were. The air in the flat the previous evening had been charged with rage.

25

Doris opened the meeting by introducing every attendee, and then asked that they switch off their phones until they finished. She saw Carl was about to query it, and she held up a hand.

'We need fifteen minutes of uninterrupted life, Carl. I promise you can switch it back on straight away.'

Luke picked up his phone, a smile on his face. Time to check in with work. The disappointment he felt when first Nan, then Kat, then Mouse's phones all went to voicemail was soul-destroying. He hoped they weren't out getting into trouble, and he wasn't there to help. He rang Nan's again and left a voicemail telling her he would ring later.

The doctor's confirmation that he could go home once pharmacy had delivered his pain relief had made his spirits soar. An appointment had been made for the day the cast could be taken off his arm, and he had rung his mum to tell her the good news.

Struggling to get on his jeans had been a bit of a nightmare with only one working arm, but with the nurse's help when it came to fastening the waist button he'd dealt with it fine. His mum had said she would bring him a zip-up jacket and a loose sweatshirt as his arm had to remain in a sling, so once the jeans were on he laid back on his bed and went over again what had happened to him.

He knew everybody would make him stay at home, not start work yet, but there was nothing to stop him going for a walk. Six and a half minutes to the Connection office – okay, maybe seven and a half in the snow. He could always say it would help clear the niggling little headache that the doctors said was perfectly normal after a head injury.

He was starting to doze – the crossword had drained him of energy – when the nurse came in, waving a white bag full of tablets.

'Time to go, Luke,' she said, and his smile lit up the room. He thanked her and picked up his phone once again, this time to ring Naomi.

'Tessa,' Doris said, 'before we get down to what we need to sort, I want to say on behalf of every single person here how very much we're all going to miss our lovely Hannah. I'm not convinced you should be here, but I know you won't stay away.'

Tessa gave a brief nod in acknowledgement of the words she knew were heartfelt, and she felt Kat's hand reach to squeeze hers.

'Carl,' Doris continued, 'don't answer this if you can't, but are the police winding down the major side of this crime? I realise you will have to deal with the issue of Todd, but Paul Fraser is dead, so is that side of the investigation closed?'

'Superintendent Yarwood says it is,' he said, but Doris caught the hesitation in his voice.

'And you?'

'Look, I'm struggling here, because Kat was up half the night, and if she feels it's not at an end, I'll back her feelings.'

'She's not the only one who was up half the night, and I think Nan should tell us what she's thinking, because if she's come up with thoughts in the same way we have,' Mouse pointed quickly towards Kat, Tessa and herself, 'then this is not over.'

'You're right,' Nan said, 'and I want Mark and Greg back at the Clarks', ensuring nobody does anything foolish until we say it's done, life can resume.'

Greg looked at Mark. 'Should I go back now?'

Mark frowned. 'No, we need to both listen, and then you need to convey to the family any perceived danger. We'll leave as soon as Doris says that's all we have. Okay?'

'Thank you.' Doris pulled her notes towards her. 'Something has been on the edge of my consciousness for a couple of days. Tessa, tell me about Edna Davis.'

'Good grief. How do you know about...' Tessa glanced briefly at Alistair, who dropped his head, hiding the faint smile on his lips. 'Never mind. I won't ask. Edna Davis is an eighty-nine-year-old lady who lives next door to Todd Fraser. She's lived there for a long time, knew Christy Brown, the Fraser boys' mother, very well. On the day we discovered the address of the house in Bamford that Todd had inherited, she was out so we didn't get to speak to her, but as the facts started to develop we did.'

Tessa took a deep breath. 'Hannah and I did. It turned out she's a pretty smart lady, and gave us a lot of information about the car that had been parked on the newly made parking area in the back garden of Todd's house. Her and her husband had owned a car sales place until their retirement.'

'Was she the one who told you about the Christmas tree?' Carl asked.

'She was. She said the tree hadn't been there when she went out that day, but when she came home it was. We went through that house checking for fingerprints as you know, but there was nothing to show that Paul Fraser had been there. But we didn't check the baubles. When we did we found prints on three of them, two of them were personalised and were Sheffield Wednesday baubles. It proved he had been in the house that day.'

'Thank you,' Doris said. 'Now we come to what's been niggling away at some of us. Todd and Paul didn't know we knew of the existence of this house, so in theory they should have both been sitting feeling comfortable when Tessa and Hannah arrived. Instead, Todd had wiped everywhere to get rid of prints, and there was nothing in the house at all to suggest a second person had been there. The car had disappeared also. This is where we temporarily leave the police investigation out of it, and go on to the Connection involvement. We had been employed to track down Paul Fraser. Once Julie's parents were killed and it was confirmed it was Paul Fraser who had murdered them, we were further employed to sort security for the house and family. Therefore our priority will always be to the person employing us, in this case Greg and Julie Clark.'

Doris hesitated for a moment. 'I take full responsibility for this next part because I was the one who made the phone call. Before I passed the information on to the police, I rang the Clark home and told them we had found a house in Bamford owned by Todd Fraser. That was the only information I gave because I didn't want Greg taking justice into his own hands. Then I rang the police. In a very short space of time, and I mean *very* short, that information was with Todd and Paul. I can only imagine that they had set up a disappearing act on a *just in case* basis, because it worked to perfection. Greg, did you pass that on immediately to everybody?'

Greg's face was devoid of colour. 'Of course I did. It was massive for all of us. But hang on a minute, Doris. Are you saying that someone I told about the discovery of the house in Bamford was in contact with Todd and Paul Fraser?'

There was silence around the table as everybody tried to digest what Doris was saying. Both Kat and Mouse pushed their notes towards Doris, who glanced through them to see that they had come to similar conclusions. Doris looked at Tessa, who held up one sheet of paper that she had folded in half and placed in front of her. She opened it and in capital letters it said **WHO THE FUCK WARNED THEM WE WERE ON OUR WAY????**

Doris shuffled through the notes, complete with doodles she had done while she let her thoughts roam through the long night, and eventually found what she was seeking.

'Okay, listen to my list of everyone who was in that house on that day.'

She paused for a moment, then spoke.

'Greg Clark, Julie Clark, Oliver... Ollie Clark, Saskia van Berkel, Tracy Worrall, Kaya Worrall, Mark Playter, Denny Evans, Ian Downes, Leila Palmer, and I can't remember exactly when we upped the security by two further people, but they're on the list anyway, Fred Iveson and Zara Ormond. Somebody on this list contacted either Todd or Paul and warned them that we had found the house. So here's what's going to happen next. Greg and Mark, you need to go back to Hathersage as soon as possible. I can't instruct you to keep quiet about this meeting, obviously, but if you tell anybody I need to know about it. I don't believe the danger has dropped at all, because somebody in that house has a connection with the Fraser brothers. Until we find who it is, there is a threat to life.'

Greg lifted up a hand almost in a gesture of defeat. 'And we've added to the problem because Petra, Saskia's sister, will be at the house when we get back. The plan was that she would visit for the Christmas period, and she arrived two days ago. She's been in a hotel, but Sas rang her early this morning to say it was okay to come to us, because Fraser was dead. She'll be there and unpacked by now, I expect.'

Mark groaned. 'We should have discussed this, Greg. I'm assuming Julie will have okayed it with my people? They won't take instructions from anyone else...'

'She will. But to be fair, after last night's news I would have okayed it the same.'

'Presumably her name is also van Berkel?' Doris added it to her list.

'As far as I know,' Greg said. 'I'll ring you as soon as we get home if it isn't. What will you do now?'

'I'm going to find the connection that links somebody on here with the Frasers. How is Julie coping, Greg?'

'Not good. I know Tracy is worried because Julie is eating very little. The sooner you come up with the name of our mole the better, Doris.'

Greg and Mark stood, asked to be kept informed, and Kat followed them out of the room. She watched them walk across to the big Land Rover that she guessed belonged to Mark, then locked the door once again. She remained at the door as the black cab pulled up outside the shop, aware of a few snowflakes beginning to fall. She really was getting fed up of the snow.

She saw Naomi get out, then move around to the other door and assist the second passenger.

Kat gave a small yelp, unlocked the door, and went outside to help.

Luke was battered. He had bruises on his face that were turning from blue to yellow, and a coat that was fastened but shielding his left arm. He limped and Kat put her arms around him.

'I'm sorry,' Naomi said, 'but as soon as he realised we were approaching home from this end of the village he insisted on stopping. I'll ask the cab driver to hang on for a couple of minutes...'

Kat laughed. 'No, get your stuff out and let's get you both inside. We can take you the rest of the way. Come on, Luke, let's go make Doris cry.'

26

Doris obliged with the tears. She couldn't help it. Luke popped his head around the door, having to lean on it because he was hurting.

He struggled inside the room and she held him, crying onto the fleece jacket he wore, her tears like rivers.

He held her, his own tears close to the surface. 'You've not forgotten me then?' he whispered into her hair.

'No we bloody haven't,' she whispered back. 'We couldn't take the risk of visiting you and bringing any other actions down on your head. Today I was coming to see you, because things have changed and I needed to tell you. And here you are, you've come to us instead!'

'Changed? They've caught him?'

'Luke, let's get you sat down. You seem uncomfortable. Coffee?'

He turned to look at his mother, who nodded. 'Ten minutes, Luke, then I'm hoping somebody can take us up the hill. You'll be ready for your painkillers soon anyway.'

He smiled. That was an extension. She'd originally said they could only call in for two minutes. Mouse poured him a coffee, then topped up everyone's cup. Naomi refused one, said she'd had enough coffee for the day, but she'd have a glass of water.

The next ten minutes were ten minutes Luke never wanted to experience again. He hadn't listened to any news while in the hospital, and knew nothing of Hannah's death, nor that of Paul Fraser, the man who had tried to kill him.

After listening to Doris, he turned to Tessa.

'No words, Luke,' she said softly. 'They're not necessary. I know how much you liked Hannah, we all loved her. We need to put his brother away for a long time, and we need to find out other things that as yet you're not aware of. By the time you return to work after Christmas it should all be tidied away, and offenders locked up in their cells.'

'After Christmas?' He looked at Doris.

'After Christmas, Luke,' she said, trying desperately to sound stern. 'And not even then if you're not fully recovered.'

'Oh, I will be. It's my left arm in a sling, you know, and I'm right-handed.'

Doris looked for back-up towards Naomi. 'Help me out here.'

'It's Luke,' she said. 'You got any thick rope I can tie him to the armchair with?'

'We can buy some out of petty cash.'

'You leave my petty cash alone, Doris Lester.' Luke winked with his eye that wasn't black, blue or yellow. Suddenly he noticed Alistair, and he stared at him.

'Luke, this is a friend from London, Alistair Glentham, who arrived alongside the heavy snow, and has wisely decided to stay until Derbyshire sorts out its roads. He's going to be helping Mouse and me with some work on the case.'

Luke gave a slight nod. 'Mr Glentham. I take it you're computer literate, extremely literate, then.'

Alistair smiled at Luke's use of words. 'I am. What's more important is I have the right passwords for the right places. I've heard a lot about you, Luke. An awful lot. In fact for the three days I've been here, you're all I've heard about.'

Naomi interrupted. 'Luke, drink your coffee, please. I want to get you home.'

A frown briefly flashed across his face, but he knew when he was fighting a losing battle, so he finished his coffee and stood, awkwardly and ungainly. 'Who would have thought,' he said, 'that bruises could hurt so much.'

'In a week's time you'll be so much better. I'll pop up and see you tomorrow unless anything happens to make it not safe yet again,' Doris said.

'Can I do anything? I have my laptop at home, you know.'

'Luke! For goodness sake,' Doris went into scolding mode. 'Go home and get better. No, you can't do anything. Go on the laptop and find yourself a new car or something.'

He laughed. 'Yeah, you're right. I'll have to lower my sights a bit, I was planning on waiting another six months, but I've got some savings. I've not even thought about a car, to be honest. Was mine totalled then?'

'Absolutely.' Kat stepped in. 'And we thought the same of you, Luke. It's good to have you back, even if you're a bit battered and bruised. I'll run you and your mum home, come on.'

They headed for the door and Doris followed them out. Kat walked across the square and drove her car around to pick them up. Naomi sat in the rear seat, and Doris helped Luke into the front passenger seat. She leaned in to help him with the seat belt, and whispered, 'Before you look for a car, check your bank account.'

. . .

187

The smile on Doris's face was one of pure joy. 'Wasn't that lovely,' she announced, daring anyone to disagree with her.

'Certainly was, and it's made me more determined than ever to track down the culprits behind this problem we have,' Mouse said.

'Right, Alistair and I will work in my office. Shall we put this room back to being two rooms now?'

'Nan, Mouse, you get on doing what you do best, it will only take Kat, Carl and I ten minutes to put this back to rights. Carl, what will you tell Yarwood?' Tessa said.

'God knows. I think I'll try to avoid him and say nothing. I've enough to be working on with the Todd Fraser aspect of this, and you know what? I think within a couple of days you'll be telling me all the answers anyway. Can I claim all the kudos for this when it comes out?'

Tessa gave a dry laugh. 'Not if you want to stay out of prison. Don't ask questions, Carl, I've found it's the best way. Let's get Mouse's desk back where it should be and she can get started.'

Doris and Alistair took glasses of water in with them, and both opened their laptops.

'You're close to Luke?' he asked.

'Right from day one. We have the same sense of humour, and his work rate is awesome. I can ask him to do anything and it's immediately done. He's good company when we do surveillance work, and he has loads of qualifications now.'

'He could take over from you when you retire? Is that the plan?'

'My plan is not to retire.'

'You have to at some point.'

'Wendy did and she died.' Doris had talked often of Wendy

and their adventures during the summer months, and he struggled for a response.

'But was she dying before she retired? I suspect she was.'

Doris shrugged. 'I don't know. She didn't tell me about the tumour because she knew what it would do to me, but I could tell there was something wrong. I didn't know it would end as it did, and I suppose retiring before you are ill is the best way to do it. I've simply never considered it.' The thought hit her like a bolt of lightning. 'Alistair, you're not ill?'

He smiled at her. 'I promise you I'm not. I'm only tired of working really. Financially I don't need to, and all my adult life has been about top-secret stuff, hiding in plain sight, keeping the country safe, and eventually it wears you down. I have a brilliant woman ready to step into my shoes, so I judged now was the right time to go. Will you visit me?'

'In London, or in France?'

'Both. I don't want to have to wait till the summer to see you again.'

Doris felt the blush in her cheeks and bent over her laptop. She didn't want to be honest with herself, she wanted to lie and say she wasn't bothered about keeping up the relationship, but this man was getting under her skin, and she knew as soon as he went back to London, she would be checking on train times. And in March it would extend to plane times, or the excitement of the TGV down to St Raphael.

'Will you take Tracy and Kaya Worrall? I'll go with Saskia van Berkel. I know Petra's there now, but she wasn't there on the day we're interested in.' Doris didn't look up.

'Smart change of subject, Doris Lester. I won't give up, though. I shouldn't have let you stay here all those years ago.'

Now she looked up. 'But you did, Alistair, you did.'

. . .

'I can't find a birth registered in the name of Saskia van Berkel.'

'She's not been born?' Alistair grinned and sipped at his water.

'If she has, I don't know where, or who her mother is.'

'How deep have you gone?'

'UK, the Netherlands, Belgium. Simply basic-level births. I'll go deeper.'

He nodded, and returned to his own laptop.

Tracy Worrall had always been Tracy Worrall, no marriage. Kaya Worrall's birth certificate showed a father, name of Adam Loxley, but further easy investigation showed a death certificate dated five months after his daughter's birth, from a drug overdose. Kaya's birth certificate showed her name as Kaya Loxley, but he quickly discovered a formal change of name for the child to Worrall. It seemed Tracy didn't want any part of Kaya to have a Loxley inheritance. They had lived in Sheffield at the same address until Kaya was five and then had moved to Hathersage.

He quickly typed in his findings, with something nagging at the back of his mind about 232 Bramall Lane where mother and daughter Worrall had lived prior to taking the carer job looking after Julie Clark. He'd seen Bramall Lane somewhere else, and he couldn't think where it had been.

'Doris.'

She looked up.

'How well do you know Sheffield?'

'Intimately. I lived there all my life until I met Kat and everything changed. Why?'

'Bramall Lane. Does it mean anything?'

'It's a street virtually in the city centre. Sheffield United ground is there. Why?'

'It's where the Worralls lived, and now you've mentioned it's the name of the football stadium, maybe I'm subconsciously linking the two. Okay, thanks.' He returned to his search, and Doris stared at her screen.

She brought up the file where everything discovered so far had been stored, and used her search to type in Bramall Lane.

Prior to Christy Brown becoming Christy Brown and moving to live at Bamford, she had lived on Bramall Lane as Christy Fraser.

'Alistair, there's a link and it's nothing to do with football.'

He smiled. 'I thought everything in Sheffield was to do with football. What's the link?'

She explained, and he typed something into his laptop. 'They lived four doors away from each other. Tracy Worrall must have known who Paul Fraser was before she went to Hathersage. Although...' he typed once again. 'She took the house on Bramall Lane in 2003, Kaya was born the following year and they lived there until 2009. Paul Fraser was already in prison at the time she rented the house, he was sent down in 2001. It's entirely possible she didn't know, and all of this is a coincidence.'

Doris laughed. 'At Connection we don't believe in coincidence. I think Tracy Worrall needs her life looking at from every angle, but I don't want to see her taken out of the Clark household, not at this stage.'

'Reasons?'

'Number one, she's the one who cares for Julie and they would really struggle without her. Number two, if we remove her from the equation and we've got it wrong, it leaves the family wide open to whoever the Fraser contact really is. Number three, I don't think she would risk losing Kaya to help Paul Fraser – it simply doesn't make sense.'

27

During the drive back home, Mark and Greg had discussed the situation in sporadic bursts of conversation; Greg wanted to dismiss it out of hand, unable to accept that people he knew and had grown to love could possibly have any connection to the Fraser brothers, but Mark had followed the reasoning with perfect clarity, and knew he had problems that at first glance seemed insurmountable.

How could he keep the family safe when it was somebody inside the family who was the problem? And the unthinkable was that it was one of his own people, his staff who had been vetted to the nth degree, leaving no stone unturned at any point in the process.

They pulled up to the gates and waited patiently for Leila to approach them. She checked the inside of the car and the boot before allowing them to pass. The Christmas tree in the lounge window glowed cheerfully, and for a moment Greg felt a sense of normality. For a moment.

'What do I do?' he said to Mark.

'Nothing for the present, if you don't mind, Greg. I need to think this through, work out how to handle it. I'm going to start by contacting somebody at the office. I want every one of my staff vetted again in case something has slipped by us. Once I can feel safe with my people, we can begin to work on yours, but it's got to be done fast, and clean. Extremely fast. I have to watch everybody. Any strange activity, I need to see it. The only thing I am sure of at this moment is that it's not me, and it's not Julie, so it's my job to clear as many people as I can, as fast as I can.'

Greg stared at him. 'You're not serious? You don't trust me?'

'I trust the findings of Connection, and the more I think about it, the more I'm sure they're right. They'll clear you first, and the second they do, Doris will ring me. I've already spoken to her and told her I need you onside. Then we watch everybody, Greg. Everybody.'

Mark's phone pinged and he checked the incoming text. It was from Mouse, and it was long, but it made it clear that Greg Clark was squeaky clean, she could find no connection at all to the Frasers and there were no black marks against his name, from any angle. He appeared to put his family first at all times, and she would recommend trusting him. She added at the end of the text that she was hoping to clear Mark Playter's name in exactly the same fashion, and she'd let him know as soon as she was certain he could trust himself.

He smiled, but knew she wasn't really joking.

Greg reached for the door handle to get out of the car, but Mark put a hand on his arm. 'Hang on a minute.'

He showed Greg the text, who read it and nodded. 'Good,' he said. 'I'm glad it's not in my head that I need to go and work out how best to kill my wife and son.'

'Sarcasm's not called for, Greg. We're doing our job to the best of our abilities, and that last bit at the end of the message from Beth Walters wasn't a joke. She has my name on her computer as we speak, and despite me running a second check on all my employees at this location, she'll be doing the same. Work with us, Greg, not against us.'

Greg hesitated for a brief moment, then nodded again. 'Sorry,' he said. 'We thought it was all over when we got the news about Fraser, but it's really not, is it?'

'Definitely not, and you have DCI Marsden and the Connection ladies to thank for spotting that this household is the weak link. Shall we go in?'

'Yes, and I need to speak to Julie on her own. I couldn't tell her anything this morning because we knew nothing, and this is going to devastate her. If there was any way we could see to her needs, I'd move her away from here...'

'Greg, we'll watch her all the time. I know Tracy has been with you for ten years, but don't make the mistake of assuming she's okay. For all we know, she could be related to Fraser, and have been waiting for his release all this time. Don't trust anybody except Julie, and I'll show you my Connection clearance as soon as it comes through. In the meantime, don't fucking trust me either.' Mark shook his head in exasperation at his own words and the two men left the car.

Luke swallowed the two painkillers his mother brought to him, and he carefully moved his arm to make it as comfortable as he could get it. He'd inspected his face after carefully brushing his teeth which were unbelievably tender, and had been slightly awestruck by the colourful skin reflected in the bathroom cabinet. They had recommended not shaving for a few days, and the stubble clearly in evidence made everything so much worse.

There was a gash down his right temple that was held together by what looked like glue and little white strips of paper, and there was a sizeable lump on the side of his head. The doctor had been at pains to explain that it was the cause of his unconscious state and if it had been bashed much harder, he would have been dead; one eye was open as normal but the other was only halfway there. The skin in general on his face and his upper body was varying shades of blue and yellow, and the stripe going across his chest from the pressure of the seat belt was almost navy blue.

His left leg and left arm had taken the biggest battering, and he had already been warned that his arm may have to have a second partial cast on it after they had removed the full cast, but that he should eventually have full use of it. His leg had showed no breaks, but the bruising was extensive; it looked even worse against his white boxers, and he had quickly pulled on his joggers. Even doing that one-handed was a chore, although so much easier than the fight with a pair of jeans.

He limped carefully downstairs into the kitchen. Naomi handed him some toast and looked him over. 'You look rubbish,' she said.

'Thanks, Mum. The girls both said the same, and if my nan says it, I might leave home.'

They heard a bedroom door close, and footsteps descend. He groaned. 'Speak of the devil...'

Geraldine entered the kitchen and looked at Luke for a long moment. 'And how's my gorgeous grandson feeling today?'

Luke punched the air with his right fist. 'Yes! I'm fine, Nan. Did I ever tell you how beautiful you are?'

She frowned, as if trying to recall a time. 'Not that I can remember. And don't get carried away, I thought I'd call you gorgeous to try to cheer you up. You actually look like you've gone ten rounds with Doris Lester.'

Tessa drove to her home to pick up some clean clothes, after agreeing to stay with Mouse for a few more days. She wasn't sure it was the right thing to do, but Mouse had said when you feel ready to go home, tell me and go.

She stopped the car outside her house, and saw the spray of flowers inside her porch. Only one person apart from her and Hannah had a key, and she knew the flowers had been placed there by her neighbour, Margie.

Tessa walked slowly up the path, unlocked the porch door, picked up the flowers and cried. She couldn't even lift her arm to put the Yale key into the lock to get into the front door. She simply stood, her arms by her side, the flower heads pointing towards the floor; she cried in the heartbroken way only the truly bereft can cry.

She felt an arm go around her, and Margie took the key out of her hand. 'Come on, love, let's get you inside.'

Within minutes the heating had been turned on, the kettle had been set to boil, and the tears had subsided to a gentle hiccup every now and then.

Margie handed her a mug of tea, with instructions to get her hands around it. 'We'll all miss her, your Hannah, you know. And I only want to say, Tessa, that whatever you want, we're here for you. We couldn't believe it when we heard her name on the news.'

'Margie, will you keep an eye on things here for a few days, please? I'm going to stay with some friends in Eyam, and I'll leave you the phone number in case you need me. Obviously, I'll have my mobile, so you can reach me on either number.'

'Tell me you're not working?'

'No, I've been removed from the case, and told not to go back in before the end of January, but we'll see. The way I feel right now, I don't ever want to go to work again.'

She sipped at the tea, feeling her eyes prick with tears once more. Hannah was here, this was the home they had created together. It had been Tessa's home, but when Hannah moved in they had completely stripped and decorated every room, bought new furniture, made it their forever home. Forever. Forever had lasted such a short time.

'Can I do anything else, Tessa?'

'No, I'll be okay, Margie. I'm going to pack a suitcase for a few days, then I'll head off back to Eyam.'

Margie stood. 'I'll leave you to get on with it then. Walt's not too good today, his chest is red raw, so I don't like leaving him too long. Leave that phone number next to your phone, but I'll not ring unless it's urgent. You need to take it easy.'

Tessa smiled. 'I will, I promise.' She uncrossed her crossed fingers and stood to walk with Margie to the porch door. Margie kissed her cheek, then left to go home to Walt.

Tessa headed upstairs and the tears started again. That last morning they had laughed as they made the bed between them, with Hannah showing what little share of the duvet she had had during the night, and the difficulties they were having in getting it to sit evenly on the bed. The beautiful lemon duvet set they had chosen together...

Holding back further tears, Tessa filled her suitcase, taking all the notes they had on the case, along with her laptop. If Yarwood thought she was going to be a good little girl and avoid contact with what was happening, he was mistaken. She knew what Doris and Mouse, alongside Alistair, were working on, and she also knew they would come up with the answer. She intended being there when that happened, and if her police work could help, then so be it.

The last thing she put in the suitcase she retrieved from under Hannah's pillow. She placed the Harry Potter pyjamas on top of everything else, closed the lid and headed downstairs.

Tessa scribbled down the Connection number and her own mobile number, leaving the piece of paper tucked underneath the phone.

She locked the door behind her, took her suitcase and the bunch of flowers and walked down the path. She could hear Christmas music playing, and quickly got into the car. Christmas would never be the same again, she knew that, and she really didn't want any reminders of it now.

Half an hour later she was back with friends who loved her.

28

'Mark, is there any possibility of finding out Saskia and Petra van Berkel's date of birth without letting on we're investigating their background? Don't answer if anybody's standing too close to you.' Doris had put the phone on to loudspeaker so Alistair could hear.

'It's fine. They're all in the kitchen. I don't need to ask anybody about that. Is nothing showing up?'

'Not under that name in the right age group. What do you mean, you don't need to ask?'

'It's the reason Petra's here with her sister. They're twenty-five on New Year's Day. They were talking about it last night after we got the news Fraser was dead. They were saying they could celebrate properly now. So I guess that makes it 1995.'

'Brilliant. That's a massive help. I'll try to produce some sort of family tree with them, let's see if there's some familial connection to the Fraser brothers. We have a tentative connection with Tracy and Kaya and Christy Fraser. They lived four doors away from each other until Tracy took the job with the Clark family. You might want to bear that in mind. I'm not saying it's a major thing, because Paul was already in prison, had been for a couple of years when they moved to that house, but...'

'I get it. I'll be aware, don't worry. It's like a morgue in the house, as though all the fight has been knocked out of them. They were so upbeat last night after the news, but deflation's the new word now. Has Mouse cleared me yet? She hasn't texted.'

'Cleared you? Are you kidding?'

'Not at all. She said she'd let me know as soon as I was kosher, her words.'

'I'll ask her to message you when she gets back. She's gone on an errand of mercy to smuggle some work into Luke, on the pretext of popping in to see how he is. He's been texting her this morning saying he needs to finish his file on the job he was working on before he was rammed by Paul Fraser. He reckons he can do it with one arm, so she's nipped up to see him. If his mother finds out she'll be down here to give us all a verbal bashing.'

'Take care, Doris. A verbal bashing's okay. The situation as it is at the moment is a lot harder than when we thought we only had a raving lunatic in the form of Paul Fraser to deal with. We need answers, and until I get clearance on my people, I can't tell them anything. I've simply said to them it's not over and they've to watch out for anything suspicious.'

'I know. The second we know anything we'll pass it on to Carl and he can remove the suspect. Even then it won't be straightforward, nothing about this has been. Speak to you soon, Mark, and you take care.'

She disconnected as they heard the ping of the old-fashioned shop bell. Mouse popped her head around Doris's door. 'He's fine, but achy and stiff. Got all sorts of aches and pains, and he's told his mum he's going to stay in his room so he can sleep when he needs to, and play games on his laptop. I felt guilty handing over that work, but he'll not settle until it's done.

He's going to email it all to me when he's finished the report, and he's asked me if I'll deliver it to Mrs Henry the Philanderer as soon as possible.'

Alistair looked up. 'You have strange surnames in Yorkshire.'

Mouse laughed. 'We certainly do. Actually, it's Mrs Little, but her husband's been Henry the Philanderer since day one. Maybe if we get this out of the way, Luke will rest.'

'Good, but I doubt that. Mark was asking if you'd cleared him yet.'

'I'll text him now. Is he worrying about it?' A small frown creased her brow.

'No, I think he wants to move things along as fast as possible, he only has himself, Greg and Julie that he isn't having to watch, and although we've found bits out about Tracy, and by reason of being her daughter, Kaya, it doesn't exactly clear them. We don't know if they knew Fraser's mother before they moved a few doors away – they could have done. We've research to do into who owned the houses, stuff like that. I know we need fast answers, but it's not going to happen. It would be so easy to make assumptions, but that's not the way we work.'

'That's one query answered,' Alistair said. 'The houses on Bramall Lane – there's a long row of them, ten in total, all owned by a company called Bramall Holdings. They've had them for... thirty-three years. The question is did Christy Fraser help Tracy Worrall get that house, or did she come across it all by herself? I think we need to be asking the question to the company.'

'I'll go,' Tessa called through from reception. 'I've not handed my warrant card in or anything, so I'll go and see them.'

She joined Mouse in Doris's office. 'I'll be turning off my phone so I don't have to tell any lies if anybody rings from work. If Yarwood tries to contact me here, tell him you think I'm asleep.'

• • •

Bramall Holdings was housed in an old Victorian house in its own grounds, and was located in Dore in Sheffield. It could only just be seen from the road; trees hid it nicely in the leafy suburb of the city. Tessa drove through the gates and parked in an area only big enough for eight cars at the most, and she guessed they didn't have many employees. She was the third to park there, and she did so alongside a Jaguar, immaculate in its pristine newness.

'There's money in property,' she mused, and walked across to the imposing black door. It opened, which surprised her. She expected to knock and wait for a tinny voice to give further instructions.

The door led into a large reception area, and it briefly occurred to her how much Luke would love this much space for his reception. A lady of middle age sat behind the gleaming desk, and she looked at Tessa with a smile.

'Good morning. Can I help?'

'DCI Tessa Marsden, Derbyshire Police.' She held up her warrant card, and the smile disappeared. That was obviously kept for clients.

'I'd like to speak with whoever is in charge, please.'

'That would be me.'

'The Jaguar's yours?'

'No, that's Mr Kent's, but he's asked not to be disturbed.'

'And Mr Kent is...?'

'The owner. Co-owner with his brother, but he's in Ireland at the moment.'

Tessa stood. 'Thank you for your help.' She moved around the side of the reception desk and headed down the small corridor.

'No, no!' Tessa heard coming from the lady on reception, but didn't stop until she located the door that said Peter Kent. She knocked and opened it.

Peter Kent was fast asleep on a sofa underneath the magnificent tall window, the sort favoured by Victorians everywhere.

The receptionist reached the door too late to stop Tessa walking over to the sleeping man; she hesitated in the doorway, thinking good luck with that, DCI whatever your name is.

Tessa held out her warrant card, and shook his arm. 'Mr Kent.'

He opened one eye. 'What the fuck...'

'My name is DCI Tessa Marsden, and I'd like to speak to you, please.'

The alcohol was coming off him in waves, and Tessa stepped back, levered the open-mouthed receptionist out of the room and firmly closed the door.

She walked over to the coffee machine tastefully displayed on an antique side table, and said, 'Black?'

She made a flat white for herself, and carried both cups across to his desk where he was slumped over, his head in his hands.

'I feel like shit,' he said.

'Would it offend you if I said you looked like shit?'

'Are all policewomen like you?'

''Fraid so. Are all receptionists like your receptionist?'

'She protects me.'

'You need protecting on a regular basis, then?'

He seemed uncomfortable. 'Look, what do you want?'

'Information.'

'Sorry, can't tell you anything. Data protection and all that, these days.'

'Okay.' Tessa stood. 'Get your coat. We'll discuss this down at the station. You might want to call your solicitor at some point.'

'Now hang on a minute...' Kent tried to stand.

'It's a murder case,' Tessa said tiredly. She didn't say it was the love of her life who had been murdered. 'I don't have a minute.'

He slumped back down in his chair. 'What is it you want to know?'

'I want you to look back to 2003, at 232 and 238 Bramall Lane. These two houses are your properties, aren't they?'

'They are, but do you think you could lower your voice a bit? I don't feel too good.'

'Mr Kent,' she said loudly. 'You will feel even worse in an interview room, believe me. Now, 232 Bramall Lane, I'll make it simple for you and start with one property at a time.'

He stared at her, pulled his keyboard towards him, and switched on the monitor.

'Drink the coffee,' she said, and he reached forward to grasp the mug. 'You live here?'

'Not usually,' he said. 'I've got a nice house, a nice wife, and two nice kids. She doesn't want me anymore, so this is my second night on this sofa. I drank that last night.' He pointed towards an empty bottle of whisky.

'The full bottle?'

'Yep. It's why I don't feel good this morning. Believe it or not, I'm usually quite professional and smart.'

'I'm finding it hard to believe, I must admit.'

He leaned forward and typed something in, then looked at her. 'Two hundred and thirty-two you said?'

Tessa nodded. 'I believe a Tracy Worrall and her daughter Kaya lived there.'

He peered at the screen. 'Sorry, I usually wear glasses. You haven't seen them, have you?'

She stood and walked over to the coffee machine. 'Saw them earlier. These them?'

'Thanks.' He took them from her, and she realised he was a good-looking man once the bleary eyes were hidden behind lenses.

He scrutinised the screen. 'That's right. February 2003 to November 2008. Nice lady, the baby was only a month old according to this. It's coming back to me now. I believe she took a live-in job somewhere in Derbyshire. I remember her because she did something strange. She handed in her notice to leave the house, but paid for a further three months. She said it was in case the job didn't work out. I agreed to the arrangement and at the beginning of March she rang me to say she was happy with the job, and it was okay to let the house. In all the years I've been doing this job, nobody else has done that, which is why it stood out. And the other house?'

'Two hundred and thirty-eight.'

He typed in the number. 'Two hundred and thirty-eight... Christy Fraser. Her two sons lived with her when she moved in back in 1995, but one of them ended up in prison, and the other got his own place. Never caused me any bother, always paid rent on time. No, nothing on here to give me cause for concern at all.'

'Were they friends? Tracy and Christy, were they friends?'

'I imagine they were, there's only two houses between the two properties, and when Tracy Worrall left she asked that any mail be taken to 238, and she would collect it from there, or Christy would forward it to her.'

29

Tessa left Peter Kent feeling slightly more human, and saying he was going upstairs to have a shower and consider the possibility of using a couple of the rooms on the top floor as his pied-à-terre for the next few weeks. He had actually said 'until I can persuade my wife to forget all this nonsense', but Tessa had a feeling he might be upstairs at the office for some time.

She stopped for a few seconds to admire the immaculate Jaguar, then climbed into her own car which needed a complete valet inside and out, and pulled out of the gates. She thought the snow was starting to melt, but by the time she had driven back to Eyam she knew it must have been an optical illusion. The roads were still difficult to navigate, and she parked outside Connection with an overwhelming feeling of relief that scruffy though it may be, her car was still intact.

The pavement outside the shop had, in her absence, been cleared of snow. Joel stood surveying his work, leaning on a bright red snow shovel, obviously contemplating carrying on and clearing more of the pavement.

'Just do it,' Tessa said with a smile, as she clicked the lock on her car.

'I was thinking, Tessa,' he said, 'how much my life has changed since I met Mouse. I would never have considered doing something like clearing snow! Sledging, yes, but physical work like this, I would have asked someone else to do it. It seems I'm relegated to being the someone else in this organisation.' He laughed. 'And strangely enough, I've really enjoyed doing it.'

'You'll be sorry when you have to go back to work.'

'I'm not going back until I know my girl is safe.'

'We'll have it sorted soon. Everything we do leads us a bit closer to solving the mystery of what's going on. Before it was about finding Fraser, but there's been a subtle change because it's not about that. Not anymore. We know where he is, in the morgue. And Todd is banged up for the foreseeable.'

'Good.' Joel picked up the red shovel. 'When you get in there, can you mention the worker outside might appreciate a hot drink?'

She smiled. She liked Joel, loved how he protected Mouse. 'I'll make one. No doubt everybody will want one as soon as I mention what I'm doing.'

'Thanks, Tessa. You're a wonderful lady combined with being a smart cookie.'

Smart cookie, indeed. Not smart enough to save Hannah, not smart enough to have found Fraser before he could use that gun.

Luke had a headache. He'd got everything ready for going to Mrs Little, all it needed was printing off at the office. He emailed it, sat back with a sigh, and picked up the two painkillers he'd been trying to avoid taking. They deadened the pain, but they sent him to sleep. Presumably that was supposed to happen, but he wanted to get better, wanted to be able to go outside, down to the village centre. To Connection.

He swallowed the tablets, opened his book and settled back on the bed, battering his pillows until they were perfect for reading. Within five minutes his eyes closed and he slept.

He missed out on the cup of tea Naomi brought up to him; she stared at her son all too aware of how close she had come to losing him. Memories of that dreadful night at the hospital when his body attempted to shut down and give in to the damage caused by the accident flooded her mind, and she sat down for a moment, simply looking at the sleeping Luke. His thumb was inside the book, as if keeping his place for the second he woke up, and she moved it gently away from him. She sipped at his cup of tea and stayed for ten minutes, then headed back downstairs, taking his empty cup with her. It didn't matter, she would happily make him fifty cups when he woke, if that was what he wanted. Her son was home.

Mouse had texted Mark to apologise for having forgotten to text him, and formally cleared him of any skulduggery in the Clark household. She had also double-checked Dennis Evans, but as Denny was still immobile at home following the random shooting by Paul Fraser and nowhere near the Clark house, that information was a little irrelevant.

Mark was quick to point out that fact, and she retaliated with she hoped he wasn't connected to anyone else in the house, as she hadn't checked that. Mark's apology was swift and abject; Mouse smiled. One–nil to her.

She moved on to Leila Palmer, and was surprised to see that her husband was a house-husband and main carer for their three children, while she did the security work for Mark Playter's company. Mouse followed Jonny Palmer's work life back, and he had been made redundant two years earlier, at the same time as Leila had started to work for Playter. It must have made financial sense to cancel all childcare for the children, with the inevitable massive costs that generated, and for Jonny to stay at home. Good for them, was her immediate reaction, and Mouse typed up her findings before sending the text to Mark.

Fred Iveson was a little difficult to trace until she realised he had moved straight from the police force to Mark Playter's set-up. There was little to follow with him; no wife, no children, no parents, both having died while he was in his teens, and he had reached sergeant level in the force. He had no Facebook account, and nothing else across the social media spectrum. Mouse tried everything to get some sort of feel for the man, but there was little to find. He was fifty-two, and he had lived a singularly unremarkable life. She immediately texted her findings to Mark, who replied with 'Boring and solid. Love the bloke.'

It didn't take long to check out Zara Ormond and Ian Downes, both equally transparent. They had Facebook, Instagram, WhatsApp and every other account, used them frequently, and their lives were open doors as far as their families were concerned. Mouse actually considered mentioning this to Mark, because it had to put them at risk in the job they were doing; they were traceable. She decided, in the end, that she was interfering in their lives and it was up to Mark to check that kind of thing, but felt uneasy at how much of themselves they were revealing.

Mark rang to thank her when she had finished clearing all his operatives, and said he had had pretty much the same results from his own people. She disconnected, and sat back with a smile. He must be one happy man, to know he hadn't slipped up when he employed his operatives.

Kat had spent the day at church. So much needed to be prepared for Christmas, and she wanted to be sure it would all be ready for the celebrations. The church possessed a large nativity scene, and it was time for it to be in place, ready for baby Jesus to be laid in his cradle on Christmas morning by one of the children.

She had minor repairs to do on two of the shepherds – one had a broken crook, and the other's lantern was looking a little worse for wear, so she had taken down everything she would need to smarten it all up. They all had a wash, and the sheep looked so much better with brighter fleeces. The crook proved a little difficult, but she managed it by clever use of a coat hanger and hessian fabric.

She had brought a bag of hay, and placed it in the cradle, scattering the rest of it around the floor of the cave-like edifice where the Holy Family gave birth, and she eventually stood back and thought how good it looked. She was about to lock up when the choir arrived to practise their carols, so she hung back for a while to listen to them. When they started to sing 'In the Bleak Midwinter' she shivered. Her favourite carol always had the same effect on her, and she listened to their flawless rendition of it.

They were still singing as she slipped out of the large doors; they had moved on to 'Away in a Manger'. She ran across the road to get to Connection, arriving as everybody was making themselves comfortable in Kat's office.

'Room for a little 'un?' she asked as she popped her head around the door.

Doris smiled at her. 'Your last words were you wouldn't be in today because you had to get the church ready. You've finished?'

'I have. The choir's in practising, so I thought I'd leave them to it. They sound wonderful, I can't wait for them to come and sing at ours, Martha will love it.'

'When's Martha coming home? You must be missing her.'

'We speak on FaceTime every night, but I'll wait until this is all sorted before I bring her home. Mum hasn't collapsed yet, so we're okay.'

Mouse handed around coffees and they all took their places around the table.

'We figured we should have a discussion on what we've found out today,' Doris said, 'and whether Tessa needs to report anything to her bosses. I suspect we're not at that stage yet, but we have a lot of progress, or so I've gathered from hearing bits and bobs. Alistair and I will go last, ours is a bit twisted and convoluted. Mouse, you start, I know you've been beavering away all day.'

'Okay. Let's start with Luke. He's doing good. I took his precious file up so he could finish it properly. He's done that, so I've printed it all off and it needs to go to Mrs Little tomorrow unless we get another snowfall.'

'I'll take it,' Kat said. 'I can't help at all on this intelligence stuff you've all been doing, but I can do the legwork.'

'Thanks, Kat. It's on my desk,' Mouse said. 'I've checked every single one of the security staff employed at the house, including Mark Playter and Greg Clark. Everybody cleared. The only one I struggled with, and Tessa might know him actually, was an ex-police sergeant by the name of Fred Iveson. He has nothing in his life. No relatives, no social media presence, nothing. Lives in a flat so doesn't have a garden, I only found really basic stuff on him.'

Tessa smiled. 'He's one of the nicest men I've ever met. He

had a girlfriend many years ago who was killed in one of the terrorist attacks in America. She'd gone there with her job, and he never got over it. He withdrew, kept himself to himself, and eventually retired. So he's with Mark Playter's outfit? Good for him, I'm glad he's not simply wasted away.'

'All the rest were pretty transparent, but I could tell Mark was relieved to hear it. He'd asked his own staff to check them out, but we needed to do it – we don't have a connection with anybody who works for him. His staff do.'

'Is that everything, Mouse?' Doris asked.

'It is,' she said and sat back, but Joel leaned forward.

'Can I say that in the absence of my beautiful girlfriend, I've cleared what seems like most of the snow from Eyam. Thank you.'

Doris smiled. She was learning to love this young man who clearly adored her granddaughter. 'Pity it's started to snow again, isn't it?'

30

Tessa lay on the bed in Mouse's flat, her thoughts wandering to Hannah, as they did every second she wasn't distracted by issues connected to the case. She didn't want to get over it, she wanted to wallow in the love she felt for her life partner, the child they had never met and now would never meet; the devastation to her life was breaking her.

She sighed and rolled over on to her side, pulling the Harry Potter pyjamas towards her. She smiled as she remembered the look of horror and shock on Hannah's face when Tessa had confessed to not having read any of the books. Part of Hannah's birthday gift to her had been the full set. Ultimately, once she had read them, they had discussed the ins and outs of the series, the criminal elements and how they would have gone about tracking down the culprits and getting them before a judge without use of wands or broomsticks. The Potter books had brought so much into their lives; laughter, love and occasionally deep discussion.

That would never happen again.

Still holding on to the pyjamas, she sat on the edge of the bed, pondering if she should help with preparing the evening meal. Her thoughts roamed towards Alistair, and she wondered if there was going to be a future for Doris with him. She hoped so. He seemed a man of integrity and boundless intelligence, but he had mentioned his retirement to France in March, and if Doris was considering being with him, that would make being a part of Connection really difficult.

Tessa straightened out the pyjamas and rolled them up carefully, before replacing them under her pillow. 'Love you, Hannah,' she said, as she did so.

'Go and sit down with Alistair, Nan,' Mouse said. 'I'll cook. I enjoy it, you don't.'

Alistair placed a glass of wine by the side of the cooker. 'You can manage that while you're cooking, can you?'

'I can manage that while I'm doing anything.' Mouse grinned at him. 'Take my Nan out of the way, will you? Bribe her with wine.'

'Doris,' he said. 'Come and sit with me. Red, white or pink?'

'We have lemonade?' she asked. 'My head's pounding, and having wine will make it worse.'

'Lightweight,' he muttered, and walked across to the fridge to investigate the lemonade situation.

Doris sat on the sofa, and placed her phone on the side table. She had been text chatting with Luke. He desperately wanted to come back to work to give her a big kiss for the money that had been placed in his bank account, there to help him get a new car that would be better than the one he would have been able to get relying on his savings alone.

She had asked him not to thank Kat and Mouse because they knew nothing about it; the money was from her and it wasn't a loan.

The texting had led on to a discussion about cars, but he

appeared to have gone quiet following his text saying he had taken painkillers so he might nod off.

She smiled as her phone pinged – she was wrong, he hadn't fallen asleep. He'd probably found a car he wanted to show her.

There was indeed a picture on her phone, but it had come from Mark Playter, not Luke. It showed Greg Clark kissing Tracy Worrall, and she didn't look as if she was fighting him off.

Doris sipped at her lemonade, suddenly angry. She couldn't say anything yet, she had to think about this. She sent a brief text back with a thank you, and asking Mark to send any further pictures if he saw them together again.

An hour later they all sat back, fully replete after a delicious meal in which Doris played no part, although Tessa had volunteered to help. The apple pie and custard had been the end to a perfect meal, and Alistair stood to pour coffee for everybody.

'Are we staying around the table, or sitting on the sofas?'

'If you don't mind, I think we should stay here. We may be about to have a discussion and it's always easier around a table. I'm going to send each of you a picture when Alistair is back with us. We certainly need to discuss the implications of it, and also what we do next.'

Alistair poured the five coffees and refilled the pot in case anyone wanted a second cup, then carried them over and handed them around.

'Okay,' Doris said, 'group message,' and she hit send.

Four phones all pinged at the same time.

There was silence as they digested what was on their screens.

'Fill me in,' Alistair said. 'I can see this is Greg Clark, but who's the woman?'

'It's Tracy Worrall, his wife's carer for the last ten years,' Doris said. 'I think we need to find out how she got the job, because if they were having an affair before she went to work for him...'

'Who sent you the picture?' Mouse's cheeks were flushed. Like her nan, her first reaction had been anger.

'Mark. I've asked him to send any others he may get, and to keep a particular eye on these two now. This opens everything up, and tomorrow I'm going to find out how Tracy Worrall ended up in that house. If it was by simply applying for a job, that's fair enough and these things happen. How many au pairs lose their jobs because the feller fancied them more than he fancied his missus, but if she got the job as part of some long-term plan and she knew him before moving into his house, that's a whole different ball game. And, of course, it opens up the question again of did she know Paul Fraser before he went to prison? Is she related to him even?'

'Nan, promise me you'll leave this until tomorrow,' Mouse said.

Doris smiled. 'I promise. Tonight we're going for a walk around the village with the choir.'

'We are?' Alistair looked surprised. 'Did I know?'

'I might have forgotten to mention it.'

'But I can't sing.'

'It doesn't matter. They like a nice crowd to support them, you can either join in or simply listen to them, and at the end of it we have mince pies and glühwein in the church.'

'Oh, in that case then...'

Tessa laughed. 'You'll enjoy it, Alistair. Hannah and I went last year, we loved it, but I'm giving it a miss this year. I'm not sure I could do it without her.'

Doris squeezed her hand. 'You'll be welcome, Tessa, but you must make up your own mind. We leave the church at seven.'

'Does Kat have this picture?' Mouse was frowning. 'I feel so angry about this, as if they've lied to us from the beginning.'

'No, I've not sent it to her yet, she's part of the choir visits, and I didn't want her to have the same reaction we've had before she heads off out singing carols. I'll send it when we get back. I'll head over to Hathersage and ask some pertinent questions in the morning, but I'll be discreet. I'll make the assumption that Julie doesn't know about this, until, or if, I am told otherwise. Thoughts anybody?'

'Only that Julie doesn't know,' Mouse said. 'She deliberately sent Greg to the car so she could tell us about Fraser raping her, and she could have told us about this little *ménage à trois* at that point. She was keen that we had all the facts, so I think that means she probably doesn't know about her husband and the hired help.'

Doris nodded. 'I suspect you're right, Mouse. I'll be careful.'

'I'll go with you if you'd like that,' Alistair said. 'I'd like to see the house, and what you've had to do to keep them safe.'

'Then that's what we'll do. I'll speak to Kat later after I've sent her the picture, but let's get this dishwasher loaded and we can head off to church. It's going to be beautiful with all this snow around.'

Eyam welcomed its carol singers with gusto. Their collecting tins for the Marie Curie foundation were soon filled, and many shots of whisky were imbibed on the choir's journey around the village.

Kat was obviously in her element, and sang along with the choir, her eyes shining. She led a short prayer as they finished at the last house before returning back to the church, as the first flakes fell.

· · ·

The church was warm and welcoming, glühwein, tea and coffee awaited them, as did multiple plates of mince pies covered with a light dusting of icing sugar. Christmas music was playing softly in the background and the choristers and supporters were reluctant to go home. There was much laughter and Doris felt relieved that Tessa had made the decision not to accompany them. The festivities would have been a step too far.

Doris peered through the door that led into the church, and Kat walked up behind her. 'You want to go in?'

'No, of course not, it's all locked up. I do like to see the nativity though, so I'll pop across next time you're here.'

Kat pushed gently on the unlocked door. 'I'm here now.'

Doris followed her through and they headed towards the altar. Kat switched on a spotlight. To the left was the nativity scene, perfectly displayed, and waiting for the Christ child to make his appearance on Christmas morning.

Doris knelt and picked up a sheep. 'It's such a beautiful set. For me, this has become Christmas, this nativity display.'

Kat laughed. 'I had to do some running repairs this year. I think it's fairly old now, and I had thought of doing some fundraising to get a new one for next year, but this one is beautiful. I think when we take the decorations down I shall pack the nativity set up and take them to George Mears, and ask him to look at everything and smarten it up. He's really good with stuff like that.'

'He certainly sorted out our security on the office, it's always worked perfectly. I like George, he has a sense of humour that's like mine.' Doris replaced the sheep in its designated spot, and stood. 'Kat, we have to persuade Tessa to come to us for Christmas Day, I can't bear the thought of her being on her own. I know they said no, they wanted it to be special for the two of them, but things have changed. Will you ask her, as we're going to be at your home?'

'I'd already decided to do that. I'll get her on her own tomorrow and talk to her. She didn't want to come tonight?'

'Couldn't face it, she said.'

'That's understandable. It's strange having Tessa with us without Hannah being there. She's going to be so missed by all of us.'

They walked back into the church hall, and Alistair waved his cup in the air to ask if they wanted drinks.

They shook their heads, and he turned back to Carl, to continue their discussion on Manchester United.

'Kat,' Doris said, 'there's something we need to talk about later. I'll be sending you a picture, and then I'll ring you when you've digested it. Don't fret about it now, we've had such a lovely evening and I didn't want it to impinge on this part of your life, but once you're home get yourself a brandy.'

'Oh Lord, will I need a prayer?'

'Possibly,' Doris said. 'Probably.'

31

The Bentley pulled up to the Clarks' gates and Leila came to check their identities. 'Nice car,' she said. 'Morning, Mrs Lester. Mr...' She checked Alistair's ID. 'Mr Glentham. One moment, please.'

She moved away and spoke into her transmitter. Mark confirmed he was a bona fide visitor, and she opened the gates with a smile. 'Nice car,' she said again, as they drove through.

'I think Leila likes your car,' Doris said sarcastically.

'*I* like my car,' he countered. 'Do I park it out front?'

'No, let's go round the back. We'll go in via the kitchen.'

'Any reason?'

'Might get a cup of tea? No, it's because we normally go in the front. Call it intuition, call it what you want, but I want to see how it is going in the back.'

They parked on snow, but it had been cleared thoroughly leading up to the door. The gravel crunched and Ian Downes appeared.

'Morning, Mrs Lester, Mr Glentham. All's quiet.'

'Good morning, Ian. Thank you.'

Ian walked up to the door and knocked. Three short, two long. 'That's today's knock, hope I've remembered it properly.' He grinned. 'I couldn't get in the other day because I was remembering the previous knock.'

The kitchen door opened, still on its chain, and Ollie peered out. He closed it, removed the chain, and welcomed them both inside. 'We'll never get used to simply opening a door again.' He smiled. 'Who are you here for? Dad?'

'Probably later. We'd like to have a word with Tracy first, if she's free. We can wait if she's seeing to your mum.'

'I'll check. Cup of tea?'

'That would be lovely, thank you, Ollie. Shall we wait in the lounge?'

'Yes, the tree is lit, even if the bastard's dead.'

Doris and Alistair settled on the sofa, facing a single armchair, and chatted quietly while waiting for Tracy to arrive. No one disturbed them, and it was warm and welcoming.

'Is your house like this?' Doris asked.

'You must come and see it before I leave,' Alistair responded. 'It's about the same size as this, but the only room I feel is anything like homely is my library. It's all shiny dark wood furniture and shelving, a proper library ladder that I bought from an auction and it cost me nearly as much as the house, leather armchairs, I love that room. The other rooms are... nice. Tidy, clean, but no soul. I'll be sorry to leave it, I've been there a long time now, but the South of France is calling me. I'll be taking on a similar sort of role to the way you went; a consultant when needed with the option to say no I can't do that. Will I get to see your cottage before I head off back to the capital?'

'We can set aside half an hour after we finish here if you like. It's about a five-minute drive, not far at all.' She looked around. 'My entire cottage would probably fill this room and the kitchen. I absolutely love it, loved its previous owner also. After she died the investigation we were conducting in conjunction with Tessa and Hannah stopped, but I was never convinced she was the person the police believed her to be. Still, all water under the bridge now, and when the cottage came on the market after her death, I jumped at the chance of owning it.'

She was sipping at her tea when the door opened and Tracy arrived, remaining half in and half out of the doorway.

'You wanted to see me?'

Alistair stood. 'Thank you. My name is Alistair Glentham, Doris's ex-boss and friend. We've a couple of questions to ask, if you don't mind.'

Tracy frowned. 'Will it take long?'

'No, not at all. Five minutes or so, I would think.'

She moved reluctantly into the room, and sat in the armchair.

Doris took out the picture from her bag and passed it across to Tracy. 'How long?' she asked.

Tracy stared at it, her eyes widening. 'When...?'

'Yesterday. There are too many eyes here, Tracy. You must have known you would be seen at some point.'

Alistair moved in. 'So, tell us how you came to get this job.'

'I applied for it, of course.'

'Of course.' He kept his voice smooth. 'How did you hear about it?'

She hesitated. Uncomfortable. 'I... erm... saw it advertised in *The Star*.'

Doris wrote *The Star* in her notebook, purely for effect and to send the message to Tracy that she would be checking it for accuracy.

'When?' Alistair didn't let it go.

'Probably sometime in January 2009. Just after Christmas.'

'Yes, I know January is just after Christmas. Had you met either Mr or Mrs Clark before? Answer carefully, Tracy.'

'I don't have to tell you anything. Julie says you're civilian consultants, or something. Not actually police.' Tracy was starting to sound defiant.

'Okay, let me explain something, Tracy.' Alistair's mild manner changed. 'I am definitely not a civilian consultant. My rank exceeds that of your Chief Constable, and I am here in my official capacity, combined with being a friend of the owner of Connection.' He turned to Doris, who hadn't batted an eyelid during the exchange. It was playing out exactly as they had anticipated. 'Maybe we shouldn't have given her the courtesy of an interview here. Is Chesterfield the nearest station?'

Doris closed her bag and started to stand. 'It is. I'll ring them to let them know you're bringing someone in for questioning.'

'Whoa!' Tracy stood, her eyes wide. 'I didn't say I wouldn't tell you!'

'You did. You said *I don't have to tell you anything*. Actually, you do, so either start talking the minute I stop, or Alistair makes it official and we take you to Chesterfield.' Doris's voice was steely.

Tracy looked at the door as if contemplating running, then crumpled in a heap in the armchair.

'I knew them both. I looked after Julie several times when she had to be hospitalised, and I became close to Greg. We used to go for a coffee when I was off duty and Julie was resting, and it grew from there.'

Doris was taking notes. 'So you met in 2000, after Julie was shot?'

Tracy nodded.

'Did Greg help you get the house on Bramall Lane?'

'Yes. The daughter of one of his clients was moving out, and he gave me the information.'

'Who paid the rent, Tracy?'

Tracy brushed away a tear, all too aware of what was coming next. 'I did. Greg paid me.'

'Who's Kaya's father?'

Tracy dropped her head, scrambled for the tissue that was tucked up her sleeve, and wiped away the free-flowing tears. 'Greg.'

Alistair and Doris waited in silence for Tracy to compose herself. There was a knock at the lounge door, and Ollie asked if they needed any more tea, before disappearing to bring three drinks. Doris thought Tracy probably needed one.

Tracy kept her head turned away when Ollie delivered the fresh drinks, and he told them to shout out when they wanted another.

Tracy sipped carefully at hers. They waited.

'Okay, details. The relationship has continued all this time?' Doris asked.

She nodded. 'It has. I taught Kaya to call him Greg, but he played a large part in her life. It was difficult when we were first here, but as we moved into the granny flat accommodation straight away, I could keep them apart. She was also at school during the day, and her attachment to him became an attachment to the family, so nobody thought it was strange. She was an outgoing child anyway, always wanting hugs, someone to read to her, she actually made it easy. With my nursing background, the job fitted me perfectly. Oh, I know he'll never abandon Julie, he'll never fully be mine, but I've accepted that.'

'Really? You're not starting to feel that after ten years of looking after Greg's wife, maybe it's time she died?' Alistair's voice was harsh.

Doris pushed a little harder. 'Did you have contact with Paul and Todd Fraser? You lived near enough to their family home on Bramall Lane. Did you become a friend of Christy Fraser, knowing the background story behind Julie's injuries? Did you text Todd Fraser on that morning when you found out that we had tracked down the house in Bamford.'

'For fuck's sake! No, I didn't! I've never had anything to do with Paul, he was in prison when I first met Christy. And I think I only saw Todd once, he wasn't living at home then.'

Alistair and Doris sipped at their drinks and waited, but she said nothing further. Her face had registered massive shock at their words.

'What will you do now?' she eventually asked. 'Julie and Oliver don't know. And Kaya definitely doesn't.'

Doris smiled. 'You seriously think Julie doesn't know? I wouldn't count on it. Make no mistake, if I am right, Julie is allowing you to have her husband, and one day she will stop you. But she needs you, so you're allowed to retain the status quo. Think about this, Tracy.' Doris dug the dagger in even deeper. She was sick and tired of philandering husbands. 'Ollie appears to have acquired himself a nurse as a potential future wife. I can see he's not head over heels for her, and probably you can also as you're closer to the family, so why is she here? She's certainly here for the financial stability that Ollie will give her, but he is a smart man who has possibly clicked on to the situation, so has brought in your replacement. My bet is an engagement at Christmas and a wedding early in the new year. Then you're out.'

'He wouldn't...'

'Yes, he would. I think next year will be a different life for you, Tracy, and I hope Kaya takes it well, or you'll lose her also.'

Doris stood, and Alistair followed her. 'That's all for now,' she said, 'try not to be caught on camera again, although I suspect you have been seen by Ollie in the past. If we have further questions, we'll be back, I promise you.'

· · ·

Doris said nothing apart from giving Alistair directions to her cottage. On arrival, she switched on the heating and turned to him. He took her in his arms and gently held her.

'That wasn't you, was it?'

'It felt like being back at work thirty years ago. I don't do nasty, not anymore.'

'I know. I thought we made a pretty good team, but she's not the one who managed to warn the Frasers that morning. Somebody else in that household did, and we're spectacularly narrowing it down to Saskia van Berkel, aren't we?'

'This puzzles me somewhat, so when we get back to the office she will be my main target. I'll know everything about her by tonight,' Doris said, enjoying the warmth and solidity of being held.

'You really think Oliver Clark has sourced himself a nurse for a girlfriend?'

'I do. Ollie adores his mum, and if Mark can get a photo of a kiss, what has Ollie possibly seen? Saskia is pretty, a bit airy-fairy, but above all else she is a nurse. And I bet I'm right about a quick marriage, which she'll fall for because she can see an easy life ahead of her where she won't have to work. Then Ollie will go to his father, tell him what he knows, and he'll threaten to tell his mother if Greg doesn't get rid of his bit on the side. Enter Saskia with her nursing skills.'

Alistair was still holding her in his arms, and Doris was resting her head on his chest. Neither wanted to move.

'Do you want a drink?' she said.

'No, I want to see around this cottage. In a minute. When I've finished hugging you, Doris Lester. Now shut up, and be hugged.'

32

'We'll have to wipe the smiles from our faces, or they'll know what we've been doing,' Alistair said, once more pulling Doris into his arms. She didn't object, merely let him hold her as he had done all those years ago. She nestled against him, trusting him, knowing she had waited for this moment for almost fifty years without realising it.

'Heaven forbid they should find out we've been here for two hours, and you haven't seen the kitchen yet.' She smiled. 'I'll have to avoid Mouse for a week because she can read me so well.'

He suddenly became serious. 'I can't let you go again, Doris. I was stupid once, but I'm not stupid now. If you won't come to France with me, or even to London and we can keep my France home for holidays, I'll have to move in here. God knows how you'll fit in my library. We'll have to build an extension out back. In fact, can we buy the cottage next door and make that into the library.'

'Let's not rush into this, Alistair.' She didn't look up at him; she wasn't ready for him to see what her eyes were saying.

'Rush? We've known each other for fifty years! I've loved you for fifty years. Did you forget me?'

'Of course I didn't. I simply thought you'd gone out of my life for ever. This is something I'd never dared to dream about, your name was something that flashed across my computer screen occasionally when you had to contact your consultant team. But I have a life here. My instinct is to pack a bag and go with you the second we've sorted this case, but that can't happen. I have Mouse, and by adoption I have Kat and Luke. And you've not met Martha, Kat's little one, yet. They are the people I would be giving up. And then of course, there's Connection.'

'You could still work as a consultant for Connection while living in France. We can have conference calls, and heaven forbid that emails would have to be used.'

She pulled out of his arms. 'Come and look at the kitchen. Mouse might question you.'

He laughed and followed her through. 'I love you, Doris Lester. I always have. There you are, cards on the table time. I want to spend the rest of my life with you, and I know it might only be two years, but it might be thirty-two years. Sometimes you have to take the risk, and at our ages, we qualify as risk-takers.'

'You've sorted it?' Mouse was sitting at the reception desk when Alistair and Doris returned, working on Luke's computer.

'It's not Tracy Worrall who warned them the police were on their way. What did you pick up from that picture?'

'That it wasn't the first time they kissed.' Mouse laughed. 'They looked so easy together.'

'Too right it wasn't. Is Kat in?'

'Yes. We need a meeting?'

'I think so. We have lots to tell, so let's get it all over with at once. I do wish Luke was here, he was part of this at the beginning.'

They discussed everything Alistair and Doris had discovered during the Hathersage visit, alongside Doris's theory about the acquisition of a new nurse in the form of a wife for Ollie.

'That's strange you've picked up on the distance between Ollie and Saskia,' Kat said. 'I felt they didn't fit, didn't interact. I thought no more about it, because he introduced her as girlfriend, not fiancée, so I assumed she was a passing fancy really. Did you meet Petra?'

'No, we didn't go there for them. We needed to clear the air with the Tracy thing. I wonder how she's going to explain this to Greg. I'd love to be there when she does,' Doris said. 'Now we'll see whether he loves Julie as much as he tries to show he does, or whether he'll put Tracy and Kaya first.'

'So what's next? Saskia? You need any help, Nan?' Mouse asked.

'No, I'm almost there. It seems to have taken ages to crack this one, and it's because of a name change. I need a code from Alistair and I'll have everything I want. They were kind of adopted, not officially but they lived, live, with grandparents in Holland. It seems to be complicated, so I have to have all my facts laid out in front of me with this one. Where's Tessa?'

'The nursing home where Hannah's mother lives rang earlier. Mrs Granger's not too good, and there's nobody else who lives anywhere near. Tessa went as soon as they rang. She's not in a good place, isn't our Tessa.'

'I know.' Doris sighed. 'It makes you feel so damn helpless. Thank God she has us.'

'Do you want some good news to lift your souls?' Kat asked.

'Anything,' Mouse responded.

'Martha's coming back later this afternoon. I'm going home about two, I think Mum's bringing her around three. All visitors tonight will be welcome, if you want to pop around. I know how much you've missed her.'

'Yeah! We'll be there, Joel loves the bones of her.'

'Nan? Alistair?'

Doris looked at Alistair. 'Of course we'll be there, I want Alistair to meet her so much, she's such a huge part of my life, but we'll not stay too long because I'm moving back to the cottage tonight.'

'What?' Mouse looked shocked.

'I think the big danger where we were under threat is gone, and I don't like leaving it without heat, so I'm going home. Tonight.'

'If you're sure... but you know you can stay here for as long as you want.'

Kat kicked Mouse's leg under the table.

Doris looked at Alistair, who read her mind and stood. 'Let's go solve this mystery of our Dutch friends,' she said, and they left Kat's office together.

'So why did you kick me?'

'To shut you up.'

'Why? What did I say?'

'You tried to stop her leaving.'

'But I don't want her to go.'

'They want to go.'

'They? Oh my God!'

'Don't take the name of the Lord thy God in vain. They, as in Alistair and Nan.'

'He's going to the cottage with her?'

'If she's any sense, yes.'

'Oh my God. You read people so much better than me, Kat. Do I need to say anything to her? To him? Oh my God!'

Doris opened her laptop and printed off the mini family tree she had collated concerning Saskia and Petra. The email with the birth certificate had finally arrived, and she confirmed this to Alistair.

'So you don't need me, then?' He smiled across the desk at her.

'Not at the moment. You need to go and pack your bags and pay your bill at the B&B, I believe. If they query it, tell them you've found alternative accommodation at Bradwell.'

He moved around the desk and kissed her, long and hard, then straightened his jacket before going to the door. Mouse knocked and walked in.

'I'm going out,' he said, a grin on his face. He closed the door behind him and Mouse looked at her nan.

'What's going on?'

'Going on?'

'With you two?'

'Mouse, I'm seventy. As if anything would be going on.'

'He's smiling.'

'Is he?'

'Joel smiles when we've... you know...'

'Too much information, Mouse. Leave me some illusions that you're not sleeping together. Get out of here, and allow me to get on with this. And tell that Kat to stop stirring it, I feel her hand in all this silliness.'

'She told me to get out.'

'Told you to leave it alone.'

'But she's my nan!'

'Do you seriously think seventy-year-olds don't have sex? Don't want sex? I have to give "the talk" to everybody wanting to get married in our church and that includes senior citizens, believe it or not. And trust me, it does carry on to late in life. So stop worrying about them, but start worrying about whether they'll see out their remaining years here or in France.'

'Oh no! Now I've got that to worry about also. I need to talk to Joel.'

'I'll buy earplugs to drown out his laughter.'

Doris stared at the birth certificates. She had printed them, and the truth looked so much more stark. Paulette Saskia Young, and Petra Christina Young. Mother: Flora Young. Father: Paul Fraser.

There was feverish activity on her part as she filled in the blanks, searched records that were available to her security level, and made notes of any she needed Alistair to check, but she felt satisfied after an hour that she had virtually the full picture. And she knew that the scenario with Ollie wanting her as a replacement nurse for his mother was probably accurate, but he had been truly led by the nose; she worked at a hospital in Sheffield, not in Holland. It simply happened to be the hospital where Julie made frequent visits to see her consultant, and to help matters along for Saskia, she worked the department that Julie attended, accompanied most of the time by her devoted son, according to hospital records. Beautifully orchestrated, Doris decided.

She looked up as Alistair returned. 'Can we get clearance to check prison visiting lists?'

'We can. Tessa said his brother Todd visited him frequently.' He looked at her. 'You think she was so fixated on Todd visiting him, she overlooked somebody else?'

'But surely van Berkel would have stood out?'

'It would, but Paulette Young wouldn't. The twins names were Paulette Saskia Young and Petra Christina Young. Their mother, Flora Young, died when they were four. Suicide. Their father was Paul Fraser.'

He sat down with a thud. 'Those poor kids. They were adopted?'

'Sort of. There's a suicide note. It seems she took the girls to her mother, who lived in the Netherlands with her second husband, Wilma and Isaak van Berkel. It made headlines at the time because when she boarded the ferry to come back home, she left her suitcase with another passenger saying she didn't want to trail it to the toilets, then went overboard. When she wasn't back after a couple of hours the passenger alerted a member of the crew, but it was much too late. Inside the suitcase was the suicide note. She said she couldn't face life with everybody knowing who had fathered her girls. As a result, Wilma and Isaak brought them up, and Petra still lives near them. They took on their grandparents' surname and Saskia changed to using her pretty Dutch name, but for anything legal they used their birth name shown on their birth certificates. I'm betting he had the odd visit from a Paulette Young, aren't you?'

'I certainly am. I'll get that information as soon as we can. Good job, lovely lady. I've had a farewell cup of tea with the staff at the B&B, and told them I'm heading back to London. I didn't say when. Doris, are you sure about me staying with you?'

'Of course. I've been sure about it since the day you turned up here. Please don't run away with the idea that anything that's happened today, or anything that might happen later, is anything to do with you. It's all been carefully orchestrated.'

He kissed her. 'I don't doubt it. I've never doubted anything you've set out to do, so why should now be any different?'

'When do you have to be back in London?'

'I have an appointment with the Queen on the twelfth of January, and everything prior to that is a moveable feast. The Queen isn't.'

'So you can be here for Christmas?'

'Doris, it's going to be the best Christmas I've ever had.'

'Mine too,' she whispered. 'Mine too.'

33

'You have lots of new words, sweetheart!' Kat grinned at her voluble daughter. 'I'm sure you didn't chatter like this before you went to see Father Christmas.'

'Mismas,' the little girl said, and clapped her hands.

'And did you like Father Christmas?'

'Mismas.' Again she clapped her hands.

'Baby.' Kat picked up her daughter. 'I don't care if Mismas is your new best friend, Mummy is really, really glad to have you back home. Shall we put this tray of little sausage rolls in the oven ready for your friends coming to see you tonight?'

'Sausage!' Again Martha clapped.

'So sausage is also a good friend?' Kat laughed and carefully balanced Martha on her hip while she slid the baking tray into the oven. She set the timer, knowing she could easily forget them if she started playing with Martha, and mother and daughter went into the lounge.

Kat switched on the tree lights, and Martha walked over to inspect it. 'Mouse,' she said, lightly touching one of the shiny dangling ornaments.

'No, my love, it's a rabbit.'

Martha struggled with the 'r' for a few seconds, then gave up. 'Mouse.'

Kat had filled the table with finger food, and it soon became clear designated drivers were required. There was a definite lessening of tension; Tessa had already volunteered to be the driver for the flat in Eyam, with Doris saying she wasn't bothered about alcohol anyway, so she and Alistair had already decided she would drive the Bradwell journey.

Martha went to bed at half past seven, collecting a kiss from everybody there, and the evening developed an ambience as thoughts of the danger they had been in drifted away. The gathering broke up shortly after nine, and Mouse watched as Doris and Alistair headed off in the direction of Bradwell.

Joel, Mouse and Tessa got into Tessa's car.

'I can't believe I'm letting her do this,' Mouse muttered. 'I believe I'm supposed to look after her now she's in her dotage.'

Tessa and Joel roared with laughter.

'In her dotage? This is Doris Lester you're talking about. The thirty-year-old pensioner.' Joel spluttered as he tried not to laugh at the expression on Mouse's face.

'It's not right. What if he's after her for her money?'

'He has a home in London, a home in the South of France, a Bentley, and a pension come January that will be somewhere in the stratosphere. My bet is he isn't after her money. I was talking to him earlier, and they were together before she met your granddad, Mouse. Alistair was sent abroad by the Foreign Office, and when he came back Doris had met Harry Lester and married him. Alistair jokingly said he hoped to reclaim what was rightly his anyway, but I don't think it was a joke. He's serious about your nan, and she's the smartest woman I know, present company excepted,' he added hastily, 'so I don't think we need have any worries. And at seventy, I reckon she's old enough to make up her own mind.'

Tessa stared at Joel. He was normally quiet, and she couldn't remember him talking for as long as that before. 'I agree,' she said. 'Your only concern should be what happens with Connection when she jets off to the South of France to live. Will she be your overseas consultant, or will she give it up altogether? Is Luke ready to step up, yet still be guided from a distance by his mentor? Lots of things to think about, Mouse, but that's not the bit that's worrying you, is it?'

'She's sleeping with him!' Mouse was clearly shocked.

Tessa and Joel, in the front seats, were hysterical with laughter. 'Oh, I so wish Hannah could hear you now, Mouse. She would probably agree with you, because Doris Lester was up there with Alistair's pension, in her eyes. She adored your nan, and probably would have thought the same about her sleeping with anybody. The fact that Alistair is a bit of a dish wouldn't have come into it. Look, if Doris is happy, properly happy, then that's fine in my book. And I think she is.'

Tessa pulled up outside the flat. 'Let's get in and settle down, and speak no more of the floozy that is our Doris.'

'Kat is a deacon, I understand.' Alistair sat at the kitchen table, watching Doris make them hot chocolates.

'She is. Reverend Katerina Heaton, as she is now. She divides her time pretty equally between the church and Connection, and of course fits Martha in along the way. The little one frequently accompanies Mummy into the office, and every so often they'll take off and go play in the park or something. Kat is our thinker. She put together the security plan for the Clark household, led the briefing, then handed over the computer side to Mouse and me. Kat doesn't do computers, except at a basic level. I've tried teaching her, but the interest simply isn't there. She always used to say she'd broken the internet, but she must be getting better because we don't hear that so often now.' Doris handed a mug to Alistair, and sat down opposite him, cradling her own drink. 'Kat was married to Leon Rowe. I'm assuming his activities ended up on your desk at some point.'

'They certainly did, and several times before things really blew up for him. I did know she used to be Kat Rowe. I always found it hard to believe that she knew nothing of his activities, but now I've met her. She sees the good in people, not the other side. That can, of course, be a bit of a disadvantage, but it can also make you into someone like Kat Heaton, and that can't be a bad thing.'

'She's certainly happy now. She met Carl during one of our investigations – he's normally with the fraud squad because he's pretty good with figures, but he's covering for Tessa.'

'Ah, Tessa,' Alistair said. 'A sad lady. She's going to need lots of support from her friends. You know, Doris, I sit on the sidelines down at Connection, which is something of a rarity for me, and I see someone still doing her job, despite being told to rest and stay at home. If she stops working, she will implode. Losing Hannah is really going to hit her eventually, but for now she is carrying on. Watch her carefully.'

Doris nodded. 'I know. We've been friends for some time, ever since she came in when Mouse was shot. I hate to see how she is at the moment.'

Tessa was crying. Now transferred to the recently vacated bedroom following Doris's return to Little Mouse Cottage, she had been asleep, and something had startled her awake. She had automatically reached for Hannah, only to be instantly overwhelmed by a sorrow so deep she couldn't breathe. She battled. Her breath was locked deep inside her and she tried to call out. Suddenly air filled her lungs and she drew in a breath with a screech that sounded almost inhuman. There was a clatter and then her bedroom door opened with a bang. Mouse was framed by the doorway, and Tessa was crying so deeply and intensely she couldn't speak.

Mouse swiftly crossed to her bedside and held her, stroked her hair, passed her tissues from the small square box on the bedside table.

'Don't stop,' she whispered to the distraught woman. 'Keep crying, Tess, it has to come out. I'll stay with you.'

And Tessa cried. For a long time. Mouse didn't move, simply held on to this woman who had become such a close friend, and who needed her more than she needed anything else at that moment in time. Unless it was Hannah. She needed Hannah, and Hannah was gone.

Finally she was out of tears, and the two women simply sat until Tessa spoke. 'I'm sorry, Mouse.'

'Nothing to be sorry for. I'm only glad you were here when it happened, and not on your own at home. I need to get you something. Something to calm you. And I'm not leaving till you've finished it. Camomile tea?'

Tessa nodded. 'You called me Tess.'

'I did. You didn't like it?'

'Hannah called me Tess. Thank you. It helped.'

'Let's get you comfortable in bed, and I'll go and make this drink.'

Tessa swung her legs around, and pulled the duvet over her. Mouse placed the pillows against the bedhead and when she returned with two cups of camomile tea, Tessa was sitting quietly, clutching on to Hannah's pyjamas.

'I'm sorry,' Tessa said quickly. 'It's the middle of the night, you shouldn't be up and looking after me. I don't know what happened...'

'I do. This should have happened, and under normal circumstances would have happened, on the day Hannah died. You've bottled it up because it was an ongoing case, but it's looking as though we'll have answers tomorrow, and your mind has given in. And don't ever apologise for something like that, Tessa. We're all here for you, and any one of us would have made you a camomile tea, and cried with you, at three in the morning. Now, I've brought you a couple of paracetamol I want you to swallow, because they'll take the edge off a little, and then I want you to sleep. Cuddle Hannah's pjs and if you want to cry, then cry. Stop being DCI Marsden and until you go back to work, simply be Tessa Marsden. If you don't want to go to the Clark house in the morning, we'll all understand. Carl's going, so if he needs to take anyone in he'll do it. It all depends on what answers we get from the conniving twins.'

'I won't go. I won't be responsible for my actions if they admit to warning Todd Fraser. If that hadn't happened, Hannah would still be alive. I'll stay in the shop, and ride shotgun on reception for you.' She picked up the two tablets and swallowed them with the last of her camomile tea, before placing the cup and saucer on the bedside table. She slid down the bed, and pulled the duvet up around her shoulders.

'Thank you, Mouse. I don't know what I'd do without all of you.'

Mouse bent down and kissed the top of Tessa's head. 'Night, God bless. And if you wake again and panic, try not to make that awful noise! I thought you were dying.'

Tessa smiled. 'So did I. I couldn't breathe. It felt as though my throat had closed up and the noise was because suddenly it was open and I had to take air in quickly. It was pretty scary, I'm telling you.'

'It sounds it. I'll leave our bedroom door open slightly, then I'll hear you if there really is an issue. Now settle down and go to sleep. Promise you'll come and get me if you need me?'

Tessa nodded. 'I promise.'

Mouse left her and closed the bedroom door quietly behind her.

She didn't go back to bed; she sat on the settee, Kindle in hand, and read for an hour, before heading back to the room she shared with Joel. Tessa hadn't woken and Mouse guessed it was safe to return to her own safe haven.

Joel had slept through the entire thing, and she smiled as she slid in beside him. It would take more than an unearthly shriek in the night-time to disturb him, and she slid her arm around him, feeling more secure once she did that.

'Night night,' she said as she planted a swift kiss between his shoulder blades. He moved slightly, as if aware she was there, then slept until they both woke at seven.

34

The two police cars pulled up outside the gates of the Clark house at Hathersage, and reported that they were in position. The six officers had picked up bacon sandwiches and coffees, knowing they could be in for a long wait, as it seemed that DI Heaton was leading this next chapter in the investigation and there was no guarantee he would be removing anybody for questioning.

By eight they were ready and awaiting instructions.

Carl left Kat giving Martha her breakfast and headed down to Connection, where he found Mouse and Joel discussing whether to wake Tessa or not.

'Leave her,' Carl said, once they'd explained the middle-of-the-night meltdown. 'I'll have Doris and Alistair with me, they have all the relevant documentation, and it's not as though I'm there to arrest anyone, only to bring them in for questioning once we know who we need to question. Mouse, you've been in on this from the beginning, do you want to be there?'

Mouse shook her head. 'No, as far as I'm concerned, Tessa is more important. You have my nan, and she's your main woman in this. I feel I want to be here for Tessa today. We've paid a high price for taking on this case, so go and finish it, Carl. Has Kat stayed home?'

'She has. She couldn't bear the thought of Martha going away again when she's only recently got her back. That's the price we paid because of this case, we had to talk to our daughter via an iPad.'

'So, you meeting Nan and Alistair at the house?'

'I am. And we'll be playing it by ear, I reckon. I know Doris has tracked down the relationship to Paul Fraser, but until we've spoken under caution to Saskia and Petra we are floundering a bit. I could have taken them into the station, but I want everybody in that family around the table when we start the discussion, because I want to see if anyone else knew about it.'

He headed towards the door. 'I'll keep you informed.'

It was obvious the snow was fast disappearing as Carl drove towards Hathersage. The main roads were clear, although gardens still had a fair amount of the stuff piled up. Snowmen were in evidence everywhere; some looked a little droopy as bits fell off them.

Christmas trees were lit in a couple of homes, but in the main it wasn't an oooh aaah journey, as he had been experiencing for some time with Kat. She adored Christmas, the pageantry, the carol-singing, her beloved nativity scene and her church work. He guessed the snow would be gone by the time they reached Christmas Eve, and he felt sorry about that. He couldn't ever remember experiencing a white Christmas.

He turned off the main Hathersage road and headed up the slight gradient towards the Clark house. Pulling up behind the second car, he sat with his engine running. He was a little early and Doris and Alistair hadn't arrived. He spoke to the lead car via his transmitter, checking that everything was okay, and was told that nobody had gone in or out, although the postman was about to put in an appearance.

Carl watched as the postman popped some mail into the postbox hanging on the wall to the side of the gates, and realised for the first time that the house had a name. It was on a sign attached to the grey metal box, and it said Dovewater. He somehow knew that Kat would approve of that; she loved the River Dove, and every time they visited a stretch of it she would say how much she wanted to walk the length of it until it met up with the Trent. Thinking of his wife always put a smile on his face, river or no river.

A car pulled up behind him, and Carl glanced in the mirror. Doris and Alistair both gave a little wave, and Carl switched off his engine before getting out and going to meet them.

Doris lowered her window and leaned out, waiting for him to speak.

'Morning, you two. There's only the three of us, but I've seen the videos, Doris, so I reckon we can handle whatever happens in there.' He grinned and kissed Doris on the cheek.

'Videos?' Alistair looked at Doris. 'What videos?'

'Not porn, I promise you,' Doris said with a laugh. 'I've had a couple of tussles over the last few years, and both times were filmed.'

'Alistair, if you want a lesson on how to take down a man when you're only five feet two, you have to see them. In fact.' He laughed, looking at Doris's face. 'I insist you see them. Then you'll always know your limits with our Doris.'

'And your limits, young man,' Doris said, 'are getting dangerously close. Now let's get in this house and see what they have to say.'

Carl took out his transmitter and spoke to the lead car. 'Ray, we're going in now. Be alert, if I need you it will be as we agreed, get in, and fast. I'll arrange to have the lock isolated on the gate, but stay this side of it and block the exit.'

'Okay, boss,' Ray Charlton responded. 'You still want Dave round the back?'

'I do. Dave? Follow me in when we go through, and take your car round the back of the property, and park close to the kitchen door. If you hear me shout "Go!" then it means I need you on the move, and stopping anybody leaving. Everybody clear?'

There was a chorus of *yes, boss*, from all the men in the two cars, and Carl walked back to his own.

Both he and Doris drove around the police cars and up to the gates, where Carl leaned out and spoke into the speaker.

Within seconds Leila arrived to check the cars and let them in; she glanced back and saw the two immobile police cars. She raised her eyebrows in query, and Carl said he required that the lock be kept off the gate for the time they were inside the house. It would be safe because one car would be following him and Doris, and the other would be covering the gate.

Leila nodded, not convinced she knew what was going on, but guessed this smart man did. To be on the safe side, she figured, she'd better report it to Mark.

Carl parked close to the front door, and Doris pulled her Jeep alongside him. All three of them exited their vehicles, Alistair carrying Doris's briefcase.

Mark opened the front door with a smile. 'Good morning, early birds. Tracy is finishing up with Julie if you're wanting her.'

'No, for the moment we've finished with Tracy. We're actually here to talk to everybody. Is everybody available?'

'I believe so.' Mark led them into the dining room, and disappeared to track down Dovewater's occupants. Alistair placed himself at one end of the table, and Carl and Doris moved to the other. Doris pulled documents out of her briefcase, laying them down in front of her.

Ollie popped his head around the door. 'You need me?'

'Everybody, Ollie, please,' Doris said.

The last to enter the room was Greg, who was on a conference call. The others talked amongst themselves while they waited, and Tracy organised teas and coffees. The atmosphere was convivial, with the family joking between themselves, glad that the tensions of the last couple of weeks seemed to be over. Doris, Alistair and Carl remained silent, knowing the chatter would soon stop once Greg joined them.

It was obvious that nothing had been said to Julie, or anyone else, about the ongoing affair between Greg and Tracy; if it had, Doris thought wryly, Julie was a bloody good actress. The arrangements for the funeral of Julie's parents had been completed, and Julie and Tracy were discussing the logistics of it when Greg walked through the door.

'Sorry I'm late, everybody. If I'd known this was happening this morning, I could have postponed that call until later.' It was clearly an admonishment to Carl and Doris.

Carl looked up at him. 'We're not in the habit of telling suspects we're about to turn up to interview them,' he said with a brief smile.

'Suspects?'

'That's what I said. Do you want to help yourself to a drink, Greg, so we can get started?'

Greg took his time pouring a coffee, then helped himself to a couple of biscuits. He finally sat down at Julie's side, and waited for somebody to speak.

Carl looked around at everybody. 'Thank you all for being here this morning. We'll try to make it brief, but that depends on the responses we get. I do have to explain that if we don't get truthful answers, or any answers, the cells at Chesterfield will be pretty full tonight. I'm not here to pander to anyone, we want the truth and we'll get it. I have lost a truly close friend because of this investigation and because someone in this house is hiding something, so it stops now. DS Hannah Granger was a remarkable woman, and an amazing officer. We know Paul Fraser killed her, but if we had apprehended Fraser earlier, he wouldn't have been in that car park aiming at Hannah's head. We didn't find him in the house at Bamford because somebody from this house warned the Fraser brothers.'

Carl paused.

'Julie. Was it you?'

Julie Clark jumped as if all the wasps in the world had stung her. 'What? No, of course it wasn't.'

'Greg. You?'

'Don't be ridiculous, man. I called Connection in to help us. I'd hardly have done that if I was in cahoots with the Frasers all along. Paul Fraser wanted to kill my wife, for fuck's sake.'

'You wouldn't be the first husband who had wanted to kill his wife and used somebody else to do it. Don't go all sanctimonious on me, Greg. I know too much.' Carl swung towards Ollie.

'Was it you, Ollie?'

'Of course not. As my father said, you're being ridiculous. We protect my mum, we don't put her in harm's way. There's nobody in this house who would want anything to happen to Mum.'

Carl looked at Doris. 'That's three who've allegedly told the truth. We're running out, aren't we?'

'We are. This could present complications, couldn't it? Maybe we should move on, see what the remaining members of this group have to say.' Doris turned her head. 'Tracy, was it you?'

'Bloody hell, Doris, leave me alone, will you.'

'No. We need an answer. Did you send a message to the Fraser brothers warning them that we had discovered the location of their hidey-hole, and were on the way to arrest them?'

'No. Now piss off.'

'Kaya,' Doris continued, fixing her eyes on the young girl. 'Was it you, or were you aware of somebody texting immediately I rang here to say we had found the house in Bamford?'

Kaya turned to her mum. 'Mum, I don't know what she's on about.'

Doris brought her back by continuing to speak. 'I don't want you to worry, Kaya. Because you're fifteen you'll have an appropriate adult to help you if DI Heaton has to take you to the station. It won't be your mum, of course, she'll be in a different interview room, but you will be looked after. Now, I'll ask you again. Did you see somebody text when Greg shouted to tell everybody the house had been found?'

There were tears in Kaya's eyes, and Doris felt sick. She was hating this, but it had to be done. They had to push to get answers.

'No,' Kaya sobbed. 'I didn't see anybody. I was up in my room when Greg shouted.'

Tracy pulled her daughter close and turned to Doris. 'Leave her alone, or else.'

Doris smiled. 'You think you can threaten me? Think again, Tracy.'

Alistair joined in the conversation, and all eyes turned towards the tall, good-looking man. 'Thank you for attempting to be honest. Shall we all calm down a little, we need to continue.'

He turned to look at Saskia and Petra. 'And then there were two.'

35

'You do not have to say anything, but it may harm your defence if you do not mention when questioned, something which you later rely on in court. Anything you do say may be given in evidence. Saskia Young, do you understand the caution?'

Carl repeated the caution to Petra, and watched as their faces turned white.

Saskia was the first to break the silence. 'What do you mean?'

'Saskia, I asked if you understood the caution.'

'Are we under arrest?'

'Have you done something you need arresting for?'

'Of course not,' Saskia snapped.

'You are about to be questioned under caution, here if that's possible, but if it proves difficult we'll take you to Chesterfield. Petra, did you send a text to Paul Fraser? Did you send one to Todd Fraser?'

Petra looked horrified. 'No, I don't even know them.'

'Saskia does.'

Ollie interrupted. 'Saskia Young? I thought your name was Saskia van Berkel.'

Carl waited, but she offered no explanation.

'Well?' he said.

'Our surname is Young.' Saskia said it with a finality, having taken into account that they seemed to know about it anyway. 'Our mother died when we were little, and we went to live with our grandmother and her husband, our step-grandfather, in Holland. He was called van Berkel, Isaak van Berkel although I expect you know that also, and to make things easier with school, Granny decided we should use their surname. We've done that ever since.'

'How do you think we found these things out, Saskia?' Doris said gently. She could feel a sense of panic coming from Saskia, and didn't want her to shut up completely. Petra simply sat and stared at her sister.

'I have no idea.'

Doris opened her file folder, and took out the birth certificate for Saskia. 'This, of course, is almost identical to Petra's birth certificate, the only difference is the Christian name. Saskia, in your case, you use your middle name. Petra, you use your primary name. Paulette Saskia Young. Petra Christina Young. Saskia, you received your father's name, and Petra, you received your paternal grandmother's name, so I am assuming when you were born your mother still loved your father.'

Body language showed how angry Saskia was. Petra sat with her mouth open, unable to comprehend what was going on.

'Your father,' Doris paused, allowing the girls to calm down a little, 'is listed as Paul Fraser.'

Julie gasped, and scrabbled to clutch hold of Greg's hand.

Ollie stood, anger and confusion vying for a place on his features.

'Sit down, Oliver,' Alistair said calmly.

He hesitated a moment, then retook his seat.

'Your mother is listed as Flora Young, but it seems although she may have given you names to link you to the Fraser family, your surnames were Young. I suspect even at that early stage she knew it might be better not to be tied too closely to Paul Fraser.'

Petra turned to her sister. 'Why didn't I know any of this?'

'*Hou je mond*, Petra.'

'Speak in English, please, you two, or we'll have you down in Chesterfield with an interpreter on board before you can say *hou je mond* again.' Carl frowned at the sisters. 'Don't shut your mouth, Petra, that would be stupid, if you don't mind my saying so. In English.'

Petra suddenly appeared to find some backbone, and slammed her hand down on the table. 'I am not stupid, but I know nothing of what you're talking about. Paul Fraser is the man who shot Julie? And he is my father?'

'He is.' Doris kept her tone civil, but she really wanted to scream at the two silly sisters, scream that he had also killed their good friend Hannah.

Petra's head dropped. 'I've never seen my birth certificate. I've never needed it. When I asked Granny years ago who my daddy was, she said she didn't know. She also said she didn't have copies of our birth certificates, and if we wanted one at any time, we could simply apply for it. Obviously, my sister did that.'

Saskia glared at her. 'You're such a wimp, Petra. Did you never wonder who we were?'

'I know who I am. I'm Petra van Berkel. It only says Petra Young on my passport because we had them from being tiny babies, and we've never changed the names, only renewed.'

'Saskia, you clearly found out what your father had done. How?' Carl fixed his eyes on her, and watched as her face hardened.

'It's nothing to do with you.'

Taking their lead from Carl, Doris and Alistair copied his actions and pulled their paperwork back into their folders.

Carl stood, allowing his eyes to roam around the table. 'Be prepared for a long day, folks. We're taking all of you in. We were considerate for your needs in holding this interview here, but once someone refuses to answer questions, it's game over. Julie, I apologise for any discomfort you may experience, but we do have an on-call doctor should you require medical assistance.'

Shockwaves flowed around the room and everyone watched as Alistair and Doris stood, picking up their files.

'Hang on a minute...' Greg said. 'I can't allow this...'

Doris looked directly across the table towards where he was sitting. 'You can't allow this? Somebody in this house has been complicit in the murders of your parents-in-law, a hotel receptionist, DS Hannah Granger, and an attack on one of our employees, and the shooting of one of Mark's men, and you say you can't allow this?'

Greg turned his attention towards Saskia. 'Tell them what they want to know, Saskia. Tell them now, and tell them every little detail.'

Ollie joined his father with words. 'Sas, fucking tell them.'

'I found a box,' Saskia whispered. 'I found a box one day when I went in Granny's bedroom. My period had started, and there was blood on my sheet. I went in the airing cupboard to get clean bedding.'

Carl, Alistair and Doris resumed sitting at the table, and waited for her to continue. 'All of it, Saskia,' Carl warned the broken woman, but he could tell she had given in. The bravado had gone.

'The quilt I took out to look at was beautiful, and I thought it might be nice on my bed. I didn't notice the box under it when I lifted out the quilt, but I realised it was a large quilt and would be too big for my bed, so I folded it and went to put it back. That was when I spotted the box. I took it out and looked inside. There was all sorts of stuff relevant to our mum and us, including our birth certificates, Mum's death certificate, the letter she posted before she got on the boat explaining why she wanted to die, and there were several newspapers with headlines concerning our father.'

Saskia faltered. Oliver's eyes never left her, accusatory and without any form of comprehension being apparent.

'Did you speak to your grandparents about it? To Petra?' Carl asked.

'I spoke to nobody.' The stiffness was coming back into her voice. 'I used the internet until I had all the answers.'

'You started visiting your father three years ago?' Carl moved the questions on.

For a second, Saskia looked startled. 'Yes, I did.'

Doris pulled a list out of her file. 'You and Todd alternated visiting sessions. Is that right? Nobody else ever visited him?'

'No, only the two of us. I visited him as Paulette Young. I told them I was his niece.'

'And what did you talk about?'

Julie held up a hand. 'Do I have to listen to this garbage?'

Tracy stood. 'I'll take Julie to her room. It's her rest time.'

Carl gave a slight nod. 'Then come back here, Ms Worrall.'

Tracy was back within two minutes and the questioning resumed.

.   .   .

'Yes, he told me of his plan to kill Julie. He fully expected to be released, and he fully expected to be caught again; he was prepared for a return to prison. He simply wanted her dead, and part of the plan was for me to become friendly with the family.'

Ollie looked sick, as if he couldn't believe what he was hearing. This woman had actually pushed in a not so subtle way for an engagement ring for Christmas, and he had almost fallen for it.

'Ollie was easy,' Saskia said, rubbing further salt into Oliver's wounds. 'He came frequently with Julie to the hospital for her treatments, and I managed to get a position on the ward. I would have found some way to bump into him no matter what, it was what my father wanted.'

Saskia's cheeks were glowing; she could feel hatred and disbelief emanating from people who had taken her into the family, welcomed her into it. Even Petra was inching her chair away from her, distancing herself from this woman who was part of a murder plot.

Doris sighed. 'Saskia, that morning when we discovered the location of the house at Bamford, I rang here before I rang the police or anyone else. I told Greg, and I heard him shout to tell everybody that a possible location had been found. Did you know that location?'

'I did. I was in contact with Todd.'

'And did you text either Paul or Todd to tell them the police were on their way?'

She paused for a moment and looked around the table. 'I've been absolutely truthful about everything that's happened, and I know I'm going to have to pay for it, but I promise you, I did not text either of them to tell them the police were on their way.'

She slid her mobile phone across the table towards Carl. 'Check it,' she said. 'I know I could have deleted it, but I also know you can still find it. There's nothing there. You might have laid everything at my feet, but you've not found the one who texted, have you? And whoever it is didn't form part of the plan as far as I was concerned, it was me, Todd and Dad. You might want to talk to Todd about it, but all I was here for was to let him into the house when the time was right, and act the horrified house guest. When you,' Saskia nodded towards Doris, 'said we all had to go into lockdown, it spoiled everything. The entry code for the house was changed, and Greg wouldn't tell anybody because he said we didn't need to know as we weren't to leave the house. I think it's why Dad killed Julie's parents – they couldn't tell him the code.'

36

C arl couldn't believe how tired he felt. Saskia's statement had been taken, and she had been charged, with a magistrates' court appearance scheduled for the following day. He had told Alistair and Doris to disappear for the rest of the day, and try not to think about the revelations that had come like chunks of ice from Saskia van Berkel, but he knew he wouldn't relax until he had some news on the mobile phone front.

Holding on to the phone Saskia had slid across to him, he then collected all the other phones, much to everyone's dismay. Kaya had been the most vocal, but he hadn't given in.

'I promise I'll bring them back as soon as our tech guys have finished with them, but we have to eliminate as much as discover.'

The technical department had prioritised; they had all liked Hannah Granger.

Alistair and Doris didn't go back to Little Mouse Cottage; they went to the office and reported to Kat, Mouse, Tessa and Martha. Martha was the most talkative, but they told the others everything that had occurred, and the story that Saskia had reluctantly told them.

'I felt there was more to it than she was saying, and I know Alistair felt the same. It's why we came back here instead of going home. Whatever she might say, somebody in that house messaged Todd Fraser, or Paul, we don't know which one as they were both there, and passed on what I had said on the phone.' Doris sounded stressed. 'Carl's collected all the mobile phones and is currently having them checked, but until we get an answer on this, I feel Julie is still in danger. What do we know about Todd?'

'Nothing much,' Tessa said. 'He's the brother in the background, isn't he. It's been all about Paul.' Tessa frowned as she tried to think where to turn next. 'I'll ring Edna Davis,' she said, and went into the reception area, seeking quiet away from Martha's chatter.

Luke was sitting at his desk.

'Oh my God. Oh my God! Luke!' She carefully pulled him into her arms. She held him, then pushed him to arm's length to inspect him. 'You look yellowish and purplish and bluish but you'll do. Does your mother know you're here?'

'I told her I was going out for a little walk. I need to get my leg muscles working properly again. It's more about my brain muscles though, I'm stagnating.'

'Right. Let me make this phone call, and we'll discuss what you're going to tell your mother and nan about where you've been, and what happens next.'

Luke laughed. 'Yeah. Let's tell my nan something. When I said I was going for a little walk, she winked at me and said "Don't go near work". I'll keep quiet while you make your call.'

Tessa smiled at him and took out her phone, looking for Edna's number. She answered immediately.

'Good morning, Edna. Were you waiting for me to ring?'

There was a tinkle of laughter. 'No, Tessa, I wasn't. I rarely answer it, but I'll always answer to you. What can I do for you?'

'First of all, I want to check you're okay after everything that's happened next door to you, and secondly, I want to talk about the men who lived there. I know you didn't know the younger brother at all, but Todd lived there for a while before Paul turned up. Did he ever have visitors? A girlfriend maybe? Anybody who ever stopped over?'

Again the tinkle of laughter. 'Hardly a girlfriend, lovely. But he did have a boyfriend. Up to two or three weeks before the brother arrived on the scene, this chap was a pretty frequent visitor. Tall, not sure of his age because I thought Todd was a lot younger than he turned out to be, but I would say he was younger than Todd. They laughed a lot when he was here – I could hear it through the walls, but before you ask, I never heard anything they spoke about.'

Tessa felt a frisson of hope. 'Edna, are you in for the rest of the day?'

'I am, lovely.'

'If I bring some pictures out to you, will you have a look at them to see if you recognise anybody who visited that house?'

'I'll put the kettle on, and make some scones.'

'I might bring a young man with me. He's a victim of Paul Fraser also, and a little fragile, but he'll enjoy the trip out to see you.'

'Then I'll feed him scones too.'

Tessa disconnected with a smile. She turned to Luke. 'I need printouts of everybody connected to this case. All the family, all the security staff, absolutely everybody. You'll have them in your files, I'm sure of it. Then all we have to do is convince your mum that you'll be perfectly safe with me, and I'll deliver you home later in a much better frame of mind.'

'Done,' he said, and switched on his computer.

· · ·

The reception area filled up rapidly once Tessa broke the news of Luke's arrival. She explained what was happening, and she was taking Luke out for the run.

Doris didn't want to leave his side; she kept clutching at his hand, checking he was okay, saying she would get the stuff Tessa required, until Luke pointed out he was a battered and bruised man with a broken arm, and he could do his job even if everybody around him wanted to wrap him in a cocoon.

Then he kissed Doris. 'This is the most fun I've had in what seems like months, even if it's only weeks. I won't be driving,' he waved the cast around, 'but I'm looking forward to moving away from this village even if it's only as far as Bamford. And I'm going to meet another smart lady who's going to feed me scones, so it's a win–win.'

Luke eased himself out of Tessa's car, ever mindful of the pain if he caught one of the more battered areas of his legs, and tried to control the slight limp as they walked up the path to Edna's home.

He felt relieved that paths and pavements all seemed to be clear of snow, and all roads currently passable. He didn't have that hazard to worry about, but he did have the hazard of a random pain in his leg forcing him to his knees. He walked slowly, and Tessa kept pace with him, chatting so that he didn't notice she had recognised his discomfort.

Edna opened the door as they approached, and her welcome was warm, as was her home.

'Come on,' she said, 'first things first. Let's have a cup of tea and a scone and then we'll look at these pictures you've brought. I've been going through my phone to see if I've accidentally caught him on it, this chap, but I haven't. I get lots of wildlife in my back garden, and I like to take photos of it all, so if I had captured him it would definitely have been accidental, but I haven't.'

She disappeared into the kitchen and Luke eased himself down into an armchair. Tessa wanted to help, but knew he wouldn't want that. She took the sofa, trying to squash her feelings. Being so close to the spot where Hannah had taken her last breath was hard, and Tessa squeezed her eyes tightly closed to stop the prickle of tears.

'I'm so sorry we've lost Hannah,' Luke said softly. 'We all loved her. And coming here, Tessa, is unbelievably brave. You're a strong woman and when you grow up you'll be another Doris, hold on to that thought.'

She turned and smiled at him. 'You say the nicest things, Luke. But I miss her every second of every day. Tomorrow I will be making arrangements for her funeral, and that is so unreal it's scary.'

Edna walked through from the kitchen carrying a tray, and Tessa jumped up to take it from her and place it on the coffee table.

The tea and scones were delicious, and Edna spoke of the life she had enjoyed with her husband. The early years had been hard; she had borne three children in quick succession and at that time they were also setting up the beginnings of their empire with their first car lot.

'By the end of our working lives I could strip down and rebuild an engine, sell the highest spec model to somebody who was passing by with no thoughts of buying a new car, and supervise all our accounts. I loved cars.'

'Then I need to take you with me when I go to buy my new

one,' Luke said. 'Mine was written off when Fraser rammed me.'

'I understand he almost wrote you off as well. An evil man. I'll be happy to accompany you, Luke. I'll tell everybody I'm your girlfriend though.'

Luke laughed. 'That's absolutely fine. I'll probably tell them that anyway.'

Edna looked at Tessa. 'He's nice.' Edna inclined her head towards Luke.

'Certainly is, but you'll have to fight our Doris for him. Let me clear away these goodies, and I'll get the pictures out. I'm not going to say anything about them, I don't want you to have any preconceptions, I'll lay them on the table and let you take your time. Luke is going to film it, if you don't mind, so we can show our colleagues the outcome of this. It's easier than telling them. In these pictures are photos of Todd and Paul Fraser. If you can pick those two out first it will be a massive help.'

'That proves I'm able to recognise people?'

Tessa nodded. 'It does. I don't want anyone accusing you in court of poor eyesight, of being mentally unable to recognise people, of simply being elderly. This video will show you for the smart, sassy woman you are, who's going for world domination. This man who visited next door may not, of course, be in this line-up, and that's not a problem as long as we know we can rule everybody out. However, you will also see some women in here, and I want you to look at them alongside the men, in case you have ever seen them visit. We're ruling out as much as ruling in. Okay? You ready? Oh, and I'll be calling you Mrs Davis, in case this video is needed as an official piece of evidence.'

Tessa stood and loaded the tray, then carried it through to the kitchen before returning to get her briefcase with the pictures inside it.

Luke took out his phone and videoed from that point, watching as Tessa laid out the photographs. He shuffled forward to the edge of his seat so he didn't miss anything, concentrating as each of the pictures were laid down.

'Okay, Mrs Davis, Todd Fraser and Paul Fraser lived next door to you. Can you pick out their pictures, please?'

Edna leaned forward and picked them up one at a time, being careful not to block Luke's filming. She handed them to Tessa. 'The first one is Todd, the second one is Paul.'

'Thank you, Mrs Davis. Now, I want you to look carefully at the rest of the pictures and tell me if anyone from the remaining printouts has, to your knowledge, ever visited next door.'

Edna remained quiet, slowly scanning the remaining pictures. She didn't immediately pounce on any one piece of paper, but went back to the beginning. Tessa watched as Edna's head travelled slowly along the two lines of photographs for the second time.

She leaned over and picked up two of the printed pictures. She held them towards Luke, individually, and said, 'These two. I am absolutely sure I am correct in this.'

37

'I'll get somebody out here to take your statement to go with this video, Edna, and I can't thank you enough for this. I'm not sure what the implications are yet, but I promise when I know more, you will. And thank you for the bag of scones, these will be much appreciated, I can tell you.'

She kissed Edna on the cheek, and climbed into the driving seat, trying to shut out the image of Hannah as she had last seen her. Tessa managed until the bottom of the road, then pulled in, unable to see through her tears. Luke awkwardly shuffled across, placed his right arm around her shoulders and pulled her towards him. 'Come on,' he said. 'Let's cry together.'

And they did.

Carl headed out to Dovewater accompanied by a large van and two squad cars. He wanted to make it obvious that major things were happening at the house, waiting patiently for Leila to open the gates. He had instructed the squad cars to use lights and sounds; this arrest situation would be obvious.

Carl spoke quietly to Leila and asked her to tell Mark that

arrests were imminent and happening, and somebody from Connection would contact him later.

She nodded, bewildered by the emerging circumstances, and hiding it under her controlled blanket of professionalism. 'Of course, DI Heaton,' she said. 'Do you require assistance from Mark?'

'No, as you can see, we're fully loaded with personnel today. Some will be staying to go through the house, authorised by a search warrant that DC Irwin has in his safekeeping, but I'll be returning to Chesterfield to interview our suspects.'

Leila watched as the convoy of police vehicles drove past her and headed towards the front door, with one of the cars peeling away to cover the rear entrance. She took out her transmitter, and waited for Mark to respond. 'It's all kicking off,' she said. 'Over.'

'Thanks, Leila. I can see it is. Did DI Heaton confirm who they're here for? Over.'

'Nope. I reckon it's that slimeball, Tracy Worrall. She must think we've not seen what she's up to. Over.'

Mark laughed. 'You have such a way with words, Leila. Over and out.'

Greg and Ollie looked towards each other as handcuffs held their arms behind their backs. Julie and Tracy were in tears, Julie demanding to know what the hell was happening. Petra stood to one side, shaking and wishing she was back home with her granny and granddad, safe from whatever shit Saskia was in up to her neck. Kaya was sitting on the top stair, watching the activity below, feeling numb. She'd liked that DI Heaton, but she wasn't sure she liked him now. It looked like being a bad day all round.

. . .

Luke paced backwards and forwards across his bedroom floor. The day had been brilliant, and he blessed his decision to go for the walk that had inexorably drawn him towards the Connection office. Spending time with Tessa had been good; she hadn't mollycoddled him, simply expected him to get on with things. Crying together had eased them both, and before they left Bamford she had filled Carl in on the two men he needed to get out of that house before something happened that was irreversible.

Dropping Luke off at home had been sensible, but he didn't want to be sensible. He wanted to be back at work, and in that moment he realised that waiting until after Christmas was ridiculous. He would be climbing the walls by then, so, decision made, he was restarting work the following morning.

Driving was out of the question, particularly as he hadn't got a car, he mused, then burst out laughing at his thoughts. Finally a laugh. He could laugh again. He went downstairs, preparing to meet the argument head on. Ten minutes later he rang Doris.

Ollie had never been so scared. It was all very well his solicitor advising him to say 'no comment', but the police were authority, probably with a capital A, and if his father had instilled anything into him, it was to respect authority.

Carl spoke for the recorder, signing himself and Dave Irwin in before adding Ollie Clark's name. The solicitor spoke his own name and the interview began.

Ollie answered Carl's questions, starting with the big one of what is your relationship with Todd Fraser. 'I love him.'

Oliver's solicitor looked at him as if to say that didn't sound like *No comment.*

'And how long have you known him?'

'Three years or so. We didn't become lovers until he moved into the house in Bamford.'

The solicitor rolled his eyes.

'What is the relationship like with your mother?'

He visibly stiffened. 'We don't get on.'

'Would you like to expand on that?' Carl thought back to the sessions around the table at Dovewater and although it hadn't seemed significant at the time, he realised that not once had Ollie sat anywhere near Julie.

'She won't accept my sexuality. Having Saskia move in made her think I'd "grown out of it" to use her phrase.'

'So why did Saskia move in?'

'We are family. Her father, as you know, is Paul Fraser. We share a bed to placate mother, but Sas knows I love Todd.'

'And your mother knows nothing of this?'

'No. It's not complicated, you know. We wanted mother dead. She's in pain most of the time, has to go everywhere in that bloody wheelchair, is cranky as hell all the time unless she's trying to impress somebody then she's all sweetness and light, and we had our reasons for wanting her life to end. When I met Todd he eventually told me all about Paul, because he discovered who I was. He said the only thing Paul thought about was killing my mother, to finish off the job he tried to do twenty years ago. It seemed like an omen to me. I knew, even then, that I wouldn't do anything to stop Paul Fraser from getting it right second time around.'

'You said "we" wanted your mother dead. Who is we?' Carl stared across the table at Ollie.

Ollie looked at his solicitor, but he simply waved his hand as if to say 'You're on your own, you've ignored everything I've advised so far'.

'My father and I.'

'I've seen your father with your mother. He seems loving, caring and solicitous.'

'That's for anybody who's watching. If you really want to see caring and solicitous, watch him with Tracy and Kaya. My mother is an encumbrance. We can't go anywhere because it's too big a job – do you know we've never been abroad? Not as a family.'

A brief smile flashed across Carl's face. 'And it could be a further few years before that opportunity crops up. So – you discussed with Todd Fraser the possibility of assisting Paul in his quest to kill your mother?'

'Not assist. I'm not that heartless, you know. No, I simply wouldn't hinder him, but he cocked everything up by dying, in the end.'

'We have results from your mobile phone that show you sent a text to Todd's phone on the morning we discovered the existence of Todd's house. You didn't even wipe it from the phone.' PC Dave Irwin spoke for the first time.

'I know. I tried to warn him, but they'd practised Paul getting out quickly, and getting rid of fingerprints, so it all went smoothly until some clever cow thought to check the Christmas tree ornaments.'

'I can kind of understand how you came to be involved in all of this, but your father? That baffles me a little. Did you tell him?'

'I did. That's when it all started to go wrong. I saw him kiss Tracy. I'd always suspected he fancied her, but never realised it was a lot more than that. He was in his study on his own, so I went in and told him what I'd seen. He admitted it, and offered me a whisky. Man-to-man chat, he said. We got legless, I told him about Todd and his relationship to Paul, and what Paul was planning. I fell into bed that night, had a massive hangover next day, and went into panic mode because I couldn't really remember everything I'd said.'

Ollie hesitated as if thinking back. 'Everything changed that morning. He wanted in. I took him to meet Todd, who relayed everything to Saskia and Paul.'

'Is Petra involved?'

Oliver shook his head. 'Not in any way. She knows nothing at all. She's only with us because it's their twenty-fifth birthday in January, and they wanted to spend it together.'

Carl gave a slight nod. It confirmed his own thoughts on Petra, that she couldn't have faked the reaction they saw when the questioning about their names began.

'Your father hired Connection. Was that his suggestion?'

'No. He knew they were good, but Mother insisted. He didn't want good, he wanted mediocre, but he got Connection and the security team they found for us. It stopped everything. Paul managed to wound one of the men, as you know, but he got nowhere near his proper target. A complete shambles.'

'So what you're telling me is pretty simple. Neither you nor your father would have done anything to prevent the murder of your mother, in fact you actively encouraged it.'

Ollie let his head drop. 'That's all true, but we didn't do anything. I haven't committed a crime, and neither has my father.'

Carl stood and spoke to Dave Irwin. 'Take him downstairs, PC Irwin, get him booked and charged. We'll start with conspiracy to murder. I'm sure there'll be other charges to follow, but that will keep him locked up for a while.'

Carl looked at a horrified Ollie who was protesting to the solicitor that he hadn't actually done anything.

'Your sexuality won't be questioned when you get where you're going, Oliver. Good luck with that.' Carl left the interview room.

. . .

Initially Greg followed his solicitor's advice, saying 'No comment' to everything, but the more Carl and Dave Irwin said about Ollie's statement, the more Greg spoke, to try to deny everything. He followed his son to the charge office, and Dovewater was left empty of men.

Tessa went with Carl to explain the situation to Julie, Tracy and Kaya.

Petra had already left for Holland, wondering how her life could have collapsed so spectacularly, and wondering how to go about finding stuff written about her father. Her dead father. She had so much to tell her grandparents.

Julie was interviewing a woman in the dining room when they arrived, so Tracy took them to the kitchen and made them a cup of tea, explaining Kaya had gone to their bungalow in the garden to put the heating on, and get it ready for their return. 'Julie is speaking to someone about coming in to help me, now that we're not going to have Ollie and Greg here,' she explained. 'It's going to be a strange Christmas this year, isn't it? A week to go, and everything is about as far as it can be from being festive. A proper unjoyful Christmas we're expecting.'

'What will you do?'

'Stay here. Julie will still need caring for, and we have nowhere else to go anyway. This has been our home for ten years.'

Tessa looked behind her to make sure the door was closed. 'You are aware that neither Greg nor Ollie will be coming home? Not for a few years anyway.'

'What?' Tracy sat down with a thud.

'They're facing charges of conspiracy to murder, and there'll probably be other charges once the CPS has seen the evidence. Does Julie know about you and Greg, and the fact that Kaya is his daughter?'

Tracy's face drained of all colour. 'No, nobody knows. Except Greg.'

'Be prepared,' Tessa said. 'If Julie does know...'

Tracy shivered. 'Happy bloody Christmas, Tracy,' she said, and picked up her cup of tea.

EPILOGUE

26 DECEMBER 2019

'We have to talk.' Alistair held Doris's hand as they sat side by side in the double bed. A mug of tea rested on bedside tables, and they were enjoying the peace of the post-Christmas morning.

'I know,' Doris said with a sigh. 'Does it have to be today?'

'We can't keep putting it off. I love you, and I want us to be together. Do you want that?'

She nodded. 'I do.'

It was Alistair's turn to sigh. 'Okay, we're agreed on that. Now we only need to decide on where we want to be together.'

'France.'

'What?'

'That's where we want to be together. It's not fair that you expect me to go live in London, because after all the beauty of Derbyshire I would hate that, as you know. I can't expect you to give up your dreams so we have to compromise. And the compromise is France.'

There was silence for a moment. 'I was prepared to compromise and move here,' he said quietly. 'Before we make the final decision, I want you to see my place in St Raphael.'

'How many bedrooms is it?'

'When it's finished it will have three on the normal bedroom level, then a further two bedrooms and a study on the attic level, up in the roof. Is that enough for you? There's only two of us, you know,' he said with a laugh.

'I want enough so that everybody can visit us whenever they feel like it. Okay, get out your credit card and book us a flight and a hotel near to your place. We can hire a car when we get there. I'll consider paying for that,' she said with a grin.

'You really mean it?'

'I do. We're seventy, we don't know how long we have left, but I want to spend it with you. And if I have to rough it on the Côte d'Azur then so be it.'

'Rough it? It's the most glorious place on this earth, Doris Lester. I'm having trouble believing I'm hearing this.' He slid his legs out of bed.

'Where are you going?'

'To book these flights before you change your mind. And when I come back, I want to see these two videos, superwoman. You thought I'd forgotten, didn't you?'

Carl sat in the middle of the lounge floor, wondering how to put the nappy on the naked doll. Martha had completely stripped Suzie, the name decided for the doll Father Christmas had brought her, but couldn't get things to go back on properly. A daddy had been required to help her.

'Kat,' he called, 'I can't do this.'

'Course you can,' she responded from somewhere upstairs. 'Dads can do everything.'

'Not this one,' he mumbled, and Martha put her arms around from behind and hugged him.

'Daddy,' she said, 'dress Suzie.'

The nappy appeared to be back to front, so he patiently removed it and started again. He looked up to see Kat coming downstairs, laughing at him for his ineptitude.

'Don't laugh. This is serious stuff. When I used to change Martha's nappies her legs bent. This doll's legs don't bend.'

Kat walked across to where he was still cross-legged on the floor and bent down to plant a big kiss on his lips.

'Okay, my handsome husband, here's another Christmas present for you. I'm sorry it's a day late but I wanted this to be only for us, and not to have to share it with everyone yesterday. And besides, this is nothing to do with Father Christmas.'

She held the pregnancy tester for him to see, and he looked up. 'We're pregnant?' he whispered. Then it changed to a shout. 'We're pregnant?'

'We are indeed pregnant,' she said, and watched as he scrambled to his feet, wincing at the aches and pains that had arrived during his half hour on the floor.

Carl held her, and they waited for Martha to interrupt them as she always did. 'Mummy. Daddy. Kiss,' she said.

'I know Nan is going to swan off to France,' Mouse said. 'I've never been without her, you know.'

'I know, my love,' Joel responded, 'but don't be unhappy. She deserves this. And she hasn't said yet that she's going. She may decide to stay here.'

'And we can visit her, can't we?'

'We can. I'm definitely up for a sojourn in the South of France though. We could get married there.'

Mouse froze. Married? Had she agreed to that in a drunken moment?

'Married?'

'You don't want to?'

'Might do.'

'When?'

'Soon?'

'Okay. That's settled. June. That okay?'

'It is.'

Luke was tapping his finger impatiently. He had sent Edna details of a car, and she had responded, telling him that she knew the owner of the showrooms, and to leave it with her. She would find out if it was okay, and get back to him.

He was feeling uneasy about the situation with his Doris. He feared that Alistair would be taking her away, and for a moment he wondered how many Ferrero Rochers it would take to bribe her to stay. It wouldn't be the same at work without her, and with no Hannah, he was suddenly overwhelmed with unhappiness.

Even Tessa had spoken of quitting the police force, but he put that down to her having heard the news of Joan Sharpe's death on the same day that she had been making the funeral arrangements for Hannah. Surely Tessa wouldn't give that thought serious consideration. He picked up his phone and without giving himself time to think, he rang her.

'Luke? Is everything okay?'

'No. I don't want things to change.'

'What?'

'Things are changing. I think Doris will leave soon, and you're talking of leaving the police... it doesn't seem right.'

'Okay. Let's lose the panic I can hear in your voice. If, and it's a big if, I leave the police it won't be yet, because I can't go *into* work until the end of January. And Doris hasn't said she's escaping to France, she's only said Alistair is retiring to there.

Nothing has changed in either Kat or Mouse's lives, so quit worrying.'

Luke sighed. 'This has been such a brilliant job, I really don't want to see it alter in any way. Do you understand?'

'I do. But that's what life is about, change. No more panic, Luke. We have your back. Now, tell me what Father Christmas brought you.'

Todd felt fed up. Bloody Heaton had been to see him, asking if he had known who had sent the text message warning him and Paul of the impending police visit. If he hadn't been cocky about it and said yes, he had known who had sent it to him, he wouldn't be looking at further charges of conspiracy to murder. For fuck's sake, these bloody police officers were too smart for their own good. But one day he'd get out…

Dovewater felt empty. Julie couldn't believe how quiet it had gone, and yet she would never have thought of the people who had lived in it as being noisy, or intrusive. But now there was only her and Monica, the woman she had been interviewing the day she had told Tracy and Kaya Worrall to pack their bags and go.

Monica seemed to be efficient, but there was no camaraderie as there had been with Tracy. Monica, however, wouldn't be sleeping with her employer's husband, wouldn't be bringing his bastard child into the household, and Julie wouldn't be having to pretend she didn't know about it.

Because she had. Known about it. She had noticed affectionate little touches, glances between Greg and Tracy, but one day Ollie had said something about how like his father Kaya was, the same shape nose, the same colour eyes and hair, and they had all laughed about it. And if Kaya wanted something, it miraculously appeared. Bought by Mum, Kaya always said, but one night Julie had seen Greg carrying a laptop box in from the car, a laptop that Kaya showed to them the next day.

Julie looked at her watch. Ten o'clock and she was still in bed. It seemed she was being punished by her new carer after the altercation as she was being prepared for bed the previous evening. She hadn't meant it to sound as it did, when she told Monica she wasn't as gentle as Tracy had been...

Ten o'clock and she hadn't seen Monica for fourteen hours. No tablets and she was starting to feel pain. She looked around for her mobile phone, and saw it was on the stand that contained her medication, plugged into the charger. Out of reach.

She called Monica's name, but there was no response. For the rest of that day she called aloud, but unable to even hoist herself up the bed, she was helpless. Hunger was gnawing away at her, and she tried to ignore the thirst issue.

After three days she stopped calling for help. There was nobody to hear her. And there was nobody to care.

THE END

ACKNOWLEDGEMENTS

As always, my primary thanks go to everyone at Bloodhound Books who are always there for me, listen to my moans, my queries, and anything else that crops up in the crazy imaginary world that we authors inhabit. It is a fabulous team, consisting of Fred and Betsy Freeman, Alexina, Tara, Heather and the publicity team.

Morgen Bailey is my long-suffering editor who constantly tries to get me to understand point of view. Thank you, Morgen, you're an outstanding editor, and I promise to try harder.

I have a four-member team of beta readers, who receive my manuscript at various points, and give me invaluable feedback. Thank you, Sarah Hodgson, Marnie Harrison, Alyson Read and Tina Jackson.

My ARC group members get advance copies of my novels, and by the time launch day arrives, they are ready to post their reviews. They are an amazing group of people, too many to name, but their feedback is awesome. I have to give a special mention to Christopher Nolan, a member of my ARC team, who begins to read the manuscript immediately, and who gives all my books their final proofread. Thank you, Chris, you don't know how much I appreciate this.

Most of my books feature readers who want to be in a book. I have three people to thank for lending me their names – Tracy and Kaya Worrall (mum and daughter), and Saskia van Berkel. Saskia also helped me out with the sentence of Dutch I use in the book. I hope the three of you enjoy the parts I allocated to you!

I have written the biggest part of this book during lockdown. Dave and I went out on 9 March and we haven't been out since. Today is 16 July. I have to say a massive thanks to Dave, because I have sat at my computer day after day after day, writing, shielding from Covid. We have remained healthy, and have had wonderful support from our family during this dreadful time. And I have written this book and started another one. I am going to take a two-week holiday in my back garden, because we also had to give up a week in Croatia.

And then there is my Trish, my help when I need to talk about plots, my Mancunian friend who will read anything I send to her, usually when I am asking 'Does this sound daft?' She is a massive support, and most of all she made me promise not to kill Doris. I didn't. Thank you, Patricia Dixon, love you.

My final thank you goes to you. If you've got as far as reading the acknowledgements, you've finished the book. My readers are the most important people in my long list of thanks, and I am truly grateful for the support that has grown with every book of mine that Bloodhound Books has published.

And now Kat and Mouse is ended. I see my reviews, and it has been a truly remarkable journey, reading them all. It appears everybody likes our three musketeers at Connection, and I, more than anybody, am so sorry to say goodbye to them. I leave them in your hands now, to enjoy.

Anita Waller
July 2020

Or maybe it doesn't end here...

Lightning Source UK Ltd.
Milton Keynes UK
UKHW011828211220
375673UK00001B/195